THE WEALDWIFE'S TALE

PAUL HAZEL

An AvoNova Book

William Morrow and Company, Inc.
New York

AVON BOOKS
A division of
The Hearst Corporation
1350 Avenue of the Americas
New York, New York 10019

Copyright © 1993 by Paul Hazel
Published by arrangement with the author
Library of Congress Catalog Card Number: 92-25069
ISBN: 0-688-12188-8

Library of Congress Cataloging in Publication Data:

Hazel, Paul.
    The wealdwife's tale/Paul Hazel.
        p.   cm.
    I. Title.
    PS3558.A889W4   1993
    813'.54—dc20   92-25069
                                                              CIP

First Morrow/AvoNova Printing: March 1993

AVONOVA TRADEMARK REG. U.S. PAT. OFF. AND IN OTHER COUNTRIES, MARCA REGISTRADA, HECHO EN U.S.A.

Printed in the U.S.A.

ARC   10   9   8   7   6   5   4   3   2   1

Faye's Book

Apology

This rather confused narrative owes its popularity to the delightful tune, which is that of a spring carol, "Tempus adest floridum," No. 99. Unfortunately Hazel substituted for the spring carol this "Good Wenceslas etc. . . . ," one of his less happy pieces, which E. Hilary Salt goes so far as to call "doggerel," and *The Dalesman* condemns as "poor and commonplace to the last degree." The time has not yet come for a comprehensive publisher to discard it; but we reprint it not without hope that, with the present wealth of light holiday literature, "Good Wenceslas and so forth . . ." may gradually pass into disuse, and the tune be restored to springtime.

—*The Editors*

Part I

The Promise

"My good woman," said he, "can you show me the way out of the wood?"

—The Brothers Grimm

Chapter One

CASTLEBURRY, HIS GRACE'S BROLLACHAN SERVANT, seeing the hour, climbed the 188 stairs to the Aviary. From the basement kitchen where, as was its longstanding habit, the brollachan took a saucer of morning coffee with Mrs. Curran, there were twelve wide steps on two levels and four more to the top of the butler's pantry. To the third floor landing there were 28. Already panting, the old servant lumbered past Miss Elva's room, avoiding the three massive bedchambers of the sons of the house, turned heavily down one of the lesser-used hallways, and then, catching its breath while it unlocked the door, began the last ascent to the tower.

The tower had 144 steps and was unheated. Sensing the frost on the stone, the brollachan thrust its shapeless hands deeper into its pockets and thought wistfully of the kitchen range filling the lower house with warmth. Queer, icy shadows curved ahead of it. It did not mind the cold, but the narrowness of the stairwell was confining. Fortunately, now and then there were windows out of which it could look into the snow-covered yard and be assured that it was climbing nearer the Aviary.

Nevertheless, it was a very old brollachan, and the stair seemed unmercifully long.

"Is that you, Castleburry?" the Duke asked when he heard the great, weary thump on the door.

The brollachan considered the two words of which it was master.

"Myself," it croaked finally.

"What do you want?"

"Thyself," croaked the brollachan, left with no choice.

In spite of his melancholy, His Grace, the Eighth Duke, smiled.

"I shall come to them shortly," he said distractedly, adding another feather to the skeleton of the parawing. Without thinking, he listened to the shapeless presence behind the door reorganizing itself for its descent.

The brollachan, if it could be said to be like anything at all, resembled a pile of animated hedge trimmings or, depending how one looked at it, a heap of wet hay which had blundered onto the secret of locomotion. It lacked a proper head (or at least recognizable features) and initially it had been impossible for anyone to determine whether it was paying attention. Such ambiguity, according to the housewomen, could not be tolerated in polite society. By way of remedy the Duke had presented the brollachan with an old tarpaulin coat which, although it was still impossible to know for certain whether the coat was being worn front-to-back or back-to-front, gave the brollachan at least the illusion of human appearance and symmetry. In truth, every now and then the Duke suspected that the coat was being worn backward. Nonetheless, he was not displeased. Lately, he had even begun to take a quiet pleasure in the small rebellion of his servant. Since his wife's death, the world of fields and pastures under his hand had grown much too solemn and orderly. He longed instead for the uncertainty of his young manhood, for the chance to pose unanswered and perhaps unanswerable questions. Above all else he longed to be in love again.

The Eighth Duke listened to the shambling descent of the brollachan and, although he knew he must soon go down to meet the barons, thinking of his amphibolous servant, he smiled once more.

The cold December sunlight came in through the Aviary windows and lit his long face and the frizz of his graying hair. He was not yet fifty and until the past year had always looked extraordinarily young. Even now his arms were strong and his carriage vigorous and sturdy.

His ancestors, the ancient line of the dukes of West Redding, were robust men, accustomed to leading the barons after the hounds and to joining the fieldmen in the meadows at haying. The present Duke had a thick rust-colored moustache, heavy brows, and, at the corners of his startling blue eyes, a pair of significant squint lines which, in a certain light and with a tilting of his head, gave him the appearance of a thoughtful badger. His given name was Rudyard Riding Wenceslas, but from the cradle his older brother, whose name had been Arthur, called him Waldo. The name had stuck. When his brother, the Seventh Duke, died of a fever, the fieldmen and serving-boys continued to address His Grace as they had when he was a lad of six. The Duke took no notice. He was preoccupied with discovering improved methods of planting barley and with ridding the river road south from Stephen's Well of highwaymen. With much the same care with which Mrs. Curran oversaw his table, he saw to his lands and the

fortunes of all who lived under his rule. For thirty years
he had presided at dances and weddings and was revered
at local fairs as a judge of dark beer and white oxen. He
was fond of old books and had taught himself to tile a roof
and make kites. He dreamed of inventing a flying machine.
After his sons were born, he got their feet wet chasing about
in swamps and bogs and kept them up too late waiting for
shooting stars. He had a prodigious memory; throughout
his life he could recall the names of each smith and potboy
and every one of the gardeners, gamekeepers, and fieldmen
who worked on the six-thousand-acre farm. Yet after his
wife died, he had to be reminded by the maids to put on
laundered shirts and, before midnight, to come down for
his supper. These last months, he had spent every available
moment in the Aviary constructing the parawing.

This device was part kite and part parachute and part
(and this was a very small part) magic. The magic was
owing to the knife with which, when paper wasps buzzed
high in the rafters, the Duke had whittled the frame. The
knife had been purchased by the Duke from a wandering
tinker, a queer, tiny man with a hunchback, who had
promised that the knife would impart to whatever it cut
the most important characteristics the carver dreamed of
while he worked. The Duke had smiled skeptically. But,
in the tower, the white curls of wood falling softly about
him, he had held in his mind, just in case, the image
of three ravens scouting over the borders of the Weald
or, when his hands grew cramped, the livelier memory
of silver fritillaries flickering above the green walks and
the gardens close to the house. In fact, it had sometimes
seemed to him that the frame had taken on a curious
lightness. Once, before he had stitched on the feathers,
he had strapped the frame to his arms and climbed onto

the table. He had almost imagined then he was flying: sweeping out effortlessly over courtyards and barns, taking the wind swiftly eastward toward the Weald where, if Mrs. Curran were to be believed, the dead slept and where, because the Duke took the old woman fiercely at her word, he meant to find his wife and bring her home again.

His wife had died giving birth to the child who shared her name, had died paradoxically, delivering a girl when she had been delivered of boys already, large squawling sons, first Harry, then Arthur, then John, each without a whimper, and then dined with His Grace in the evening. Her hair had been as black as a raven's and as slippery, when the Duke drew his hands over it, as feathers. In the daylight she had worn it braided and coiled. But in the evening as he was mounting the stairs, she unwrapped the long tresses. In their bed, combed out with ivory combs, her hair lay about her white shoulders like a cloak of finest sable.

Night after night as he settled down next to her, he had nuzzled into her neck. They had seldom slept, not in the bright summer moonlight, not when the growling winter storms vanquished the high, wheeling stars. At sunrise, before he left her, they would rest quietly in each others' arms, fully awake, counting the hours until it was night again.

The Duke fixed one last feather into the outer skin of the parawing. As he withdrew his hand, his fingers softly brushed the vanes. He held himself still.

"Elva," he whispered.

In the yard there was the clattering sound of a carriage. From one of the rooms below came the muffled chorus of young men's laugher.

★   ★   ★

Harry edged the door open enough to see his father's graying head disappearing below the landing. He did not know whether it would be safe to go on, for there were a great many things about which it was impossible to be certain, too many things, especially when he had always to consider His Grace. He knew that he had disappointed his father, had disappointed him somehow from the very beginning, long before he had been sacked from St. Berzelius. The debts had been petty, nothing that could not have been tolerated from a duke's son, and any number of boys might have fathered the scullery maid's brat. (In fact, he had not once so much as kissed the girl.) Certainly, he was far from the least attractive boy in the school, but as the rector explained rather sorrowfully, he lacked industry. Nevertheless, Harry was the oldest, and although dimly, he recognized his place. Putting on a brave front, he pulled the door shut, then turned again to his brothers.

"We shall have two hours," he said.

"Except if Da has an argument with the b-barons," said John, who, being the youngest, was inclined to think about being caught. "If there's an argument, he is s-sure to come up again."

"There is always an argument," Arthur said wearily. Although he was the middle son, Arthur was already the tallest. He had his mother's black hair but his skin was bad, and because he read too many books, he squinted.

"There is *always* an argument," he repeated, assuming a learned air. "Da likes arguments." He blinked in the general direction of the brollachan and tried, unsuccessfully, to determine whether it was looking back. "Trust me," he said. "They'll be yelling for hours."

"W-we won't h-hurt it?" John asked.

"No way of knowing."

"You won't be h-hurt?" John continued, appealing directly to the brollachan.

The brollachan lay on its side in the light of the grate, looking as if it were dead. At least it looked as if it had given up struggling. The convulsions of the brambles which somehow served as its feet, having been bound for ten minutes with a leather cord, had stopped. Harry reached for a stick which had been left in the coals. Away from the fire, the sharpened end burned with a dull, unsteady flame. Harry drew it as close as he dared to his mouth and blew on the tip to make it hotter.

"Y-y-you won't actually burn it?" John said.

"*We* won't actually do anything," Arthur answered truthfully. "The point is to see what it does when we bring the flame near it from different directions. The question is which part of it is the front part."

"I d-don't suppose that every p-part of it is the f-front part," John said.

"Not if it thinks," Arthur said with assurance.

John meditated on the coals in the grate and looked puzzled. In spite of the fire, the room seemed to darken about him. It was a large room, filled with oak chests and dark worm-eaten panelling. He turned his head. Through the mullioned windows he could see the shadow of his father's tower. "I d-don't really see w-why," he began.

"Still, it's obvious," Arthur said. "The very business of thinking requires selecting some things and excluding others. If the brollachan saw everything at once, it could never decide what was important. It would have no understanding of cause and effect. In short, it would never . . ."

"But it *does* think," John concluded, interrupting him. "B-because it speaks." He paused, knowing that, given the nature of the brollachan's speech, this was a less than perfect example. "Anyway, it d–does things," he said, "when you a–ask it."

Arthur smiled victoriously. "Which just proves the point. Because it thinks, some part of it is the front part."

The brollachan lay motionless.

"Can't we start, then?" asked Harry. Listening to his brothers always made him impatient. In one motion he pulled the brollachan upright.

The brothers took up positions in a circle and Arthur waved silently to Harry to bring up the flame.

From that moment the experiment was a failure. At the other end of the room the door opened. A small black shape came tumbling over the threshold, small, that is, for a man, but not at all small for a woman. Yet it did not seem to be a woman particularly, but a squall of black hair. It came quickly. In an instant it was on them, sobbing and trying to pry them away.

"Elva!" Harry shouted, grabbing hold of one of his sister's flailing arms with one hand and struggling with the other to keep himself from getting burned.

"Don't you dare hurt it!" she cried. "Don't you dare!"

Frightened she would scratch out his eyes, Harry let go of her and guarded his head. "Oh, please stop," he whispered.

Elva was not certain who she meant to kick, but she kicked Arthur. His breath went out of him. Falling, he knocked Harry's arm; the flaming stick, crossing the little space of air, plunged toward her cheek.

For a terrible instant everything seemed to stop. Afterward Harry found that he recalled certain details which, although they were fixed in his memory, had simply not happened. He remembered, for instance, the furrows of his sister's flesh opening and the sickening cloud of her black, melting hair.

Suddenly, instead, a strange substance was descending on the backs and arms of her brothers, falling lightly on the broad bed and the floor. The dark chests looked as if they were being dusted with a darker, vaguely membranous snow. Elva stood just out of reach, unhurt, brushing the sooty fragments of unnameable matter from her gown. Harry, an excuse half-formed on his lips, looked directly into her large, gray eyes, but instead of accusation he saw only a confused watchfulness.

It was Arthur who noticed the smouldering hole in the middle of the brollachan. Clots of fibrous soot escaped between the lapels of its coat. Somewhere inside, the brollachan was burning. Arthur pulled a blanket from the bed, hoping to smother whatever it was that burned. John ran for the water bucket. When the contents of the bucket were poured in, the brollachan made a kind of grunt. It made no other sound. A moment later, after a shaking of branches, an oily froth ran from under its feet.

Elva knelt in the ash and the puddles. Her hands moved in several directions. "Poor Castleburry," she cried, tearing away the leather cord and smoothing and straightening the disorder of its brambles. "Poor, valiant Castleburry."

The brollachan stirred. With something that was not quite a hand, it reached the edge of her crow-black hair and, in a manner at once curious and sad, for a moment held fast to it.

"Thyself?" it asked. Its voice, Harry remembered, seemed almost tender.

From that time her two oldest brothers hated her.

★　　★　　★

The Duke took off his spectacles, folded them, and put them hastily into his shirt pocket. The spectacles were a concession, an unwelcome reminder of the advancing years. He used them for aligning the feathers. He did not need them to meet with the barons, and yet, had he required them, he would not have worn them into the hall. He gazed at the blur of the parawing. "Vanity," he thought. But as he closed the door of the Aviary behind him he thought: "Christ, I'm still young. Everything is possible."

At the top of the tower stairs he stopped for a moment and looked out over the roof. At a distance of a hundred feet he could make out, where the wind had cleared the snow, the edges of a few individual black slates and, in the yard, the fine white stitchery of the ivy iced to the well house. Just as clearly he could see Mrs. Curran, her stout legs plunged into a pair of too-small boots, wading angrily into the drifts in pursuit of one of the ever-vanishing servingboys. Some of his weariness passed from his face. He could see well enough from a height and at a distance. He would need such sight, he knew, in the morning when, whatever the judgment of his barons, he took the parawing for its first flight over the wood.

The Duke started down. He had lingered a little in the Aviary, but the brollachan was slow and the Duke expected to meet it, if not in the tower, at least on the landing. The stairwells, however, were empty. As he descended to the main floor, he heard a door close behind him and, with much on his mind, took no notice.

He was aware of the children in the house, but it had been years since his wife's death. Even the youngest, Elva, was now a young woman and had, he imagined, concerns of her own. Nevertheless, if by chance he met her in one of the sitting rooms, he paused and remarked on the color of her gown. He had made frequent suggestions for her reading. On Wednesdays and Saturdays, as long as the weather was decent, he went riding with his sons, a good ride from which sons and horses returned panting. Except for the nights he stayed in the Aviary, everyone met for dinner. From his place at the head of the table he tried not to lecture more than was necessary about the duties young Harry was heir to. He had taught every one of them as much as he knew himself about clarets and how to address His Royal Majesty if he were to come to visit. And he had let them fight. They fought about the value of priests and about the likelihood of angels; about which was to be more desired, "love" or "respect"; and about the necessity of algebra (especially for John) and whether Elva, at eleven, on the afternoon of the spring ball should have been permitted to watch the wife of the hereditary mayor of Devon being dressed by her maid in the upstairs bath. (The Duke had been agreeable, but Mrs. Curran intervened.) They had been long hard fights and sufficient, the Duke had always thought, to satisfy any obligation he may have had for parental instruction.

He never heard the commotion in Harry's bedchamber. By the time he had walked into the great hall, there was silence.

The priest half rose from his chair. The barons were already standing. The Duke smiled. Some of these men he had known since childhood. Their formality was not for himself but for his station. He had crossed to the head of the table before he noticed that none of the barons had returned to their seats.

"There is no need of ceremony," he said mildly, not watching their faces, unaware there was a cause for that.

Instead, thinking of their journey and remembering two bottles of especially fine malmsey that had been set aside in the pantry, he clapped his hands for the boy. "Perhaps some refreshment?" he said.

"And a stretcher and bandages," the priest added dryly.

"A casket's more likely," complained Gwenbors.

For the first time the Duke looked at the men about him.

"I think we had all better sit," he said unhappily. "You especially, George. Before you crumble."

George Gwenbors frowned. He was the most senior of the barons—almost as old as the priest—and the frailest. His nose had grown sharp, and his knees, even under his leggings, looked as thin as a wren's. His claim to importance was that he remembered His Grace's father, having shared the same schooling at St. Berzelius and a war (with the Indians and the frog-eating French) and could, as a result, give His Grace long accounts of the braver, simpler world that had been.

"In my day," Gwenbors said, "we never believed the law of gravitation could be done away with."

"Sit then," the Duke said, his voice hardened.

There were six barons. The youngest, Hob Franklin, was the son of Sir Robert, the Duke's friend, who had died from eating bad sheep's-milk cheese at the spring fair in Carrick. Hob, who had the slow, perplexed temperament of a sheep himself, was not the equal of his father. He would have preferred to be off somewhere with Harry and had been invited solely out of courtesy.

Jack Bermoothes and Morgan Potent-Matthers were clear-headed and quiet, farmers by nature as well as inheritance. They were big men with broad backs and grown families. Between them they divided the properties for twenty miles south of Devon. Their interest in the Duke's flying device was entirely practical. Before the Duke got himself killed, they wanted certain guarantees about boundaries. Ben Taynton, on the other hand, having had some experience with death (a favorite sister taken by influenza, a nephew drowned in a drainage ditch), was caught between the unlikely hope that the Duke might be successful and the more certain knowledge that things generally were what they seemed. The priest, of course, maintained that flying, whether possible or not, was ungodly and that in any case the Duchess was not to be found in the Weald.

"Pray for her soul," the priest admonished the Duke. "Pray to heaven."

"I don't need your approval," the Duke said.

"You called for a council," protested Hob, not knowing when to be silent.

"It is about the Weald," said the Duke. "I wish to talk about that."

There was firelight behind him. The boy had rolled fresh logs into the hearth before breakfast. The fire had been lit for three hours and refed. Now up through the center of the house the hollow throat of the vast old chimney roared thunderously.

"Tell me what he said," demanded George Gwenbors, suddenly unable to hear.

"He wants to talk about the Weald," Bermoothes shouted.

"I thought it was flying."

"He's already decided that."

"What?"

Bermoothes fished in his pockets for a scrap of paper and wrote the thing out for him.

"There's no cause for going into the Weald either," Gwenbors muttered when it had been read. "A queer, bad place, my father always said." He scowled across at the Duke. "In eighty years I've had no reason to alter that opinion."

"Nor any others," the Duke said half aloud.

"Be civil, Waldo," whispered Ben Taynton.

"A cruel wood," Gwenbors kept on doggedly, since when he spoke he knew what was said. "A wood full of wolves and wicked trees. The worst sort of trees, thick, old and staring . . ."

The Duke barely listened. He knew this part. Everyone who lived within several days' journey knew the reputation of the Weald. Its brooding presence was used by the villagers to keep boys from staying out too late and young women from wandering far from the roads and the cattle tracks. The Weald, or so the cottagers maintained, was the home of outlaws and giants. In its gloom, creatures with several heads (or no heads at all, only reeking holes in their shoulders) lurked under stones, waiting to drag to their dens the corpses of luckless travelers. Such tales were commonplace. The Duke had heard much the same stories about an overgrown orchard at the edge of Doogan's Crossing and, nearly word for word—although men swore to their truth—about a bit of ruined parkland Potent-Matthers owned west of Devon. They were not only lies, he had decided, they were worse than lies. For they cloaked the truth with conventional horror, keeping it distant and, therefore, unconsidered. And it mattered. For there was, he was certain, something dreadfully wrong with the wood. This wood and, as far as he had been able to tell, no other. Only no one spoke of it. What they spoke of were made-up horrors of vampires and hunchbacks when the fault, as simple as it was inexplicable, was that the wood had but a single edge, and only one entrance, to the east of his lands.

He had tried often enough to enter it elsewhere to know the impossibility without question.

The trees which could be seen from the house were deceiving. The first stands of birch and oak could be picked out easily from any of the lower windows. From the tower one could even begin to see the curve of its southern boundary. The difficulty only became apparent when one traveled further south and met, branch by branch, the same stands of trees, the same leafy curve of the horizon. There was no improvement in going north. Once, following the margins of the Weald, he had ridden the better part of a day in the direction of Camelopardus, the double pole stars, turning west only in the last minutes of daylight. And after a day of hard riding, in less than a quarter of an hour he had returned to his own courtyard.

The Duke sighed.

"Murderers," Gwenbors was saying. "Highwaymen, thieves."

The old priest nodded in agreement. "In the eyes of God . . ." he began.

"Rubbish!" the Duke cried out sharply.

Chapter Two

Propped up on the bench, Elva listened to Mrs. Curran shuffling across the kitchen's worn stone. The brollachan waited in the corner. By now the blackened mass in its chest (or one of its sides or its back) had separated into a tangle of new woody stems; it no longer trembled. Assured of its recovery, Mrs. Curran gave the brollachan a single perfunctory pat; from a pot on the edge of the stove she poured it one final saucer of coffee. It was for the girl she remained troubled. Mrs. Curran pulled a fresh cloth from her apron.

"Don't you weep, miss," she ordered, scouring the girl's wet cheeks for the third time. Her old woman's breath came in short, angry snorts. "You'll see, love," she cried. "Your brothers will pay for this."

Mrs. Curran shuffled again to the stove. Reaching into back shelves, she pulled down a half-dozen little crockery vessels (each with handwritten labels) and two paper cones filled with twigs, the contents of which, when the big kettle started to boil, she added, following an order known only

18

to herself. As she worked, she kept looking back at the bench. She had no formal schooling, but her art, like that of the most skillful of physicians, resided in an outpouring of sympathy. When a child laughed, she smiled; when it cried, she wept just as bitterly. If among the women of the house she was counted wise, it was because she was a mirror.

Reflecting on the callousness of the brothers and the cold-heartedness of men in general, she stared into the fire.

"There'll be toads under their pillows and owl shit in their breakfast," she promised. "Arthur's a prig and Johnny's a baby. But Harry, although I can't say he knows any better, deserves to be whipped."

As if she meant to see to it herself, she gave a violent stir to the kettle. The steam came up in a cloud and licked at her face.

When the mixture had thickened, she ladled a portion into a mug, then placing it into the girl's trembling fingers, settled down on the bench beside her.

Elva brought the mug to her lips. The strong brew smelled of tar. It tasted of mullein, but beyond the first shock of astringency, it left a curious warmth. It tickled her throat, and while at first she had seemed inconsolable, in time Elva leaned her thin shoulders into the cook's heavy breasts.

Mrs. Curran was a very large woman. Because of the weight on her lungs she breathed like a dolphin. Her knuckles were reddened, her palms calloused, and on her neck there was a mole the size of a beetle. But while she had never been pretty, she was open and sensible. After the death of the last of her four husbands, she had come into the Duke's service and, for a month or two after the loss of the Duchess, his bed. Yet, whatever her life had been, lately she spent her days in the kitchen. At present she was well past sixty. Once, while managing the entire household, she had kept an eye on the Duke's sons, and she had raised John. But now she was mistress of two hulking stoves, a single cold pantry and a line of black pots. The boys had long ago escaped from her skirts. It had been a different matter with Elva.

The girl stirred on the bench. "Why are my brothers cruel?" she asked. Her voice was weary and uncomprehending. It was much the same voice with which from the earliest years, tugging at Mrs. Curran's apron, the girl had plagued the old woman with questions. But the girl was a child no longer. Her big eyes were darker, her body at once leaner and fuller. She was gray-eyed and black-haired, with a beauty both shy and defiant. Sooner than anyone wanted the sons of the best houses had come courting.

Mrs. Curran sighed. "They are trying to learn to be men," she told her.

Elva considered the men she knew. "Da isn't cruel," she said.

For a long minute Mrs. Curran examined the front of her dress. Yet whatever thought she had on the matter she kept to herself. "I don't believe he ever meant to be," she said softly.

"Except," the girl admitted, "to the barons."

"And priests." Mrs. Curran gave her a pinch. "Certainly it is permissible to be cruel to our priest."

In the grate the fire had blazed up. All at once Elva discovered she was smiling. Leaning into the cook's comforting bulk, she had a feeling of ease and luxury. Among the living hills and valleys of the big woman's flesh she was safe again. Only she could not keep herself from thinking.

"Wouldn't you say . . ." she persisted.

"I know, child," the old woman whispered.

"But . . ." Elva started again.

"It's the Weald," Mrs. Curran corrected her.

Elva gazed at the clump of twisted brambles repairing itself. "I know Da found it there and then brought it out. But it isn't . . ."

The cook's knobbed fingers gripped the girl's arm. "But it *is*. It's the one thing, child, you must always remember. The brollachan was never just something found and brought away. Castleburry is the Weald. And the Weald, God help you all . . ."

Elva looked at her strangely.

"Oh, I'll admit it's not like any other wood," Mrs. Curran said. "Wild as folk think of it, they haven't yet come close to its peculiarity. Very wild and very queer it is and it might hurt you badly. But the wildness and hurt were never in the trees. No more than it's death in the grave."

But at the mention of death all Elva could think of were the damp steps down to the cobwebby darkness under the house. She had never been all the way to the back, but she knew what was kept there.

Mrs. Curran saw the old terror in the child's face.

"What need do any of you have of demons," she asked almost harshly, "when you have yourselves?"

In the distance they both could hear voices. Like the grumble of an approaching storm, the deep voices of the furious barons shook the charged air, the sound suggesting darkness and torment, the terrible consequences of anger. Caught up in sympathetic vibration, the little lid of a pot rattled noisily on its shelf.

The old woman's heart softened.

"Come," she whispered, now kindly. "While there is still a little time, lay your head in my lap."

"Leopards!" Gwenbors cried, waving his arms and spilling the wine.

Young Hob's eyes had grown wide.

"Lions," Gwenbors continued. "Any kind of dreadful monster."

"Godless men," the priest chimed in, as though giving a sermon. He looked challengingly at the Duke. "Hell's hounds," he shouted. "Devils!"

Through the long leaded windows the Duke was watching the Weald. For many minutes, while the men argued, he had observed the trees. He had seen the spurt of flame rising suddenly above the topmost limbs and had almost cried out himself when, as mysteriously as it had begun, the red patch inexplicably vanished. Not for an instant had he considered the brollachan.

With a show of reluctance, he turned toward the barons. Careless of their opinion, he drew another measure of wine. "Your business," he said, "is to tell me what you know. What you have seen with your own eyes."

Hob merely stared at him. "Your Grace . . ." he began.

Potent-Matthers, who had plans of his own and had run out of patience, got to his feet.

"It's a little piece of land I'm looking for," he said bluntly. "It would be less trouble if you and I could agree on it. But when you've been dropped on your head, I'll have it anyway." The hounds he had brought in with him slunk away at his heels. His hobnailed boots clomped on the planking; doors banged behind him. The priest looked smugly into the solemn faces of the men remaining.

"You see how they feel," he said, his words full of somber authority.

Bermoothes crossed himself.

The Duke's face turned the color of the wine. He banged his cup on the table. "The truth!" the Duke shouted angrily. "I'll tell you the truth. The truth is that nobody knows. And the reason nobody knows is that no one goes there."

"But no one can go there," Ben Taynton said quietly.

"Ah!" the Duke cried. "Now we come to it."

"Come to nothing," said the priest. "This is no fit subject for Christian men."

The Duke's upper lip twisted. "Where is it written?" he demanded.

"It is an unholy wood," said the priest.

"Name the sin."

"We are enjoined, Your Grace, to avoid evil. For no other cause the Weald must be shunned."

The Duke looked down the line of the table. "What is the purpose," he asked, "of shunning what cannot be had?"

Ben Taynton nodded. "It is true, Father. No one can go there. Walk under the trees and you find yourself coming out. Ride in, and the horse becomes skittish. In the end it won't move, won't turn and has to be led out backward."

"And there's no other side," Bermoothes muttered. Filled with uncertainty for having spoken, he crammed his beard into his mouth. "At least," he said tentatively, "no reasonable man knows what is beyond it."

The Duke placed his palms on the knees of his trousers. "The only question," he said, "is why we have as little idea as we have. Is the Weald two miles deep or two hundred? I cannot tell you. Nor can Gwenbors. Nor could his father.

Like our priest, they never dared ask. In such circumstances
the one thing . . ."

"Your wife . . . ," the priest reminded him, "is dead."

"What would you have me do?" the Duke shouted.

"Stay home," said the priest.

The Duke leaned his heavy shoulders into the chair,
pushing it gently into the wall. He hung there, on two
chair legs, listening to the jingle of bridles as the barons'
deep-chested horses rode from the yard. He hadn't been
certain what he expected. All the same, he had expected
more than he got.

He sometimes wondered why it was that men not lacking in physical courage were so often brought to a standstill
by spiritual uncertainty. No one was more incomprehensible to him than Ben Taynton. He had lain in wait with
the man on the river road. Together, waving their pistols,
they had stepped out of ambush into the path of not less
than a half-dozen horsemen who had made a habit of
helping themselves to the purses of travelers. Perhaps his
teeth had chattered a little, but his hand and his voice held.
And twice with Jack Bermoothes—mild Jack, encased in
gaiters and heavy brown flannel—he had made the harsh
trek into the fields north of Ware and both times raised
a boar and killed them too, the last with the blunt end
of an ash-plant instead of rifles. They were good men and
brave. Of that he had no question. But when it came
to the Weald, intelligence and honor abandoned them.
They made excuses and gave themselves over to childish
imaginings.

"You are fools," the Duke said unhappily, thinking back
on the men who had left him. Then, believing himself
alone, he smiled faintly. "Or I am."

But in the quiet he heard the unmistakable draw of her breath.

"You are all fools," the old woman said.

The Duke did not move. "Did you speak as cruelly to each of your husbands?" he asked.

"Only to those I cared for."

Mrs. Curran sank down next to him. Side by side in the silence, they watched the chairs where the men had been. The yard before them was empty. To the southeast, over the Weald, there was a small ragged cloud. It rose high above the trees. The Duke was reminded of the plume of flame he had seen, which had vanished.

"Of course, the barons are right," he acknowledged. "I don't know what will happen. Though they are wrong as well. All they can think of is the lies of their fathers. But all I know is what you have promised—and every bit of that seems unlikely."

"That a woman . . . ?" She paused.

"That a particular woman," he said emphatically. "That my dear wife could, after sixteen winters . . ."

Mrs. Curran put an arm around his neck. "I've come to tell you about Elva."

The Duke looked away.

"Tomorrow I may be dead myself," he rushed on. "That is the simplest possibility. Then she and I both will be only memories." He frowned. In his heart there was a terrible kernel of uncertainty. "But I have tried to think," he said, "what I would do, if going into the wood, I discover only trees. If I go and search and do not find her, I shall be lost beyond hope."

"It's a damn fool time to go courting," said Mrs. Curran.

"The parawing is finished."

"You have never flown it."

"I will fall from the sky if I must."

She watched him, knowing, in part, what must be; knowing as well that whatever she said to him he would not listen.

"Your going," she said, "is an act of sentimentality."

"I have told myself it is an act of daring."

"Which is sin enough," she said, "when it is put in the service of what one wants."

"You told me she was there."

She smiled. "You are not to be inconvenienced by sin?"

"Is she there?" he repeated, ignoring her.

"And if she is here as well, Your Grace?"

The Duke poured out another cup of malmsey. "Under a stone," he said bitterly. "In the ground," he said, staring out of the window toward the Weald. The wood was the one final obstacle. Like death itself, he could not see through it; he could not get to the other side, and no matter what any man or woman said, it remained solidly, imponderably in his way.

"She is not here," he said finally, feeling Mrs. Curran, as solid as another wall beside him.

He felt the pressure of her fingers on his neck. The cook's hands were as strong as a man's. Her face was as ugly as any woman's face he had seen. Twice the age of his wife when she left him, she was an enormous gray-haired old woman, smelling of suet and garlic, the cold pantry smell of greylags and the fat of aged mutton hanging heavily from hooks in the ceiling. Her arm had come down hard on his shoulders and hugged him.

"There is the child," Mrs. Curran said. "There is Elva."

"That is not enough," he told her.

"It is always different," the old woman said. "But it is always the same. You were better than any of my husbands.

Yet there were times, when you had me, that I called out one of their names."

"I wept when I heard it," he said.

"And whose belly was in your thoughts then?" she asked and smiled. "And when you wailed, did you ever imagine whose tears I half remembered or how much sweeter they made your cries?"

Although it was a direct question, the Duke did not answer.

Sometime after she had gone, His Grace fell asleep in the chair. In the vast, complicated wood of his sleep he imagined it was snowing. But, except for the ragged cloud, the sky had been clear when he woke. He looked at the sky, thinking how it would be, soaring high over the yards. He admired most the kale yard—because he had dug it out with his own hands—and several of the lesser outbuildings whose construction he had ordered. The rebuilding of the estate was endless. Year by year stones loosened in their mortar, timbers rotted and fell. "This is my trust," he thought, and wondered, as he often had, whether Harry would be able to care for it. Without thinking, he returned his spectacles to the bridge of his nose.

He did not understand at first why he felt so uneasy.

"Dead is dead," he thought, knowing the argument. "If she is not there, I shall be as I am."

The cloud he had seen had gone higher, had turned bright-edged vermillion against the falling sun. It was a real cloud in a real sky. But in his mind's eye he could see her more clearly. In just a few hours, in a glen, with the ancient trees crowded around her, she would raise her dark head. She would be the same, he decided, for how can the dead change?

It was then that he understood his fear.

She would place her smooth hand on his cheek.

"You have grown old, my husband," a voice whispered inside him, her voice, familiar and unexpected, sharp as the tinker's knife with which he had whittled the frame of the parawing.

Chapter Three

ARTHUR WAS LYING ON HIS BACK AMONG THE PIL-
lows with John at the end of the bed. Harry was standing
in the middle of the room, swearing. He had removed his
shirt and his trousers and had put on a clean dressing-gown.
Still, he did not feel any better.

"You must have left the door open," he complained
when he had run out of curses. He kept looking at the
soot on the chairs and the carpet and the puddles in front
of the hearth. "Elva saw us," he decided, "and then she
rushed in."

"The door was shut," John remembered more accurately.

"Not that it matters," said Arthur without lifting his
head. He didn't much care for his sister. In truth, he
tolerated his brothers only when they were useful. Of
course, Harry was nearly always useful because he could
be made to do anything. Hating to be laughed at and
never knowing whether he was measuring up, Harry was
defenseless against Arthur's prodding. John, on the other
hand, was prone to attacks of conscience. He brooded and

29

stared into fires, and whenever Arthur proposed one of his schemes, his lips quivered. "No," he would say. "Never!" But he was too old to run back to Mrs. Curran, and in the end, against his will and ever alert to the possibility of failure, he usually went along.

"If only you hadn't . . ." Harry persisted.

Arthur sat up on the bed.

"What does it matter," he exclaimed, "whether the door was open or shut? Elva, certainly, doesn't matter. She's fine. You both saw it. Nothing at all wrong with her."

Harry stared at his brother, waiting for Arthur to explain what to think.

"But have you ever seen such a thing?" Arthur cried excitedly. He was spellbound, enraptured. His head filled with plans, he stretched his arms and swung his long legs down from the bed.

"But I s-smelled her . . . her f-flesh," John stammered. "And her hair . . ."

"Y-yes," Arthur mimicked him. "Y-yes." He was grinning. "We all s-smelled it."

Harry was standing in front of him, moodily scratching his chin. It was a large, stolid chin, chivalrous and square, arguably his best feature, and he rubbed it, instead of his forehead, whenever he was uncertain.

"How do you think she managed to . . . ?" he began.

Arthur laughed in his face.

Arthur's own face, at that moment, was glowing red in the afternoon sunlight. It was a cruel face, but cruel-ty is a matter of course among brothers. Harry was not surprised by it.

"I don't suppose," Harry said bleakly, "that you can tell us how it was done."

"*How* is a mystery."

"But you have a theory?"

"None at all. What is clear is that we must continue the experiment."

"I don't care what part is the front part," said Harry.

"Nor do I really," Arthur admitted. "What is interesting is that a walking hedge could do it."

"W-we could ask M-mrs. Curran," said John.

"Do what?" asked Harry, because he had not, even then, understood that it was not Elva herself but the brollachan that had performed the miracle of saving her.

Arthur ignored him. "We could try to shoot her with arrows," he suggested. "Or . . ." He stared out of the window. "We could bring her up to Da's tower and then throw her off."

"I will not," said John.

"Not actually," Arthur went on enthusiastically. "But, if we seemed to and the brollachan watched?" He paused, thinking. "There must be a limit, of course. Something that a hedge wouldn't or, perhaps, could not do, to protect her. We would need to proceed carefully."

"I think we should ask Da," John said.

Arthur turned on him. "If he hears anything," he cried angrily, "anything at all, we're sure to get whipped."

"I did not m-mean her any harm," John said.

"I'll not mind being whipped," Harry said unexpectedly.

For the first time in a very long while he faced Arthur squarely. "It's God's truth, we deserve it." He pulled on his chin. He was not as clever as Arthur or as moral as John, but he was his father's heir, and as far as he was able, he meant to live up to it.

"Tonight at least," he said bravely, "I shall take whatever I must from him."

It was not until then that either of his brothers remembered that in the morning their father meant to strap a device of wood and feathers to his shoulders and, from the Aviary tower, leap into the air.

The nights in December came suddenly, like a winter storm pushing its head down a chimney, snuffing out the evening fire in a single violent puff. On the hills there was a stirring of ashes, and the light was gone. But inside, the candles blazed on sideboards and tables. After the Duke had returned to the Aviary, Mrs. Curran had gone again to the hall. Extra candelabra had been fetched out of storage and the sconces and hanging fixtures polished and refitted with tapers. The kitchen-boys spread tablecloths on the great table and the sideboards. Rushing in all directions, the downstairs maids placed crystal and silver, each piece of which the old cook, issuing admonitions and exhortations, had checked twice for water-spots and tarnish. The dogs, having caught the excitement, had been locked outside. The page, who had disgraced himself by dropping a platter, was banished with them, to be kept out of harm's way, because Mrs. Curran had decided that the dinner, possibly being the Duke's last, was to be a dinner of exemplary splendor.

The table looked as though it had been prepared for a wedding. There were two sour soups and one sweet one; a cold pheasant pie; hot roasted pork loin, and a tile-fish cut into pieces like flowers; two curries, and a salad with apples and walnuts brought up from the cellar. There were four side dishes and six kinds of bread. When the Duke saw what had been done, he asked Mrs.

Curran to sit with him. She acquiesced reluctantly, between courses, although she was too exhausted, she said, to try more than a mouthful. Elva ate silently. Her black hair had been brushed and coiled in braids on the top of her head. The Duke did not notice her or the smudge of soot on John's ear or even the strangeness in Harry's complexion that made it difficult for him to look up from his plate.

But when Mrs. Curran brought out the custard, the Duke turned his sad, solemn gaze on them generally. The maids had withdrawn to the kitchen just in time.

"I will be bringing your mother home," he informed them.

There was the kind of silence made deeper by a chair's creak, the unintended rattling of spoons. Elva found it unbearable.

"I dreamt about you last night," she said quietly. "You had fallen into a tree; your back and your arms were broken and pierced with sharp branches." She paused. Frightened by the naked announcement of her fears, she continued irrelevantly, "It was the first time I dreamt of you. When I dream, it's usually of strangers."

"I bet she dreams of Hob Franklin," said Arthur.

Although she had never dreamed of anyone so unremarkable, Elva blushed.

"I often dream of your mother," the Duke told them.

John looked as though he were about to be sick. His mother was dead and he didn't want to hear of his father's dreams of her.

"W-we almost killed her," he stammered, his eyes sliding dangerously toward his father's. He no longer cared what would happen. He knew only that somehow he must get his father to stop about his mother. "We never m–meant to . . ." he said, "We n-never m-meant. We were only t-trying an experiment. . . ."

Harry's mouth had dropped open. Arthur looked as if he had been shot.

But Elva sat rigid and silent. Even Mrs. Curran, although anxious, held her tongue.

"What happened?" asked the Duke.

Elva's brothers waited for her to condemn them.

"Well?"

"We fought," Elva said stiffly, her face drained. She was watching him, knowing this was likely the last night she would have with him. "We fight," she said, forcing her voice into a show of indifference. "We always fight."

The great log fire was behind them. The table crystal reflected the flames. In each of the goblets there was firelight. If one looked very closely, there were faces, small and distorted, a man's face and a woman's, the faces of four dark-haired children, each unaware of its imprisonment.

"It will be better," the Duke said, "when she is home again."

With an appreciative nod to Mrs. Curran, he stretched his long legs under the table. He looked at the flames.

The dinner was over, but Elva did not want it to end.

"Tell us a story," she said quickly. "Tell us how you rid the river road of highwaymen."

"Or the one," said Arthur, having recovered from his fright, "about Elva trying to watch the mayor's wife being strapped into corsets."

"Tell us," Mrs. Curran said in a low voice, looking straight at Arthur and watching him squirm, "about how you found the brollachan."

"Yes, that one!" cried Elva, not above enjoying her brother's discomfort.

"It's a hard story," observed the Duke. "One I am far from understanding myself."

"You were trying to get into the Weald," said Elva, beginning it for him.

The Duke smiled. "It seems, child, that I have always been trying to get into the wood." He settled again into his chair and, with the slightest movement of his hand, caught the attention of the servingboy. "There is a bottle of malmsey," he suggested, "left over from this afternoon." The boy appeared more perplexed than unwilling. "Ask Castleburry," the Duke ordered. The boy vanished. For a moment the Duke's gaze returned to the table, only to slip away to the windows.

The Weald stretched around his life as it encompassed his lands. Its presence, changing as the year changed, held him in a kind of mesmerized infatuation.

"I was seven," he said, "when I first tried to enter the trees. My father's herders had lost a ewe which the dogs were unable to discover. They came back whimpering and intractable. 'She's gone to the Weald,' old Alf told my father, making it clear that the ewe was lost beyond reclaiming. But, although I knew what he meant, it seemed to me foolish. When I had finished in the barn, I went myself down the long pasture and across the walls, out to the very last field at the wood's edge."

"And you saw him," Elva said.

"Yes."

"Not the brollachan," said John. "That was later."

The Duke smiled. "Yes."

"But a boy," said Harry, "the very like of yourself."

"The exact image," John said, "only . . ."

"Altered," Harry said tentatively. "Somehow changed . . ."

"Inverted," said Elva, who, obsessed with the story, remembered each word. "With his hair parted wrong and left-handed. Like someone seen in a mirror."

"Yes."

"Carrying the ewe," John said.

"And when you brought the ewe home to your father," Elva continued, hurrying the story on and foreshortening it, "and when he asked who had found her . . ."

"I answered . . ."

" 'Myself'!" Elva, Harry and John cried out in unison.

The Duke gave a roar of a laugh. They were his children, and it pleased him to have his words remembered by them.

"A prefigurement," he said. "And a mystery. Of course, I didn't understand then about the brollachan, hadn't met it. But whatever happens, you know, is implicit, don't you think, at the start?"

Because he distrusted everything about the story, Arthur snorted. His mind needed order.

"Grandda lost a ewe," he said, starting over. "And you found it."

The Duke smiled at the phrase. "Myself," he admitted.

The brollachan came through the door, bearing the remaining bottle of malmsey. Offended by its odd, scrabbling gait, Arthur grimaced.

"How could there be another, the exact like of you?" he asked.

The Duke poured out a glass for Mrs. Curran and himself and, because he was the oldest, an equal measure for Harry.

"How can that be?" the Duke repeated. He was looking straight at the brollachan, not at Arthur.

The brollachan tilted its head as though formulating an answer, but remained silent.

"Your exact self," Arthur continued uncharitably. "Your exact self . . . but backward."

"Yes." The Duke brought the glass to his lips, smiling and accepting the glass all at once. "Yes, for all I know. But I never saw him again, although I went back fairly often. Some afternoons I would go to the end of the field and sit on the wall waiting for him. Or, after nightfall, I would crawl out of my bed and come down to sit here by the windows. I would watch the clouds race and the moon floating up through the branches, as if it, too, had come from the Weald. Usually I fell asleep. Before morning, your Grandda would find me and carry me up to my bed."

He stopped.

"Your Grandda smelled of owls," he said. "Did anyone ever tell you that? Smelled of owls because he kept them. That is why, you know, we call the tower room the Aviary."

"You were telling us how you found the brollachan," Mrs. Curran reminded him.

The Duke chuckled. "Not found. I was myself found by it. I had gone to the edge and got myself lost. Just the edge, mind you, not far in because no one has ever done that. Less than a quarter mile probably. Still, I didn't know where I was and I couldn't get out. Because of the thickness of the branches, I could not see the sun. I had been going in circles, coming back to the same place. There was a stream and a rock, and I thought, because I had seen it before, that I must have dreamt of it. But I hadn't, and so I was puzzled, for I felt I had some knowledge I couldn't explain. I sat on the rock and threw stones at the stream. The stones were black, and the water, touched by evening, was becoming dark. Every stone sank. Then it came to me. '*He* knows this place,' I thought, 'and, because he is myself, I know it as well.' "

The Duke regarded them carefully.

"Children, I suppose, are always thinking. But it was the first thought I ever remember as a thought, and it had an extraordinary effect on me.

" 'I have made a discovery,' I called to the Weald.

"The wood failed to answer. The black water ran. The crows were settling into the trees. I could hear them calling loudly and unpleasantly among themselves. Nevertheless, by the time I could see the moon's first crescent, except for an occasional cough, they were quiet. You must remember I was only a boy. Staring into the night, I imagined terrors. I recalled fragments of the tales I had heard from the housemen, wild old songs and dark ballads, the usual nonsense. But it was men and not demons I thought of, but men drowned or beheaded or burned, dead men in their fury slithering on blistered stomachs, lumbering on stumps, to reach me. When I heard the crack of a twig, I jumped out of my skin.

" 'Who's there?' I shouted."

The Duke glanced at the brollachan, which had stationed itself behind Elva.

"It was smaller then," he said. "Not more than my own height." He waited. "It has grown since, as I have grown. It has grown old."

Mrs. Curran shook her head sadly. "There are years ahead of you, Your Grace," she said.

His hand reached out suddenly, clutching hers. All at once they realized he was crying. The movement of his chest was soundless; it was terrible. The children had never imagined that their father had fears of his own.

The brollachan stirred.

"It would have been better had we never been found," said a voice. It was not an extraordinary deep voice, but it whirred and it rattled, like the voice of something that hadn't spoken in a very long time.

Chapter Four

"IT WAS ARTHUR," JOHN WHISPERED, "I AM c-certain." Not wanting to be seen by his brothers, he had crept into Elva's room slyly, bringing what was left of the malmsey. In the confusion after the brollachan had seemed to speak, it had been an easy matter to filch the half-empty bottle from under the eyes of the houseman. But he had managed only a single cup, which he turned out of his pocket and placed in front of his sister as though it were an offering.

Elva sat in her nightdress before the mirror, intent on something that could not be found in the glass. Her mouth twitched. Her smooth brow had wrinkled. She was still furiously cross and, therefore, determined not to look at him.

"The voice was not at all like his," she complained, tossing her head in a superior way.

"Oh, but he's c-clever," said John, who had already given some thought to the matter. "And Castleburry's a h-hedge. I mean, it isn't as if you see anything moving when it speaks. There is just sound. Anyone c-could, if he w-wanted—" If he had doubts of his own, he ignored them. "B-believe me," he said, "it was Arthur."

"Why?"

"H-how should I know w-why he does anything?"

With a gesture of impatience, Elva pulled her robe over her shoulders. "Why should I believe *you?*" she corrected him.

With his red face and unruly red hair, John most resembled their father. But unlike him John hated a row, and this Elva had always found disappointing. A man, she believed, should make a little noise, not a great noise and not continually, of course, but enough so that it was clear he was thinking. On the other hand, John was the only one of her brothers who had come, and although, timid as he was, he must have hated doing so, he had stolen the malmsey.

"Why can't it have been Castleburry itself?" she asked.

John took the cork from the bottle. "For one thing," he said, "the brollachan never would have admitted that it was wrong to be found. Not with Da so hopelessly pleased to have f-found it." He poured, being careful not to spill a drop on the bedclothes. "It was Arthur," he said, "b-because it had to be."

As she raised the cup it seemed to Elva that so mundane an explanation was hateful. She had never been in love with simple truth and would have much preferred it if the brollachan had spoken, whatever it meant; even if, when she had thought everything through, it meant things she did not want.

"I don't believe you," she said. "But if it was, it was a very cruel thing."

"It was c-crueler," John said, "if it was the brollachan." Her eyes flashed. "You are all cruel!"

To her surprise he looked quickly away. Whatever his failings, her youngest brother, she realized, still cared for her. "John . . ." she began softly, faintly embarrassed.

He peered through the bedroom window into the darkness and blinked. "*She* was never cruel," he said obliquely, finding the thought inside him.

"Only Harry and Arthur remember," she answered carefully.

He stood motionless, leaning on the casement. "And s-she was beautiful," he said.

"You don't remember."

"I can see her."

"You were a baby," she said. "We were both babies."

His stare was fixed.

"Even Da forgot," she said.

"He did n-not!" he said with indignation.

But she knew. "Ask Mrs. Curran."

Her brother did not turn, but she could see his eyes reflected in the window glass. She rose from the chair and stood behind him. "She *was* beautiful," she said. "But even Da forgot. I know because Mrs. Curran told me. He made her go with him down into the vault. Because, brave as he is, he was frightened and had to have someone with him when he moved the stone."

She stopped.

In the silence which followed they both heard the creak of the stairs and Harry's loud whisper and Arthur trying to quiet him. In an instant Elva had gone to the door. Peering out, she saw her two older brothers skulking off down the hall. Arthur was holding up Harry, who, having gotten into something more potent than malmsey, was unsteady. By all appearances, Arthur was in no better condition. They were headed, she realized, toward the tower.

"Can't they leave him alone!" she cried.

It was his time to be superior.

"L-let them be," he said hoarsely.

"No, I won't!"

By the time he had pulled himself up and managed to follow, Elva had already turned the corner and gone. Grumbling to himself, John plodded after.

There was only a single smoking lamp, and beyond the first corner the hall was in darkness. John advanced slowly, drawing his fingers along the dry, papered wall. His heart told him to mind his own business. "I do not like this," he said to himself, feeling a queer apprehension of things unknown, things better left as they were.

There was no sound ahead of him.

"No, I do not like this at all," he thought with a shudder.

The tower stairs turned like a corkscrew. In the darkness there were more steps than he remembered. His legs ached and his heart fluttered, and when at last he came upon his brothers and sister, it seemed almost by chance. They were huddled together on the landing, pressed silently before the half-opened door, all the differences among them forgotten.

"Hush," Elva whispered, although he had not made a sound.

The Aviary was filled with lamplight and candles, which threw shadows, like the wings of owls, on the ceiling. Inside, their father was making final adjustments to the parawing. Mrs. Curran lay in his bed. In spite of the cold, she had undone her apron and pulled open her dress. Her large, distended breasts quivered like a pair of big jellies.

"Whatever happens," they heard her say, "it's time you understood life."

The Duke was arranging the feathers.

"The fact is," he said, preoccupied, "life let me down."

"Because there is death?"

He shook his head. "No. I expect it myself, at the end, when I have finished. All I ever desired was to be given a sporting chance."

"That's an ingenious thought."

He had made up his mind and didn't wish to be bothered by a display of her sympathy.

"Once," he said. "Just once, although you will think me ungracious and impotent."

"I know how you loved her," she said. "You will remember I had several husbands myself."

"And had you a favorite?"

"Listen," she said. "I will tell you a secret."

The Duke smiled. He had fought with the barons and, except for the final work on the parawing, did not mind contending with her. With little before him but an empty bed, there was at least a half pleasure, whoever was bested, in wrestling with a woman nearly as stubborn as himself.

"In small measures," he said with authority, "as many times as you like. But only once grandly."

The cook disagreed. "However wrong-headed," she said, "we love over and over. And normally for much the same reason. Even if it is no more than a turn of a smile or the rustle of a length of dark hair, there is something, and we are helpless before it."

The children listened as hard as they could but it seemed to them that their father was arrogant and that Mrs. Curran was rambling. Or, it may have been, listening equally to their father protest and the immense, half-naked old woman speaking of love, they were merely too frightened to comprehend.

★   ★   ★

When the Duke woke in the morning the place beside him was no longer warm. His hand traveled over the jumble of blankets. To be honest, he was not certain why he had welcomed her. The skin of her back had been rough as dry leather, the roll of fat beneath it paludal and free-floating, unattached to the bone.

The Duke raised himself on his elbows.

He was a large man, but the woman was a mountain. And the mountain had heaved, clouting him. From her first touch, his shoulders hunched, his thin legs straightening, he had fallen. Wide hands had pushed at him. Before he thought, the vague white expanse had opened and swept him in.

It was preposterous, of course. And yet, settling his feet on the cold Aviary floor, the Duke felt strangely alive. The night which would have passed fitfully had flown. His dreams, which lately had been of death, had been filled instead with images of white fields and white roads running over them and the sound of the wind. Toward morning he had dreamed of the high barley meadow. His young wife beside him, they had stopped for a moment to look down at the house. It was beginning to snow again. He had drawn her dark head to his shoulder.

The Duke smiled reminiscently.

He shaved with the water left in the pitcher and ignored the cut he made on his chin. He was much more concerned with the state of the parawing and had checked each rib twice and combed out the feathers.

He did not go down. He had said his good-byes in the evening. He squatted and looked up at the under-rigging. When he was satisfied, he went to the window and, with a heave, raised the bottom sash. Climbing through, he brought out one wing, then the other. Going back to the Aviary one last time, he took a knife and a compass, stuffed a length of replacement cord into the pocket of his greatcoat and in less than a minute was standing alone in the middle of the snow-mired roof.

It was early. The sky, which had changed little from his dream, was somber and cheerless and pressed on the wood, obscuring it. It was not the sort of morning he had hoped for, but he buckled the harness. In his mind he was reviewing the stages of flight. He mustn't leap. He must reach, as ravens did, both wings thrust forward, clasping the air, driving it rapidly under him. He locked his knees and straightened his legs. The wind came over the roof peak. A single leaf, blown from under the eaves, circled irresolutely in front of him.

In the house below nearly everyone was asleep. Mrs. Curran, remembering one of her husbands, rolled over in her bed. The kitchen-boy, who was not actually awake, stoked the first fire out of habit and sat dreaming by the grate.

Because it did not sleep, the brollachan had left the butler's pantry while it was not yet light and had gone to the well house to have a clearer view of the roof. With a tremor of anticipation, it noted the thickness of the clouds and the direction of the wind. It paused momentarily by the stable. The cold that had finally awakened Elva under her blankets was to it a matter of indifference. The snow-laden breeze moved in its boughs without complaint.

Confused by the grayness, an owl hooted among the barns.

Elva, believing there was plenty of time, was brushing her hair by the window when she caught sight of the great complexity of legs and feathers rising away from the house. It was only the brollachan that saw the first clumsy step from the roof and, at the last possible moment, the recovery.

Without moving, it studied the frantic, heavy, desperate beat of the wings. It stood quietly waiting. And it continued to wait, ice and snow crusting its rustling branches, keeping watch on the wood, one day to the next.

Chapter Five

Unable to control his speed or direction, the very best the Duke could do was keep himself from tumbling. Tentacles of air coiled around his legs; masses of air, without warning, tipped the edges of his wings. The Duke clamped his eyes shut. For a moment of panic he was no longer a man. Neither, perhaps, was he anything particularly conscious, merely gibbous and free falling, as agile on the cold morning breeze as a plummeting stone.

He swung up his arms.

If in the tower he had had a plan, in the middle of the air he had quite forgotten it. The horizon was on his left; to his right there was literally nothing. Yet he was surely looking the wrong way, so the absence of the ground was scarcely reassuring. Whether he saw it or not, he knew that directly under him there was a contrivance of ropes and pikestaffs for Mrs. Curran's laundry and, beside it, the massive stone spouts of the drains. He did not have to imagine what would become of him if he struck either one.

Aided by desperation, the Duke gave two terrified kicks

48

with his wings. Because he felt no difference, with a great deal more strength than he had ever been capable of, he pulled them down.

The effect was slow. The consequences were wobbly and imperfect; and yet, although it was still not flight, somehow the world below shifted. The sky rolled.

He reached out.

Where he could not see, there was a shelf of air. (Even in his distress he was becoming aware of the sky's palpable topography.) There were invisible ridges and diaphanous mountains. If only for an instant, escarpments rose unpredictably, achieving a moment's solidity and then, as suddenly and still invisibly, vanished. He dragged himself to the left and, by catching the rising edge of a column of air, regained a kind of equilibrium. But the wind, which must have been blocked by the tower, as soon as he had moved beyond it, swooped around from behind, tossing him up like a child on a swing.

His heart pounded.

Yet there was nothing to be done. He was looking straight out into the sky. The wildness of the clouds made him giddy. It was an alien land, distorted and driven by wind. Its coldness burned his skin; it reddened his eyes like a ferret's. Feeling a rawness in the pit of his stomach, the Duke dug his fingers into the sky. He twisted his shoulders.

When he had straightened and was able to look down again, he was crossing a wide, open meadow. Below him a pair of his fieldmen ploughed through the drifts, driving the hounds before breakfast. He watched them stop and look up in amazement. The smallest, a red-faced boy, clambering to the top of a wall, waved his arms in daft imitation, and then, because the wind had snapped the

Duke past him, either out of perversity or simple disappointment, stuck out his tongue.

And then he too was gone!

Only the wind filled his ears.

It was not like his dreams. There was no sense of wonder. His own arms pumping valiantly, the Duke rowed against the dreadful force of the wind. It little mattered; the field was displaced by a barn, by a muddied paddock and then by the snow-burdened fields again. Suddenly the treacherous chimney stacks of his laborers' cottages rushed toward him. Fumbling, the Duke scraped his legs on a chimney pot, recovered and scraped them again. But at the very last instant, and not a moment too quickly, he gave a powerful kick.

And the town fell behind.

The Duke no longer looked back. He was soaring over the lych-gate, over the cemetery avenue that led past the caretaker's hut and away from the cottages, until no other habitation was near. The faint jigsaw of hedgerows and cattle-tracks slipped gradually into the distance. To the east a low, gray bank of cloud was building, its long shadow advancing before it, darkening the contours of the meadows. With a grunt, he bore down on his wings.

Already there was a pain in his chest. Because of his weariness, his body shook uncontrollably. To keep up his strength, he thought of his wife smiling quietly under the trees, waiting.

He had not meant to think of her, not in the cold nor while he struggled. Yet he found himself remembering how she had looked asleep in their bed, her round arms draped outside the white coverlet. Now, like a lover, the Duke leaned forward in impatience; his breath came more sharply.

The trees came up all at once.

From the air they were more menacing than they had ever appeared from the ground. He had worked himself toward them by tacking to the end of the field, back to a gate and then out again. All the while he was climbing. But the old trees rose like a wall, like a city of walls, like a mountain. And no matter the height, looking over the earth, nothing was clear.

Only occasionally there were knots of white evergreen. For the rest, the huge, ghostly trees melted, becoming indistinguishable from the towers of thick swirling vapor. To the north the cloud cut off the view of the horizon. To the east there seemed only a relentless tangle, corpse-white and shadowed, its only brightness the occasional shimmer of ice.

In spite of the sky's immense cold, he sweated like a galley-slave. Hot tears scorched his cheeks. The heat of exhaustion seared his lungs. Yet sharper than the physical pain, a sense of forlornness had come over him. "One more hill," he thought desperately. But all he saw was the mist. Twice he had almost fallen. Saving himself by inches, he pulled himself over the uneven crowns of the trees, aware only that each frantic thrust of his arms somehow preserved him. Now, haltingly, the blurred shapes of the wood passed ever nearer. Toward the end he imagined the ragged shafts of their branches entering the soft parts of his belly, driven into him by an army of small men in snow-colored cassocks, each with the priest's face.

"She is dead!" the cold priests were crying, reawakening him to the world of pain.

He was not at all certain when he opened his eyes again. When he did, the same brooding trees rose out ahead of him, as impenetrable now as they had been from the beginning.

The wind tore his face. But as he twisted his head, for an instant, out of the tail of his eye he thought he saw two tiny figures in the act of vanishing. Then, just as suddenly, melting into the wrack of trees behind him, they were gone.

The stubborn line of his jaw hardened. With extraordinary labor, the Eighth Duke of West Redding dragged up his wings.

"I've no intention of staying here longer," the young woman said, hugging herself with her thin, bare arms. She had begun to cough again. Her gown, designed to show more of her than was decent, gave no warmth. Her slippers, which had been made for the dance floor, had already frozen.

Ignoring her, Avle squinted up through the branches. Having no cause to conceal her ugliness, she had pottered down the icy lane from the cottage in a pair of thick cattle boots. Her hands were wrapped in mittens and had been thrust into her pockets. Her sharp eyes fixed on the sky, she gave a sudden deliberate sniff, inhaling the smell of the wood. "On the contrary," she predicted, "it will be an exceptional morning."

"I am sure to catch my death in it."

"You are certain to catch nothing at all," Avle warned, "unless you stay where he can see you."

The young woman dropped her chin. Left with no other protest, she began to cough once more.

Avle watched her.

Except for her character, which was abominable, she had to admit that the transformation, of which she was the sole cause and architect, had been nothing short of remarkable. The girl's face was so pale that it seemed to conceal a layer of ivory beneath the skin. Her teeth had been straightened with wires, her eyes brightened with belladonna. Her hair, now black and lustrous, was the result of dyes and a tribute to long empty evenings with a brush and comb.

Avle smiled to herself. It was not a task she would have gladly repeated, but, in the end, the artless, squalling child had grown into a young woman who, so long as she held her tongue, might take her place in any of the grand country houses in Redding.

"You remember the steps of the quadrille?" Avle asked, just to be certain.

"My feet are cold."

"Answer me."

The young woman pouted as much as she dared. "I shall do wonderfully."

"Good."

"As long as my partner is an old woman in cow boots."

Avle grinned. "Soon, love," she clucked, "you shall dance with the best of all men."

The young woman considered what she had been told about men, about their heavy legs and big shoulders, the bristly hair on their faces. "And if I do not like him?" she asked.

"I shall send you back to the tinkerwoman from whom I stole you."

"I don't remember her."

"She was small and mean-tempered and she cheated at cards. Her husband was a hunchback."

"I bet you're lying."

Removing a hand from her pocket, Avle brushed the frost from the young woman's hair. "Your mother," she whispered, "was a renowned courtesan and your father a priest's seventh son. As for myself, I'm a duchess."

"Why do you always lie to me?"

"You haven't the heart for the truth."

"I've a heart," the young woman complained, "like anyone."

Without a word, Avle rubbed the young woman's shoulders. To bring up their color, she pinched the tops of her breasts. "Come away from the tree," she said finally, "where he can see you."

"But what if he hates me?" the young woman asked.

"He has only to look at you," Avle said. "And you, Elva, need only keep your mouth shut."

But she couldn't. From the beginning Elva had been filled with complaints; she complained about the tedium of her life and the monotony of Avle's lessons. Night after night alone in her cot she mumbled. In the glen, watching the clouds drift toward the mountain, she talked to herself.

It was the silence that goaded her. Except for the wind that came up just before evening, the wood was unnaturally silent. It was an odd wood. Even in the summer no flies buzzed and the larks rarely sang. Inside the cottage it was much the same. On the long dreary afternoons Avle worked on her sewing, her figure bent, her hooded eyes brooding. Staring into death, Elva always thought, or, the gray pupils hard as pebbles, watching nothing at all. Avle's hair was cut to her shoulders and left plain. It was impossible to tell whether she had ever been pretty. Except when she spoke of the man, the stillness of her face was overpowering.

"Why should he come here?" Elva demanded.

"Be still," Avle whispered, "and look at the sky."

Elva glared back at her defiantly.

So it happened that only a crow perched on the topmost branch of an elm, its feathers puffed against the cold, was watching the heavens when the man fell from it.

It was dark when the Duke woke. The evening was quiet. Fighting a numbness already well advanced in his fingers, he began untangling himself from the parawing, snapping the main brace and sawing with excruciating slowness a branch with his knife. He could see almost nothing; but a branch, he knew very well, was pressed into the small of his back. As he worked, he tried to fix his thoughts on the knife, ignoring the leg that was dangling.

Although he was mostly alive, everything that mattered had come to nothing. He had seen something almost certainly, just at the end, but what was a matter of conjecture. He did not deceive himself. He had been feverish and perhaps dreaming and there had been an intolerable ache in his chest.

Somehow it had been his own children (especially his odd, dark-haired daughter) of whom he had been thinking when, racing just above the tree-tops, his arms flapping wildly, he had attempted to cut the sharp inside of a turn.

He worked now in silence, with the seemingly impervious sense of detachment that came with the cold and the dark. After a very long time he heard the limb crack, followed by a great clattering. Like an avalanche, shawls of wet snow and timber came cascading after him.

Later he sat on the ground amid the wreckage of branches, ruffled and nursing his wounds.

Of the great fall, when he tried to recall it, he remembered nothing at all.

He had never meant to sleep again, surely not in the cold and not with the chance that the wind might sharpen. He huddled at the base of the tree, hiding a dreamer's smile when he felt a small hand slip warmly beneath his waist.

"Why did you leave me?" he whispered.

But when her fingers caught hold of him rudely, alone in the dark, he laughed aloud gratefully.

Avle bolted the door.

"Not yet," she scolded.

Elva stared restlessly at the hardened dirt of the floor.

"But he saw us," she pleaded.

At least, she had seen him. Amid the branches and the whirlwind of feathers, Elva had glimpsed, if only for an instant, half an arm and the wonderful jutting bravery of a jaw.

"Suppose he dies," she said. "Do men die?"

Avle said nothing. With a queer urgency, she rearranged chairs. She stood by the fire and peered needlessly into the kettle. After some minutes, Elva asked her again.

By now the day had gone; in the west the light was seeping away. Avle's back stiffened a little as she watched its going. "The morning will be soon enough," she said.

"I could find him."

"No."

Elva slipped her arms out of the sleeves of her gown. Across the room there was a mirror in which she could watch first her shoulders and then the little brown patch of one of her nipples. Her eyes shifting, she turned to examine her back. "Wasn't he supposed to see me?" she asked. "Wasn't that the point of everything."

"Never you mind."

The lamp was put out.

Avle sat down at her table. Slowly, taking a breath, she unwrapped the rag from her head. With only the fire's uneven light, it nearly seemed that the graying strands were black again.

"What will he say to me?" Elva asked from her cot.

Avle was silent.

"Will you tell me one thing?"

"I will tell you a story."

"No."

"Once," the old woman went on, ignoring the child as she always did, "there was a duke whose wife died, leaving him alone in the world. But because he would not accept her death, he went into the Weald seeking her. There it happened, in spite of his courage, that he became lost, and believing he would die himself, he soon gave himself up to despair. But a woman who had a cottage there found him wandering.

" 'My good woman,' the Duke asked, 'will you show me the way from the wood?' "

"Why is it always the same story?" the young woman interrupted.

"It is the one I know."

Elva turned her head toward the wall, but the old woman went on with the telling.

One by one, the lingering coals darkened. Elva slept. Awake in the darkness, Avle dug in the ashes. Removing a lump of charcoal, she began to blacken Elva's slippers, hiding the water stains. She worked carefully, relieved by the stillness. The silence made her linger, thinking, listening to the gentle scraping of the hedge branches which grew outside her door. Beyond the hedge there were fir trees and rowans, leaning over the cottage and sheltering it. At fifty yards the cottage seemed little more than a tangled grove. Living there, Avle thought, was like living within a second mystery, a secret at the heart of the Great Wood, private and puzzling and known only to herself and the young woman.

On his own the Duke would not find them. Here the snow was deeper, the trees higher, the very air so cold that it hurt. He would sink into drifts; roots, hidden in his path, would trip him and send him sprawling.

Avle thought of his anguish. But above everything she sat listening to the whisper of the wind in the chimney. The night was long, but it did not seem endless, because what she had waited for was near.

In the years before, it had been hard to wait, difficult to linger while the child grew and was transformed. Such a mean child, and an embarrassment, deprived of the benefits inborn in the gentry, too fat at first, endlessly prattling and almost blonde.

"I am going out," Avle said in the morning when Elva lifted her refurbished head. She was aware of the young woman's troubled gray eyes turning toward her. Avle drew on her boots.

"Do not build up the fire," she ordered, "or he will find us himself. And when I am gone, go into the lane and sweep away my footprints."

While the morning sun drifted higher, Avle climbed down the snow-streaked face of the rock and out onto the floor of the Weald. She moved slowly, breaking her way through the undergrowth. In the night it had snowed again and the trees were covered well into their branches. She picked her steps carefully over the strange, uneven ground. She knew the wood, but after the snow, everything seemed vague and alien, as if, without quite knowing why, she too had become a stranger.

It was some time before she found the first footprints.

Further on she discovered the place where they crossed. Thereafter, certain that her husband was walking in circles, she hid herself in a thicket and waited.

For a long time it seemed there was no one in the wood but herself. She crouched down, listening to the familiar breath of the wind and the scuffling of rabbits. "He will make a much bigger noise," she thought, knowing that she must keep very still and not betray herself. She was waiting for a marvel. She had waited sixteen years. But although she had hardened herself against the moment, she forgot everything when she saw him crashing through the hedge.

"You are frozen," she whispered.

The Duke believed it was the voice of the wood speaking.

"I have been a day and night here," he said.

His face was broader than she remembered, paler and grayer and gone to flesh. His eyes, hidden by a pair of twisted wire-spectacles, were clotted with ice. But he was himself, not a trick of her memory.

"You will die in this place," she said, pitying him.

"Never."

"You only delay it."

He stared angrily at the trees. The wind, passing overhead, scooped snow from the branches and sent it hissing around him. "I will live to tell this," he promised.

"If I help you."

His eyes traveled again over the thicket and saw nothing. And yet there was a quality in the voice. "I had a wife," he said, his own cracked voice filled with longing.

The snow under his feet was unsettled, an eerie snow that might shift or, like a bog, swallow him. Nonetheless, he tried to walk again.

She watched him fall.

"I will show you the way out," she said. "But there is a condition."

The Duke sat on the ground and did not answer.

"I have a daughter," she continued. "Her hair is as black as a raven's, her skin as fair as the pale winter sun. If you will make her your Duchess, I will show you the way from the wood."

The Duke's jaw set. The thicket filled his eyes. The wood was immense; it was immeasurable. Surely, in such a place anything was possible. He knew that to be true, for had he not, long ago, found, or been found by, the brollachan? There was a power here, he thought, joined to the wood or perhaps even the wood itself. There was wildness and strangeness and hurt. But, although the wood spoke with a woman's voice, it was no one, he was certain. At least nothing human.

"It is an odd sort of bargain," he said.

"You are the greater oddity. Since this wood was," she said, "you are the first man to come into it."

"Still, it lacks courtesy."

"If you do not agree," she told him quietly, "the cold will have you. Then, at least, I shall have your corpse to lug home for my daughter to stare at. Even dead you may please her, for she has never looked at a man."

He made himself stand. He was certain he was dreaming. Although momentarily weakened, he was powerful. As far back as he remembered, whatever he wanted he did. It was only death that had crossed him. But he had found his way around it. He had gone where no man had, into the place where she must be. A voice that was only a voice could not destroy that. It could only be that he was delirious. He began to laugh, a warm deep laugh, freeing himself from illusion.

"Why do you laugh?"

The Duke put a frozen finger to his lips. "Shhh," he sighed. "You are nothing."

It was as though he had finished the bottle of malmsey and a bottle of whiskey as well. He could feel their fire rising inside him, a great fire, and he was basking at its heart. He did not need to move. Elva was near. She would come to him.

"My love," he cried. In his joy he shouted to the wood. "My darling!"

Her head dipped, assenting. There would be no test. This was proof enough. She did not need to show him the girl. Because he had rejected the bargain, her heart leapt. Gladly she pushed her way through the thicket. With a sudden reawakening of vanity, Avle brushed the snow from her head-cloth.

As she came through the branches, he saw only that she was a woman, plain and middle-aged, wearing a rag on her head. He did not comprehend why she smiled at him.

"You must tell me your name," he said.

Chapter Six

THE DUKE WATCHED THE OLD WOMAN PLUNGE INTO the trees, first her head, buried in a rag, followed by her trailing coat and then all the rest of a tattered skirt, not gathered into the tops of her cattle boots, scraping the snow-crusted branches, skirting a ditch and then, without so much as a look back, angrily disappearing along the side of the hill.

The Duke wiped the ice from his moustache. Staring at the empty tracks, he swore again: the oath antiquated, theologically suspect and one he had used all his life. Certainly he hadn't expected such a reaction; he hadn't expected much of anything at all. He had been thinking of Elva.

"Let her go, then!" he thought.

Since she had come out of nowhere, she could very well go back to it.

Having no intention of following, the Duke set out himself in the opposite direction, blundering his way through the briars and the thick, splintered wood. Branches snapped;

snow creaked infuriatingly under his boots, *neek-neaking,
neek-neaking* unceasingly. For all that, the sound was a relief
after the voice of the woman.

Take the daughter, indeed! It was like one of the fool
tales the old men were fond of recalling, stories in which
the sons of the well-born were warned against falling in
love with kitchen maids or the daughters of strangers,
women in any event who, once married, changed directly
into ravens or flew off as swans (and escaped with the silver
besides!). Marry the child of the hag of the wood! The
muscles of the Duke's neck tightened.

It was just as well he was done with her.

He would see for himself what there was to be found.
The dead, after all, were simply dead, not Gwenbors' mon-
sters. Preyed on by loneliness, like the living, they would
not keep to themselves. If he searched, it was more than
likely he would end up on a wide avenue lined with
houses or a village built round a green. At the very least he
supposed there would be public inns or meeting halls, some
place held in common where the women could gossip and
the men, after hunting, settle in by the fire. (Of the exact
nature of its accommodations, he remained uncertain.) But
there, in whatever that place turned out to be, among so
many gone out of their lives in gray old age, surely someone
would have heard of a woman dark-haired and young.

He crossed to the other side of the ridge. Below him a
small stony river spilled between outcroppings and boul-
ders and then, in the disorienting manner of the Weald,
meandered away into shadows. Among the few streaks of
poor sunlight, he could see little footprints out on the
ice.

"God's balls!" he cried again, turning his back on what
could only be the same woman, for he was certain there

would be plenty of others. "No," he thought. "Never." But a great misshapen hedge grew up on his left. Its overgrown branches leaned over him like a wall and stretched, as far as he could tell, from one dreary hill to the next. The Duke jabbed at it manfully, but the hedge was sharp with burdocks and knotted with brambles, and it had been clear from the start he would never be able to pull himself through.

Yet the way he had come was no easier. He might have considered this complication, but he had thought only of Elva. Yet, damn her, Ada Curran had promised. And he had felt . . .

Unable to check the force of his feelings, the Duke held his breath. The memory of his wife, his life with her for over twenty years, rushed over him like a physical spasm.

He would not go back. Without her he could never take up his old life again. He had closed the door on that empty life. He had closed it himself, deliberately and forever.

Unable to settle his thoughts, the Duke tried instead to concentrate on the stones hidden deep in the drifts. But his feet would not connect to his head and, when he began to descend the slope, his mind was already wandering. The morning air had grown colder, the sky grayer and unclear. While it no longer fell from the air, snow switched from branches pelted his shoulders; an icy dust tumbled in front of his eyes. He could not decide where to put his hand for support or how to secure one boot before moving the other. He looked to the left and the right, an expression of acute distaste passing over his features. But in the end, the best he could manage was to follow the hill downward.

He did not remember how he had turned around. Even when he reached the river, the Duke took no notice.

The ice, swept clear by the wind, shone in dull patches. He did not raise his head. He was too numb with grief and never felt the shudder where, thinned by a change in the current, the milky glass under him opened a window on the weed-covered rock beneath.

Walking stiffly, he was the better part across when what had seemed no more than another half-sunken stone turned, keeping watch on him.

Yet, before he thought, the Duke thrust his hand into the river. Beneath its coat and kerchief the stone only stared at him.

He leaned out over the water.

"Reach out!" he cried. But although the body was slight, its coat was sodden and heavy; the Duke fished about uselessly, prodding beneath the slippery wool until his frozen fingers realized, if he did not, that the woman was definitely a woman, not stone.

"Take hold!" he shouted, groping and pulling with all his might. The woman did not bother to struggle. But with one last surprised grunt, he managed to drag her up on the ice.

The woman remained perfectly still. Her face was blue but her teeth did not chatter, and she might have easily become a stone again when, in a most unrocklike way, she poked an elbow into his chest.

"As you might well imagine," she said, shaking herself from her reverie, "left to myself without hope, without a man's warm arm under my back in the evening, I have grown desperate for talk."

Because he was bewildered, he did not seem to catch the words.

"You've had second thoughts," she suggested.

"What on earth?"

She pressed her elbow deeper into his ribs. "You are thinking," she added resentfully, "what it will be like to have a much younger woman in your arms."

The Duke scowled, anger forcing his brain to work again.

"What I think," he said sternly, "and what I feel are no concern of yours."

Her unhappy eyes fixed on him without listening. "The child is young," she continued. "And, at least as they used to judge such things, she is pretty. She can dance the saraband and the quadrille. I have seen to that, although she was a poor student and it meant a great deal of trouble."

The Duke removed the elbow that once again had dug into him.

The woman's neck was like a twig; her head like a small, peeled skull; even then, in spite of her ugliness, the Duke was not without gallantry.

"Can you stand?" he asked.

But the woman would not be hurried. "You must listen to me," she kept on.

"I am lost."

"And I know the one way from the wood."

The Duke shook his head. "I have given my answer."

"More's the shame then."

"Where am I?"

"Where do you wish to be?"

He grunted his disapproval. He might have turned away in disgust, and yet he had never before spoken to the dead. It was like talking to the dying and filled him with the same sort of helplessness and embarrassment.

"If," he started uncomfortably, watching the lines that rose oddly at the corners of her mouth and wondering. "If, apart from that, there is something . . ."

"Will you take her?" she asked.

He fell silent.

He needed to get in some place warm and build a fire. But she was already talking again. Trying to rid himself of the sight of her, he ran a hand over his face.

Nevertheless, although he had pulled away from her, something had touched him. Without a kick or a wiggle and above water, he had swum into a net.

"If," he began once more, tentatively.

"I thank you from the bottom of my heart, Your Grace," she said, interrupting him in a voice whose bitterness he could not measure, half heard and then vanishing.

Even when he heard her strangled cry, given up to his own thoughts, he did not at first look up. When he did, there was only a roiling pool. The woman had sunk beyond sight.

"Twice gone is forever," he thought, relieved to be free of her and yet, strangely, not in the least bit happier to be left to himself.

He made his way to higher ground, into the rocks above the river. Water had gotten into his boots and, because it had already frozen, walking was painful. The snow itself was a kind of river, softly inhibiting his limbs. He pawed and scrabbled against it, refusing to let his legs falter. When he made the ridge, the wind came straight at him. Now each step forward came more reluctantly. It was as if an incomprehensible maze had opened before him, and although he had stepped into it voluntarily, believing as he always had that he could master anything, he found he could not even begin to understand what he needed to know. He hugged his chest. He blew on his hands. But the cold, the water and the wind, he was beginning to suspect, were the least of the hazards.

He pushed himself on and, because of his uncertainty, felt the cold and the wind all the more. The flank of the ridge rose higher above him. Clenching his fingers in his pockets, he forced himself on. Finally he came into the winter shade of an oak, standing alone on the boundary between an unexpected clearing and the rest of the wood, its immense leafless branches reaching up hopelessly.

The woman hung directly in front of him. Her spindly legs dangled. Her thin neck was broken, her features preoccupied, as if death itself were too small a matter to keep her undivided attention.

"Good day to you, Your Grace," she said to him.

"Good day yourself," the Duke said, "although little benefit it seems you take from it."

"What can the dead take? Everything that was mine has slipped through my fingers."

In annoyance the Duke dragged himself back.

"Why are you limping?" she asked.

"I have lost several of my toes."

The little skull rolled sadly on its neck. "It must grieve you," she said.

"My grief is my own."

"Then you would have done better to have stayed where you were. For among the dead there is grief enough."

The Duke's long face darkened. "I do not know your troubles. Still," he paused, as if half regretting his harshness, "I will grieve a little if my words do you injury."

But in fact he had had quite enough. "I have been delayed too long already," he said.

She looked down from the tree. "Is it so small a thing then that troubles you?"

"I'll be saying good day to you," said the Duke.

The dead woman sighed. "I had a husband once," she went on, not quite meeting his eyes. "But when I died, he turned his back on me. It may be so with husbands generally. When the road's full of stones or the wind blows too much from the north, they all give in shamelessly and head for home."

"Why do you not let me be?" the Duke asked.

"Because it is plain, Your Grace," she replied quietly, "that you are in need of a woman."

This time it was he who left her, climbing higher among the rocks and closing his ears against the cries that came shrilly after him. He told himself there was no use in cutting her down. She was strong enough to have climbed from the river, to have lifted herself into the tree; and he doubted that she would soon tire of showing him versions of her death. The great mistake was speaking with her in the first place. His best weapon, he decided, was silence. Nevertheless, he went quickly, each footstep echoing under the branches. The wind had died, and the air, weighted with the odor of decomposing flesh, had become still as the air in a crypt.

He climbed with his eyes on the ground, taking care not to look up, lest she be hanging there ahead of him. There were no paths. For many minutes he tried to keep to the ridge only to find his way blocked by walls of ice. Above the ice there was a shoulder of stone and above the stone a canopy of darkness threaded with branches and thatched with brown leaves. He could no longer go forward. Unable to tell the direction, he turned. But the snow had made nests in his sleeves; it had crept into his boots and his trouser legs. He paused for a moment, irresolute, feeling like the boy who, long before, had first found himself lost and afraid in the wood.

For a long time the wind had been quiet. Immobilized, it had slipped below a whisper, then beyond hearing. He trudged on in a cocoon of gray twilight, listening like a man who has dropped a pebble into a well and waits for a sound. But there was nothing. The wood was so empty that in the moment something at last caught his ear, a whimper so distant and thin it might have been no more than the wind returning, he believed he must have imagined it.

He had given up walking and stood, simply holding himself upright, when a gray hand from the snow gripped his ankle.

"Did you not hear?" the dead woman asked.

She was lying behind him, her tattered skirt lifted, her wide pregnant belly lolling into a drift. Already there was a yellowish liquid splattered on the snow.

She dug her nails into him.

"Did you not listen?" she cried.

The Duke had never been shy of birth. But what he saw he was certain was an illusion. Yet, when she lifted her haunches, he saw the sweat standing out on her forehead. Out of compassion he slipped his rough hand along the blade of her shoulder.

At his touch she broke down altogether and wept.

"Did you mean to let it end here?" she asked.

"Madam," he whispered, "I have seen you drowned and hanged."

Even then, feeling the uneven warmth of her flesh, he found himself thinking of Elva. Even now the memory of the childbed still hammered him.

"There was a woman," he began, unable to help himself.

All at once she thrust herself forward. Suddenly all the skin of her belly was moving.

"What am I to do with the child?" he heard himself say.

Instead of answering she made a dry noise as a second convulsion passed over her. When the convulsions came again, his raw fingers felt the soft skull butting into them. Helplessly, he lifted the infant. For a moment, he held her before him.

It was another moment before he realized that, although his hands appeared bloody, he held nothing but air.

A brittle coldness, sharp as tears, had fallen against his cheek.

Then another.

A few large flakes came blowing over the wood. Drifting high up among the firs and rowans, they avoided the ground. Looking north through the sudden whiteness, the Duke saw the outline of a sagging roof. The crooked path that led up to the door of the cottage was buried in a drift.

The woman was standing against the bars of the gate, staring back at him. She was thin as a rail and small, even in her thick coat and cattle boots, and well beyond the age of bearing. He had not seen how she had left him. Now as he watched, she did not move but waited for him to come along the path, her features cold and disdainful, as unforgiving as the gray winter evening with the sudden snow flying.

Chapter Seven

THE DEAD WOMAN LIFTED THE LATCH.

Not knowing where he was, the Duke pulled himself in behind her. After the apparition and the snow, his senses were muddled, and although he had heard the sharp yelp, he could detect only a thin length of pinkness leaping away from the cot.

But to Avle one darkness was much the same as another, and she swore.

Elva tugged the gown hurriedly to cover her nakedness.

"You were scarcely gone," she cried miserably. "There was barely a moment . . ." She reached for her dancing slippers.

"There'll be no need of them," Avle said curtly.

The Duke dragged a hand over his face, disrupting his spectacles. There was a crack in one lens, and yet he saw clearly enough the curve of one breast just as the gown slipped down over it. Half in a panic, the young woman pushed back the great tangled weight of her hair. Its crow-black strands were neither braided nor coiled and, although wild as a heap of unwashed wool, reached to her waist. The Duke stared, dumbfounded.

"Your Grace," she said with open amazement, noticing how he looked at her.

"See to the fire," Avle ordered.

"I will make tea," said Elva, who, in all her life, had never made anything unless threatened.

Yet she stayed where she was.

He was ugly, of course, his lips cracked, his skin peeling. When he blundered into the room, he had knocked over the oil lamp and broke it. But neither the cold nor his hurt could hide the size of him. It would take two of her, Elva thought, standing side by side, to make as little as half of him. His bigness was mysterious; it was frightening. Steeling herself against disaster, she reached out to touch him.

"Have a chair," she whispered. "*Please* have a chair," she added, remembering for once what the old woman had taught her.

Nevertheless, pulling him as roughly as she dared, she maneuvered him into Avle's.

Just by sitting in the corner he filled it. It was like inviting a bear into the cottage, only there were no bears in the wood. Not any longer, although once, long ago, there had been a bear in the camp by the river. It was one of the few memories that drifted into her mind from the life before Avle had stolen her.

Now, like a bear himself, the Duke shook his head. He turned his face, unshaven and plated with ice, following her as she bent over the fire, blowing an uncertain life into the embers. The cold had been driven into him like nails. His knees were encased in ice; his chest was a glacier. When he shivered, snow fell from his hair. None of that mattered.

"What is your name?" he asked, unbelieving.

Avle heard the longing in his voice, and her heart filled with anger.

"She's intractable," she said, "and will not go to the well without threat. Or wash unless I beat her."

The Duke only stared.

"And she lies," Avle said, aware that he was not listening.

"And is proud," the dead woman added, "and unfeeling."

The Duke continued to stare.

"Tell me your name," he repeated.

"Give me your coat," Avle said. "And your boots and your stockings. Come, Your Grace. It is a bare kitchen, yet in the Weald it will soon be dark again. On such a night a man might do worse than warm his feet by my hearth."

She had gone to stand by the window. She had pulled a leather patch from the glass. In the dying, snow-darkened light she was older. Her outline was swollen in some places. It was sunken in others, but her general impression was meager; even in the last of the daylight, a shadow. The Duke's eyes lingered on her briefly, uncomprehendingly.

"Have you begun lately to hate yourself, Your Grace?" she inquired.

"I'm afraid I don't . . . ," he began vaguely. He had been watching the young woman daintily twisting one foot around the leg of the table.

"What sort of man have you become?" the dead woman asked spitefully.

She had turned, but he had not bothered to look.

The sight of the young woman's ankle under the edge of her dressing gown, looking very pink and shiny, seemed to fill him with merriment.

The old woman coughed, but he was not paying attention.

He barely heard her move toward the door. Although at first she was merely a dozen yards from the cottage, he never heard the sound she was making. Elva pretended it was the sound of an owl screaming. But, in fact, the Duke heard nothing at all, nothing that is, but the dark-haired child whispering, perhaps a shade too quickly, a name she had never, until that very moment, been certain was her own.

"She's a witch more than likely," Elva continued, filled with triumph to be left so long alone with him.

For the first time in her life, airing the full weight of her many grievances, she grinned. "A witch or a troll woman."

She sat near the fire, although it meant her own chair, so that she could add another log when it was needed.

"She's as plain as a witch," she went on, "and as ugly as a turnip. And she makes me stay in during the day, instead of coming and going. And at night I must sleep on the cot and listen to her snoring."

When she stood to return a pot to its shelf her hip brushed against him as though by accident.

She had made him a sort of dinner, as well as her untested abilities permitted, and, because he was famished, its simplicity had pleased him. It had been hours since Avle had gone, but this was the first time either had spoken of her. Mostly he had asked about herself, where she had come from and how she had lived. Overwhelmed by the intensity of his interest, she had answered more or less honestly. Never before had anyone wondered about her. Although she did not mention the bear, she told him about the camp by the river.

"I could hear the water," she explained. "There were bushes close to the wagon that smelled of cat. Avle says they were tinkers and even uglier than she is, with hunchbacks and flat noses or else noses that stretched down to their chins. They did odd jobs and told fortunes and, when they could, they took things. Sometimes they stole children. So it was no crime when Avle took me. It is likely I was stolen myself from one of the great houses they passed in their travels. Certainly, the people of the towns hated us and often chased us away. When we camped, it was right up at the edge of the wood, where the men who lived all their lives in houses were too frightened to come. There is not much I remember: the river and the wagons, the trees at our backs. To the east a fair valley spread in front of me, a patchwork of green fields, smallholdings, stone villages and farms."

For a moment she leaned back blissfully in her chair.

"There is nothing, Avle says," she continued, "to match the beauty and peace of the great valley of Redding."

"To the east?" he said, making it a question. "The valley of Redding?"

She nodded inattentively.

The breath came abruptly through his teeth.

She smiled, not knowing the marvel he had heard.

"Where the sun rises," she said matter-of-factly.

He let her go on.

When he had thawed, he did not look so peculiar. His eyes sharpened. They were blue eyes and they looked at her boldly. She did not remember the life in the big house and did not understand the pieces of glass bound with wire he wore in the middle of his face, but shortly they had been returned to his pocket. He sat now leaning on one side with his head propped in his hand, watching her. Away from the hearth the rest of the cottage was dark. The snow had begun again and then turned to sleet. She could hear it battering the window.

"She has been teaching me," she said confidentially, "how to dance and to curtsy. Both seem so foolish: hopping up and down while she hums; bending one's knee with one foot swept forward. Do people really do such things?"

"Yes."

"I was certain they were spells of some kind."

He thought of his guest hall, the chairs moved to the corners, and his wife in her finery, sweeping across the polished floor to meet him. "A dancing woman," he said, "is not without witchery."

She had seen Avle dance, watched the weaving of her legs and the pointing of her elbows. "Why?" she asked.

It was not an easy question, he decided. He said, "There is witchery as well in a handsome young woman sitting by a fire."

That there was witchery was without question. It was half magic that he had flown the parawing; it was magic pure and simple that he had not broken his neck. But Elva, her name actually was Elva, was a miracle. Still, he was not deluded. She was not the Elva he had loved. In a hundred ways she was different. She was thinner and younger; her hair, although as black, was undone, uncombed, the waves of it tangled and, in the cold air, electric, sticking out in all directions. She shared none of his memories. Her eyes, though filled with excitement, lacked recognition. Yet in more ways than could be counted she preserved reflections, intonations, details too insignificant to be classified. Added one by one, the effect was overpowering.

He sat up. Feeling was seeping into his legs again. Warmth was invading his chest and arms. Blood stirred under the roots of his hair. She watched, fascinated.

He smiled, but in coming back to himself the smile faltered and became the smile of a man who has looked inward and discovered that much of what had always pleased him was not worth seeing.

He gazed at the poverty of the cottage.

"I live in a great house," he said, "with summer bedrooms and winter bedrooms, a guest hall and a tower. It was my father's house, the house of his father and the wonder of the province. But lately it has been full of echoes and shadows."

Even in his own mouth, his words seemed remote.

"So you went away," she said eagerly, thinking how grand it would be to leave the place where one must be. "You taught yourself to sail above the trees."

"I dreamed about flying and made a sort of kite, but I taught myself nothing but how to glue feathers. When I jumped from the roof, except that the wind held me, I was a dead man."

"But you're here."

"I was lost. Until your mother . . ."

"My foster mother."

"The woman . . ."

"Avle," she corrected him. "Her name is Avle."

His brain, coming unexpectedly on something he had nearly missed, stopped.

"She promised," he said after a moment, "to show me the way from the wood, if . . . There was a condition. Did you know that?"

Carefully, she lowered her eyes. "It was her plan, Your Grace. It was the reason I was stolen."

"Plan?"

"From the beginning."

"What plan?"

"To draw you here."

"Why?"

The answer was so obvious she never considered lying. "Because she hates being dead."

In the Duke's face there was no understanding.

"I believe," he said, "they all must hate it."

"All?"

He considered what it must have been for her, a living woman, here in this place where the dead came, where they gathered.

"The multitude," he said, recalling the one chance, the single impossible hope Ada Curran had given him. "The numberless dead," he sighed, "gone from the better world into this dark one."

She stared at him oddly. "But she is the only one."

It was as though the words had been roared at him. The blood had come into his face. "Do not play with me!" he cried.

"But I'm not."

But he wouldn't listen and she had to say it all over again: how she had been as far as the river and been stopped by the hedge. How she had climbed the terrible slope of the mountain and looked out on darkness. And there was only the snow, she said, only trees and the cold and the one ugly old woman who had stolen her.

The Duke shut his eyes. Blindly, his hands, needing something, wrapped around her.

She tried to make him look up, but his fingers, clutching her knees, were like iron. When he trembled and cried out, she was afraid she might be torn in half. But she sat erect, waiting.

She was still waiting when late in the evening the old woman came back, shutting the door on the weather and bringing a much fiercer storm inside with her.

Elva moved her hand protectively to the head in her lap.

"Hush," she whispered, "he is finally sleeping."

"What has he done?"

"He has cried like a baby."

Avle's own eyes were red. "Do you know the reason?"

The child grinned to herself. "Because in all the wood," she said gleefully, cradling the head of the man like a great coal warming her legs, "you are the only dead."

Chapter Eight

It was evening. Under the high burning stars, old Gwenbors, although he should have been too frail to stand, was digging kales in the garden. His spade went up and down, starlight and moonlight glinting on the metal. Unaccustomed to labor, the ancient gentleman grunted and snuffled. But he did not spare himself. Working toward the middle of the rows, he threw the large, ripe heads over his shoulder and turned each time to watch them fall. Sometimes the kales were kales; more often they were soft green skulls. One of the skulls, before it smashed on the stones, smiled at him.

"Elva," it murmured; but by then the Duke knew he was dreaming.

Like sparks in the wind, the images drifted away into shadows and were gone. Evening gave way to morning, to evening again. On a dancing floor that was at once his own hall and the barn at Doogan's Crossing, a girl with a hat like a listing frigate held him tightly. When he squeezed her, she bit him on the chin.

Startled, the Duke sat bolt-upright.

Both women looked up from the hearth.

"See, you have wakened him!" complained the old woman.

"I didn't."

"You did."

The Duke groaned. Although his head throbbed, he had kept his eyes open and the sight of a young woman in a ball gown and dancing slippers struck him as so improbable that, for an instant, he considered the possibility he still slept.

Her cheeks flushed, as if she too had just awakened. Her eyes were deep and too large for her face. Her hair, in much the same way, seemed unreal.

"Do not blame me," she whispered. "I have nothing to do with this."

"Or anything else," said the old woman.

The young woman rose from her chair. Coming across to him, she lifted the blanket and crawled in beside him.

"I will tell you your future," she promised.

"She don't know it," the old woman protested.

The girl ran her fingers along the inside of his leg.

"Once there was a great king," she began, stopping appreciatively.

"He is not a king," said the old woman.

"In any event, he is rich, which is nearly as important. With a great house and lands."

"That's not the future."

"I am getting to that."

"No, you can't!" the old woman cried suddenly. "You were never meant to get anything!" She turned accusingly, facing him. "Tell her," she demanded. But since the Duke did not seem disposed to answer, she went on herself.

"Weren't anything at all, only a test!" she cried, "since men are so fickle and their memories short. And I had to be certain."

She had already risen and rushed toward the bed.

But by then Gwenbors had stepped up behind her. It took only the gentlest tap of his spade and her head bounced on the floor and rolled to a stop before the fiddlers, where it lay on its side, staring with an expression of unutterable sadness. Gwenbors came down with his spade again. The head moaned. Hearing the commotion, the wife of the hereditary mayor of Devon pulled herself from the arms of Ben Taynton and cried out in alarm.

"Do not blame me!" she was crying.

The young woman, bending over his cot, jigged up and down. She was not wearing a hat although she was dressed in a ball gown. "Do not blame me," she sighed. "Dreams are strange here. I have nothing to do with them."

Peering into the poor, cramped room, the Duke blinked.

It had seemed at first he was in one place, then another. But now, although the room resembled many of his laborers' cottages, he was certain it was no place he knew. There was one small unwashed table, two chairs and, in the space that was left, a tiny cold hearth with no mantel.

He struggled onto his side, hoping to sleep again. But the young woman laid her freezing hands on his neck.

"I meant to see to the fire," she said earnestly. "But it's no use, for if you use up the wood, you have to go out for more. And the wind blows so frightfully."

As if feeling the wind in fact, she had climbed in beside him and pulled the blanket under her chin.

Pressed against him, her raven hair spilled over his chest. He breathed in the smell of it. The stirring of its tendrils and the rank, sweet odor of her scalp made the blood bound along his veins.

As though to defend himself, the Duke made an effort to think of his children. Trying to recover their faces from the ambiguity of his senses, he lifted his head. But, except for the hearth, he saw only the blurry shapes of the rowans. Beyond the casement, a single ragged branch scratched at the glass, making a sharp crackle like the sound of musketry off in the wood.

He lay still, reminded now of dog-handlers and beaters, and listening to the branch which, more and more, he confused with a *phutt!* and then another, quite loud and close, until the guns seemed right under the window and he felt himself in danger of falling shot.

But when he opened his eyes he found himself watching the pine knots exploding in the grate.

"How long have I been here?" he asked.

The old woman waited in the shadows, brittle and small, like something hung drying from the rafters. She was delicate and shrunken, her features wizened, brown and unpleasant.

"I have made you an offer," she said. "That is the way of it, or so my old gran always said. When you're too shriveled to be wanted, put your trust in a foxy-faced wanton. Give him a bit of youth. Only make certain you throw yourself into the bargain."

He was unable to think what she meant. For a moment he hesitated, waiting for the cottage to be transformed again to a kale yard or dance floor or the barn at Doogan's Crossing. The old woman glared at him.

"Tell her!" she insisted.

The Duke swung his thin, naked legs to the floor.

"How did I get here?" he asked.

"You flew," said the old woman.

In a moment the girl was hovering so close that one of her breasts touched his arm. He could feel the quick draw of her breath under her gown. Her fingers moved, unaccountably, along his back.

"Not that we saw you," she said. "Who has ever seen a man fly?"

"You saw him fall," snapped the old woman.

"You walked," the girl answered.

"In circles," the old woman added. "You dragged yourself about like a cripple and you should have been dead. Only *I* took pity on you."

He looked very hard at her, trying to imagine why she hated him.

"Who are you?" he asked.

"Tell her!" the old woman shouted.

He limped painfully away from her. He was stiff from sleeping, and apart from his leg, he had probably torn a muscle in his back. If he would have looked in a glass, he would have seen that his moustache had become more grizzled. He looked around for his belongings.

"Perhaps," he began. "Of course," he said awkwardly, "I appreciate your hospitality."

With a sudden fierceness the young woman locked both arms around his neck. The Duke took hold of her waist. Although he could feel its smallness and the tightness of her skin beneath her ribs, he had meant to set her aside, but as he lifted her, the pair of her round legs crushed into him.

"Elva!" the old woman hissed.

It was then, like the sudden pulse of a heartbeat, that his memory returned to him. The Duke found himself in a bare room without privacy or shelter, with no one he knew.

"I am going home," he said hoarsely.

He gathered his coat. A few seconds later he had struggled into his boots and was working the latch.

Between the strands of her graying hair the dead woman watched him.

"The shame is mine," she said softly. "I had thought, out of love . . ."

The Duke understood nothing of her words.

"I do not know the custom of this place," he said. "But in the world I left . . ."

Elva's eyes laughed, stopping him.

For when he opened the door, she had felt the wind blow powerfully against her, lifting the hem of her gown as it had when he had taken hold of her waist.

"Your Grace," the child whispered, crying out to the first and only man she had seen.

"Odlaw!" the dead woman called to him.

But the door before them both now was empty.

The memory of his wife overwhelming him with longing, Rudyard Wenceslas who, man and boy, in the world outside the wood had always been called Waldo, walked away from the lane. It was not just his back that was twisted in pain.

The insistence in his trouser leg was foolishness. It was not merely the touch of a woman he wanted, but Elva. But she was gone. Even in his dreams he could no longer hold on to her.

"It is done," he thought. "It is finished."

He would go home. There would be nothing more. He had gone nowhere. Coming back from nowhere, he would take up his life again. He had been the worst of fools to think what was over and done with could be made to start over. In time, he supposed, like his father, grown impatient and slightly baffled, he would stare belligerently at his dinner and wonder whether the servants talked behind his back. Now, without resolution or hope, one day would be the same as all other days, except with each morning and evening infirmity and death would come just a little closer.

But it made no difference. He had been obsessed by the thought that the love that had been robbed from him could be regained. But it would never be. Now whatever he did in the few or the many years that remained to him, whatever he thought or wanted or planned, it would all come to nothing.

It was like being dead.

He stood for a few moments longer, looking across the little patch of the yard. He could see the trees, formidable and endless against the cold sky. As always, it was beginning to snow again.

The river, he imagined, was somewhere to his left. Although he had not even started, he was weary. As he began to walk, an owl, hunting over the hill, sailed within a yard of his head. It dipped low over a broken stand of hazels and then, its wings beating sullenly, rose until it too had gone from his sight.

"If I could fly again," he thought uselessly, out of habit, knowing it made no difference.

"Done," he thought. "Finished."

When he looked back through the snow, he could no longer see the smoke filtering up from the chimney.

He put out his hand. There was a strand of long black hair on his sleeve. "No," he thought. "Never." But he made no move to brush it away. There was no need of that. He had made his decision and trudged on toward what he hoped was the river.

The next ridge was steep and, under the roof of spruce wood and oak, so dark he felt, even as he was climbing, that he might as well have fallen into the pit of a colliery. If there had been a track to follow, whatever had not been blotted out by the snow, in the gloom would have been just as invisible. For the briars, however, he needed no sight at all.

There were briars everywhere, sticking to his coat and his legs and leaving their welts on his neck. Shouldering into them, he realized, too late, he had found his way into the hedge. Now, whichever way he went, he only became more entangled.

Also he was bleeding. Except where the coat padded him, there were cuts, especially his shins, where, because he could feel the spreading stiffness, he knew his own blood was freezing. He understood that he was in danger of dying and was not surprised. The thought, looking ahead at his life, no longer shook him. So great was his despair that if he had been able to find his way back to the cottage, he might have thrown himself before them in supplication. For what did it matter? They might do with him what they liked. Nothing would ever be the same. But for one thing. Even now, he could never bring himself to look again at the dark-haired young woman who was not Elva.

Elva!

He looked for the black hair on his sleeve, but it had blown away.

With all his heart he wished for a bottle of malmsey and for his children gathered around the table, although there had been times, perhaps in these last years too often, when he had never given a thought to them, had forgotten to go down to the hall and ignored the dinner that Ada

Curran, her faithfulness greater than his own, had made for them.

The fires of the hearth smoked in his memory: Ada hovering; Harry, always less than he had expected, confused; John sulking; Arthur announcing ruin; Elva, his own wonderful daughter, dressed, from the moment she had discovered the difference between men and women, unsuitably, her baby fat bulging pleasantly out of the top of her gown.

He wished he could have better explained it to the barons. But it always sounded sentimental whenever he put it into words. It was not just his beloved Elva, although, of course, she was, although she had been everything. Even when he explained it to himself, the words appeared foolish. But the intensity of his feeling was undeniable. From him, from them both, husband and wife, man and woman, life sprang, different and changed, and yet, standing at the back of the hall, watching, and sometimes not paying attention . . .

His foot caught.

Just within the limit of his hearing someone swore.

The Duke was so weary he thought perhaps he had spoken himself. "If I could be free of this," he thought in anguish.

"God's balls!" the voice swore again.

A cold that had nothing to do with the wind crawled through the Duke's flesh.

"Stand forth!" he demanded.

"By Christ, I shall do what I like!"

"You shall do what I tell you."

"I did."

It was almost his son's voice, and the Duke turned into the snow's blankness in wonder.

"Where are you?" he asked.

For a moment the only sound was the wind in the hedge. And yet, when he began to walk again, he heard the equal of his own helpless blundering close beside him. Behind a bend of the hedge he thought he saw a patch of a gray coat vanish. He lowered his head. Bent almost double, he pushed his way through. Only there was no one. He was certain something was playing tricks on him, beckoning him on. Yet it was the sting of a hundred hooked thorns that persuaded him he ought to wait for a moment. Nonetheless, when he stopped, his invisible companion halted as well.

"Why have you come here?" he asked.

The voice, although normally impatient, faltered a little. "I thought there should be one last word between us," it said quietly.

"Why?" the Duke burst out, the pain of his wounds driving away any sense of gallantry.

The voice waited.

"There is always something else," it said finally. "Nothing important, when there were so many years we might have spoken. Only I was not ready when you lived."

The Duke knew before he answered there was some mistake. But the error had opened another chance and he grasped hold of it desperately.

"You may be disappointed," he said.

"Will you not speak to me?"

In spite of everything, a whisper had broken into the Duke's mind. Among the phantoms of his memory he had met a face.

"When I was a lad," he began carefully, the words coming back, "years and years ago."

But now a fire ran through his veins. "My father's man

had lost a ewe," he said. "I had gone out into the Weald to find her."

He did not move. In his heart suddenly he was certain.

"No," the voice answered curtly.

"Surely."

"Not 'years and years.' "

Longing preyed on the Duke's mind. "You know," he said fiercely. "You remember."

"Not myself."

By then, in spite of the thorns, both were running. Even in the cold the Duke felt the sweat on his face.

They came out of the hedge not two yards apart. The other, his snow-streaked face bearing the sudden force of a revelation, pushed the soaking mass of red hair from his forehead.

"It was my father," the youth panted, surprised and then certain. "I thought it only a story."

He was tall and long shouldered, about the age of Harry and not at all like him. Watching him, the Duke had the disquieting sense of being in his own company. "Tell me your name," he said.

Eyes, blue as the Duke's own, burned in the long, restless face. "It would seem, Your Grace, that there is more than one of any of us." He paused. "It is 'Your Grace'?"

"Yes."

The younger man reflected a moment. "I thought. I had planned to meet my father. I had come into the Weald to find him. It is a wood like no other and since his death . . ."

The Duke looked stunned.

"After my mother . . ."

Before he thought, the Duke placed his hand on the youth's shoulder. But although the other shook it away, it was not without gratefulness. The world was simply stranger than the youth imagined. He turned his head.

"You, of course," he said thickly, "were a preoccupation. My father swore that in the valley across the wood there was another. And if . . . You see, he thought, because there was another like him, there might . . ." Something had crept into his voice.

The Duke felt that he was dreaming again. He wanted to speak, yet he dared not in case he should break the spell and the youth vanish. But the lad was near and he could feel the dampness of his breath.

"He told me," the young man went on, "on the morning we carried her corpse beneath the house. He thought he could fly to her. What he did was fall from the roof to the paving stones."

"He had made a device . . ." the Duke managed.

"Out of feathers."

Snow-driven shadows filled the slight spaces and crevices behind the dark trees.

"Why do you blame him?"

This man was not his father, yet the youth's face warmed. He said harshly, "Because I was not ready. Because there never was a chance . . ."

"How long?"

The young man glared at him.

All around them the icy light was fading in the snow. The wind, which had strengthened as they spoke, hissed in the branches. The Duke looked out through the trees and found, whether dwarfed by the winter or perhaps some unkindness in the ground, that the trees were less, their gnarled trunks thinned and set apart, their ingrown branches given space and air. Indeed, what was left of the wood straggled away to an ordinary field, its hop-yards and barley meadows encased in ice. One of its stiles was engulfed in a drift.

The house, although distant against the white hill, he recognized at once, as a man knows his own face in a mirror. Except, like an image in a mirror, the house was turned, the mews and the tower moved to the right of the chimney shafts, the high hall windows and the barns shifted left. His Grace looked back quickly. He found the young man staring.

"You'll be my guest," the young man said. Then, although he had not done so before, because there was wonder in both of their faces, he nearly grinned. "I'd give a hundred pounds," he said, "if the priest were there waiting when you walked into the hall."

"He's a cruel, sour man," the Duke answered without thinking. "My father's man. I never understood why I kept him."

"To argue with."

The Duke couldn't help smiling himself.

"Then you must come!" the young man cried. "Give me an hour and I shall roust him out from among the women and set him down at the table. I shall give word to the kitchen-boy to bring you in directly when you knock on the door."

He stared at His Grace. "You will come?" he asked.

With a sense of relief Rudyard Wenceslas thrust his cold hands toward his coat pockets. Only his hands seemed put on wrong. He did his best to dig his fingers into the slits which had become unnaturally angled. "God's balls!" he whispered.

While he struggled, the youth, assuming the Duke's acquiescence, cleared the rest of the brambles. Plunging ahead, he had already jumped a deep rushy lough close to the wood's edge, and, without looking back, had entered the white field beyond. Shortly, mounting his strawberry roan, he was riding across it.

Under the trees far behind, the Duke fought on alone with his greatcoat.

The difficulty seemed to him both fatuous and inconceivable. It wasn't a problem that could be solved by the application of force or by logic. Unable to dislodge the desperation turning his stomach, he made yet another assault on his pockets.

"A judgment," taunted the woman suddenly beside him, watching him fail.

"Still, I wouldn't blame yourself," said the girl.

"It's fate," the old woman clucked, taking hold of his sleeve. "Don't you think, though," she asked, dragging the coat from his shoulders, "it is thoughtful of us to be near?" Expecting no answer, she lifted the coat and turned it around.

"You were wearing it backward," explained Elva.

The Duke could feel the pressure of her fingers as she helped him once again into it.

"Of course, you can't renege now," Avle said.

But a dullness eddied inside him. It was not until they were refastening the buttons that he looked up and saw the vague, receding line of the hill. Something had shifted. Far off where the sky melted, were the roofs of his mews and his stables, moved round again. Through the wet mists of snow he could just make out the bleary lights of the farm.

"A bargain . . ." Avle was saying.

"Can't we just get on to the house?" complained Elva. Dressed in her ball gown and dancing slippers, she was shivering terribly.

Chapter Nine

WHEN HIS GRACE HAD COME ONTO THE CATTLE
track, his legs were numb. Snow stuck to his mouth and
clung to his nostrils. As he stumbled into the yard (where
the brollachan waited, itself like something belonging to
the night and the storm), more like an ice hill than a man,
he had fallen. Somehow the women had lifted him. Or
else, his head listing over his boots, they rolled him over
and over like a stiff, frozen wheel. Whatever the method,
in the morning the snow between the barns and the well
house appeared so scrambled that it looked as if a score of
huntsmen had chased an equal number of foxes across the
yard, and then back again.

Whether in spite of the method or because of it, the Duke
could not remember how he had come into the house. The
front door was a mystery, the inside hall a bewilderment
which, although he must have passed through it, swallowed
any trace of recognition. No voices had greeted him. As far
as he recalled, no housewomen sniffed excitedly at his heels.
It was as if the end of his journey had happened to a duller,

less critical version of himself, or to someone else entirely. He had merely been grateful when he had been given a chair and, when he sank into it, had let his eyes close.

In fact, it was late. And while in the main rooms and downstairs corridors word of his return rang out like the blissful note of a christening bell, in the wall's thick plaster it had been dampened, and between the heavy flooring it had carried no more than a whisper. The dogboy, let in because of the severity of the weather but unaccustomed to being indoors, cocked his puzzled head, listening. But, as no one came for him, he lay back, finding what warmth he could in the rumps and haunches of his hounds. In the cellar, the steward went on with his reading, waiting for the hour when he too might go to his bed.

It was one of the maids who brought the news up the winding backstairs to Mrs. Curran.

"And there's two women besides," the girl announced breathlessly. Mrs. Curran, who had suffered acutely since the Duke had tumbled off the roof and into a sky filled with gray-shrouded storm, heaved her ankleless legs over the bed. "Is he dangerously ill?" she cried, holding her own balance precariously.

"He's sleeping sound," the girl answered.

"But are there wounds?"

"Only bruises. And cuts like a pincushion. Seems to have been pulled sideways through a blackberry hedge."

"Anything broken?"

"I think not. Apart from the cold, the women seem to have managed . . ."

With half an arm into the shoulder of her robe, Mrs. Curran stopped. "The women . . ."

"Oh, they seem fine too. I shouldn't think . . ."

Mrs. Curran winced. "For godsakes!" she cried, her thoughts suddenly enlarging. "What are they doing?"

"No more than I would do myself in their place, come into the great house for the first time. Just walking about and looking over the furniture."

Mrs. Curran turned. Hearing at last what had been blotted out by the suddenness of the Duke's return, she set off at once toward the stairs, her pounding heart caught in a panic between wonder and dread.

Out of the endless warren of linen rooms and pantries the housewomen filed into the guest hall, but no one except Mrs. Curran touched him. She dried his hair and pulled off his boots. She had taken a blanket from under the settle and wrapped it over his shoulders; but, because he looked so pale, she hadn't dared strip off his greatcoat; it wasn't until much later that anyone noticed that he was wearing it backward.

"It's not the coat," said one of the women who had come with him. Her dry, sour features twisted as she spoke. "It's himself."

She had left on her damp head-cloth. Cowled, dressed in brown, shapeless wadmal, she looked as much like a monk as a woman.

The Duke's children didn't know what to make of her. While they rushed about and sent into the village for the doctor, she pinched their cheeks and peered strangely into their faces. Her own face puckered with shadows, and her hooded eyes squinted, as if she were trying to make out a jigsaw with too many pieces. Yet the trek through the cold had, it seemed, almost no effect on her. Even the other, younger woman, although demanding new logs for the fire and first one goblet then another of hot, spiced wine,

appeared surprisingly undaunted. Soon she was happily trying the chairs and fingering the silver. Arthur had given
her a carriage blanket from a peg in the hall. He seemed
uncharacteristically pleased to have done it and followed
her back to the hearth. Under his appreciative gaze, letting
the warmth and the rosy light bathe them, she raised her
bare legs.

Gradually, the men came and stood quietly in the doorway. His Grace, looking older than they remembered, slept
with his head slumped on his chest.

The shriveled old woman had taken the chair next to
Mrs. Curran.

"He was just about frozen," she was telling the cook,
"and should have been dead. Only my dear child found
him wandering and brought him into our cottage. I'll tell
you this honestly, it was a pleasant sight: a gentle maid
restoring the health of a fine strapping man. A grateful
man, I shouldn't wonder."

Before Mrs. Curran could move away, the old woman had placed a hand confidentially on the cook's gouty
knee.

"It will do a mother's heart good," she said, "to see the
child so bountifully rewarded."

Elva looked up, her big, red eyes startled. Although her
father never felt it, she had been stroking his palm and
rubbing his frost-bitten knuckles. Until that moment, mad
with worry, she had ignored the strangers. There were
always guests of one sort or another. Even in midwinter,
her father's house was seldom empty. There were plenty
of bedrooms and the Duke never minded. The tenants
wandered in at all hours; hunters, lost, waded up to the
porch through the knee-deep snows; neighbors, taking the
long way home after drinking in the village, appeared with

paint-pot noses and knocked on the door. The Duke hadn't the heart to suggest a bolt or a padlock. He had directed Mrs. Curran to keep a supply of ironed nightshirts with the extra bottles of malmsey in the butler's front closet.

Elva gave a hard squeeze to the Duke's fingers.

"What does that mean?" she asked.

"You would be his," said the old woman, as if answering a question of her own. Yet, whatever the answer was, it seemed to leave her more puzzled.

Elva regarded her suspiciously.

"You are to have a new sister," the old woman announced, as if edging another piece of the jigsaw into its place. Yet her wrinkled brow continued to be a mocking imitation of Elva's.

"You are to have a new sister and, if His Grace is a man of his word . . ."—she smiled thinly, her hands trembling ever so slightly—"a new mother."

"You never said such a thing!" protested the young woman at the hearth.

"Merely a detail."

"You never said anything of the sort." All at once the young woman looked very hard at Elva. But perhaps, for all the intensity of her staring, she was not actually looking closely. There were more people in that one room than she had ever seen and, it may be, more than she had ever imagined there might be, however wide the world was.

But in spite of her confusion, her face wore a petulant expression, like a child from whom a promise had been cruelly and unaccountably withheld.

She turned toward the old woman.

"You said I was to be a duchess!" she complained, "and live in a great house. You never said there were children."

"We are not ch-children!" stammered John. "W-we are older than you are." The pain was clear in his face. "You m-must n-never," he cried. "You c-can n-not . . ."

The young woman's eyes darted over the rugs, the rich leather chairs and the banks of glass windows protecting the room from the night, and she felt herself drawn into dimensions of comfort beyond her wildest yearning.

Her fingers squeezed the narrow stem of the goblet.

"I shall do what I like," she said firmly.

The doctor arrived before midnight, just after the priest, woke the Duke briefly and ordered him carried up to his bed.

"B-but his bed's in the t-tower," stammered John.

"And too far," said Arthur.

"And much too cold," agreed Elva, her eyes filled with pity.

"Then it had best be the old bed," said Harry, who was old enough to remember the room where long ago the Duke had slept with their mother. It was now seldom entered, but before anyone could protest Harry, who until then, for all his usefulness, might not have been present, sent the maids running for linen and a boy for wood and another for coals and a warming-pan. While they waited for the room to be prepared, the doctor opened his bag. He removed a collection of little glass vials which, when spread on the table and uncorked, smelled of phosphorus. Elva screwed up her face. The doctor, who was ancient and courtly, gently shook his gray head.

"It takes some bad," he said sympathetically, "to drive off worse."

"Takes tar and rock-salt," said the old woman, her sharp nose suddenly poking over his shoulder. For some time

she had been sitting quietly in her chair, her meager chest
breathing soundlessly as the scurrying of mice behind the
wainscot.

"A smear of one," she said, one eye disappearing as she
gave him a wink, "and a pinch of the other. The same as
for foot 'n mouth."

The doctor, occupied with His Grace, noticed her for the
first time. "I'm sorry," he said, "but I do not believe . . ."

"Few have," the old woman answered. "None, to tell
the truth, these sixteen winters. But for His Grace, of
course, and the child."

He became aware of the pretty, dark-haired young
woman sitting by the hearth, and although through
the forty years of his practice he had learned as much
as a dozen men knew of revelation and wonder, his
jaw fell.

The young woman looked back at him appraisingly.

"Your Grace!" he began. Then, realizing the impossibility, he held his tongue.

"Tar and rock-salt," the old woman repeated, so softly
now that only he heard. "Much the same for you, David
Rendcombe," she whispered, "as it's plain you both suffer
from one malady."

In spite of a stout heart, the doctor's pink face turned
gray.

In the same instant, the Duke cried out in his sleep.
Elva ran to him. Rendcombe, looking over his shoulder,
followed. Soon after, the maids returned and, when the
serving-boys reappeared, the Duke was carried out of the
hall, half of the household trailing behind him, everyone
warning everyone else to be still and therefore making a
great deal of racket. Rendcombe came along at the end,
his thoughts barely able to return to his patient.

There was a fire in the old bedroom, but it was a new fire and the uncompromising cold lingered. A maid had taken a broom to the floor, but the dust soon returned to the shelves and sank again to the mantel. What was left in the air imparted to objects seen through it a dense, unearthly hue, like shapes seen at a distance or in a cold forest shade. Rendcombe objected. Yet, as the sheets were fresh and or because Harry, whose idea this was, had insisted, or simply out of an all-embracing courtesy, Rendcombe saw the Duke safely under the blankets. He administered the contents of the vials, one bitter drop after another, perfunctorily. Then, mumbling a word of encouragement to no one in particular, he left His Grace in the care of his children.

When he came back into the hall, Mrs. Curran had cleared out the kitchen help; the others had gone to their beds. Only the priest waited. His gaze met Rendcombe's blandly.

"He'll live, I suppose," the priest said.

Rendcombe shrugged. "A few decades more than you or I. He's scratched. And he's had a bad chill. No more than that."

"They have plans to warm him," said the priest.

Rendcombe had no need to ask who "they" were. He had watched them, studying the girl at first more closely than the old woman. But it had been the woman, finally, and her whispering in his ear that had buffeted his imagination. More brutally, now that he had thought about it, than even the wind had clouted him as he had ridden into the yard. In order to calm himself, he opened his bag and began checking the vials, with their inscriptions in his own hand in Latin and Greek, to be certain the tops were sealed and that their contents would not go spilling out.

"Did you notice?" he started, although he had not meant to.

Filled with his own thoughts, the priest turned away. "I warned him," he rumbled. "I told him what would come of this."

"Would you mind if I asked you a question?"

The priest did not answer. He had been priest and confessor to the Sixth Duke and the Seventh. He had known the Eighth Duke since his birth and had disliked the boy from the beginning. But he hated the man. "Yes, yes. I know," he replied at last gloomily. "She's the image of the Duchess. But we both can see that she isn't. She is too young for one thing. For another, she's at least an inch too short. For a third—"

"So it would seem," Rendcombe said, deciding to end it there. But the priest took off his skull-cap and, some other business in mind, rubbed the middle of his forehead. "He's *badly* bruised, I imagine," he continued.

"No."

"Well then, perhaps it was luck."

"He flew," said Rendcombe. "So I've been told. His daughter saw him."

"Then she ought to be quiet about it."

Rendcombe snapped his bag shut.

The priest pretended not to notice. "You were going to ask," he began again.

"It's late."

"The storm's not any less." With a sharpened eagerness, the priest held out a glass to him. "You might pity your horse, if not an old man's curiosity."

Reluctantly, knowing the hour and that he would not in any case soon be seeing his bed, Rendcombe pulled out a chair. "We are both getting on," he said presently.

The priest nodded. "We will be a great loss, you and I," he said.

Up close Rendcombe could see the milky white of the priest's irises. "It's not the pretty one," he said quickly, relieved to have spoken, for he wished to tell someone, even, God pity him, such a man as this priest. "I thought it might be for a moment. Like you, I rejected it."

The priest smiled. "Then he failed."

"No."

"And why not?"

"He went somewhere."

"A day's journey to the north or south," said the priest. "A morning to make the rounds of workhouses. Even in these days, I am given to understand, there is no lack of young women of a certain sort." His lips parted cynically. "Perhaps the better part of an hour to come to an understanding. And a day, in this weather, to bring her back."

"The girl, I admit, might have come from anywhere."

"Then you take my point."

"I can't see why His Grace would bother to go through the trouble."

"Because he wishes . . ." A vein began to stand out on the priest's forehead. "Because he has always wished to confound us."

Rendcombe shook his gray head. "The reason," he said, "pure and simple—"

"My dear Rendcombe, *she* is dead."

Rendcombe looked around for his coat. The storm was trying the doors and the windows. In the hearth the fire had shrunk finally to embers. Wearily, Rendcombe pulled himself up. Nonetheless, partway across the floor, he turned and asked suddenly, "Would you mind if I gave you a prescription?"

"I do not see what relief might be gained."

"Take my advice, Father. The malady's pervasive."

"And the cure?"

Rendcombe stopped by the front windows. "By the time I'm home," he thought to himself, watching the snow falling heavily, "I'll be stiff from Dan to Beersheba."

"You were about to prescribe," the priest said.

Rendcombe tilted his head. "Tar and rock-salt."

The priest looked perplexed.

The old doctor smiled. "Oh, I shouldn't worry," he said quietly. "It's the common prescription for foot in mouth."

Without opening his eyes, the Duke realized that he was alone again. A single dim lamp shone from its high bracket, reflecting, although he had not bothered to look, on panels of rose-and-gold lacquer, on windows still blackened with night. He knew where he was, knew intimately the amber-hued hangings and the one rough plaster patch in the ornamental ceiling, knew and recognized at once and could, in his mind, reconstruct every detail, because he remembered the bed.

The headboard was as tall as a man, the mattress eight feet across. Molded to the shape of his back, it had borne the brunt of twenty years of tossing and tumbling. Much of what he was he had learned here, learned more deeply and a great deal more honestly than in any of the lessons he had had from his teachers in St. Berzelius. In this bed he had discarded a young man's willful carelessness and with it the conviction that in all the world there was no other like himself. Accustomed to having his own way, he hadn't realized that in her there could be the same eagerness. When on their first night together she had stretched out her round arm to draw him closer, he had been frankly astonished. Remembering that night, and the continuing amazement of a thousand others, the Duke put out his hand.

"I'm a simpleton," he said, finding the space empty.

"You are merely rash."

The room smelled of damp earth and moldy hedge trimmings. The Duke did not open his eyes. "Merely?" he wondered.

"Go back to sleep."

"I do not wish to dream again."

"You were not."

The Duke allowed himself to imagine the black cloud of her hair wavering in the air just above him.

"There has been a misunderstanding," he confided. "I was angry. Preferring the cold, I walked away from the cottage. I never agreed to the conditions."

"Then you have simply to deny it."

"I am ill!" he cried savagely, clutching the place where she was not. He felt tired and lost. He was immobilized by self-pity. "Who can say how many days I will seem to lie here, unable to say a word?"

"Three."

"As many as that?"

"Yes."

"Then you can appreciate the danger."

"Not off-hand."

The Duke's lips wrinkled in disgust. "That horrible woman," he said, recoiling. "In three days there'll not be a maid or, by Christ, even a kitchen-boy she hasn't told that I've promised to marry the child."

"When were you ever concerned about kitchen-boys?"

"I always meant to be. Anyway, I was speaking hyperbolically."

"To be fair, you are not speaking at all."

"It's true, in any event," perhaps the Duke said.

"Why are you telling us this?"

"You see what no one else sees."

"We see what you see, Your Grace."

What he saw, the snow and the wind nearly forgotten, was the cottage under the trees. The young woman was sitting on the cot. In spite of the cold, her shoulders were uncovered, her white arms, aquiver in the hearthlight, shaking with the novelty and terror of having a man close beside her.

The Duke shifted his disheveled head on the pillow. "I know myself," he said seriously. "Therefore, I'm afraid of irrevocable harm."

"You fear you will marry her?"

"Not entirely."

"Then, you are afraid you will not."

The Duke's nostrils twitched. Seeking a fragrance that eluded him, he poked his nose out of the blanket. "It cannot be just coincidence," he said. "There must be a reason for the things that happen."

"We cannot help you."

The Duke tried to follow the progress of the shadow as it dragged itself slowly past him, and could not. "And why not?" he asked.

"No one can help anyone else."

"Then why have you come?" the Duke asked scornfully.

There was no answer. For a long time the Duke lay without moving. Cold gripped his belly, and he felt a dreadful pinch in his chest and feared that the warmth of life had abandoned him forever. "I will never look on the world again," he thought ominously. But toward morning he opened his eyes once more. With an act of deliberate effort he studied a brilliant star through the frost of the windowpane. The weather had cleared, and the star, brighter in that moment than any other, seemed to him a messenger from another realm. He hauled himself up and, staring over the barns, found himself thinking of the strange, long-shouldered boy.

"Do you think he can see it?" he asked.

Again, there was silence.

"On the other side of the wood," he repeated more sharply, "are they the same stars?"

In the yard a dog barked. Already the sky had grown paler. Entering over the sill, the new light crept across the cold floor, encountering a mass of mired leaves and branches which partially resembled a foot, or several.

"At least you might tell me what you think of her."

"We think," said the brollachan, its stern, sad voice fighting among its conflicting selves for a single thought, "that it is for you, Your Grace . . ."

Out of filial embarrassment, the hedge tried to turn. But while the oldest wished to comfort him, the second attempted to crawl toward the door. The youngest, the delicate bulge of its leaves suddenly incandescent in the sunlight, torn between one and the other, merely trembled.

"God's balls!" the Duke shouted, unaware of any revelation. "Look at me when I speak to you!"

"I am thinking of property," the priest said to Morgan Potent-Matthers, saving his most persuasive argument for last. He smiled emptily at Jack Bermoothes and Ben Taynton and glanced around solicitously at the rest.

"Property, you must agree," he continued, "is imperiled by a confusion in personal relations."

Gwenbors sat at his right hand, the old woman at his left. He had consulted with both as soon as Rendcombe, reluctant but under the circumstance feeling obligated, brought the news to him. Gwenbors had acknowledged the need at once. As far as he was concerned, decency permitted nothing else. The old woman, it must be said, had proposed the solution in the first place. Now, as though unable to contain her enthusiasm, she had risen twice to look out the window. But, although the grooms had been sent quickly, it had taken the better part of four hours before the last of the barons had gathered.

The very last, Potent-Matthers, settled his long legs under the table. Unbuttoning his waistcoat and patting his forehead with a handkerchief, he glared across at the priest with a farmer's practical skepticism. He was a big man, with a broad back and a thick swarthy face. When it came to his neighbors, except for flying devices, he was inclined to keep his thoughts to himself. And yet, he understood property and the chance that its orderly inheritance might be called into question dismayed him. He wished the Duke had been more careful. Nevertheless, he felt any man (and especially a man with six thousand acres) was owed the right of consent about whom it was he was expected to marry.

He examined the cup that one of the boys had poured for him.

"Well, I don't quite know," he said thoughtfully.

"It is merely the announcement of engagement," said the priest. "His Grace may, if he recovers, forswear it."

Potent-Matthers frowned. It did not matter what privately he thought of His Grace. "I'm no lawyer," he said. "Neither, thank heaven, am I a priest. Yet, it does seem—"

Poor Jack Bermoothes, sitting uncomfortably among his companions and terrified by the course of events, snorted nervously. He poked a finger into the air. "If he had made the announcement himself," he said, his voice rising. "Had he spoken so much as a single word on the matter. That is something a man should be held to."

"He spoke to me," the old woman said.

"You will forgive us our uncertainty," said Ben Taynton, not unkindly. "We were not there to hear it."

The priest looked into the faces of each of the barons. "None of us were," he said meaningfully. "Which is exactly its beauty."

"Precisely," Gwenbors added with conviction. "The Duke may, if he wishes, set the record straight. Or he may not. It is his business and in the end he will have to decide it. In the meantime, this young woman's honor is intact."

"And if he dies?" the old woman asked.

The priest peered over his small folded hands. "Rend-combe says he is certain not to," he said, smiling dryly. "But in such an event, your daughter would preserve an unquestioned status. Not as the absolute inheritor, of course. After all, there are children. In the final accounting most everything goes to Harry. But she would have a position."

They were all silent a moment.

"It is good of you," the old woman said, "to be so direct."

Ben Taynton's gaze rested on the Duke's empty chair. "He'll not die," he exclaimed forcefully. "Nothing," he said, "ever stopped him."

Potent-Matthers grinned. "Well, that's just the point, isn't it?"

Ben Taynton said nothing.

"Still, you have to admire him," Potent-Matthers broke out afresh. "A man in his sick bed. And asleep! It's that, damn it all, that beats everything!"

The young woman, certainly, was not herself to be blamed. It was a noble impulse that had driven her to the Duke's chambers. No one had thought to question her about it. A woman's place, clearly, was by the bedside of a stricken man. No one doubted that she had been startled to find herself pulled under the blanket, much too amazed, she had explained afterward, to cry out. And he *was* asleep. As to that, Rendcombe, coming into the bedroom to re-examine the patient (unfortunately, just a moment too late), had been adamant. "A man's natural energies," he maintained, looking straight at the priest, "are encouraged by his dreams."

"And his coordination?" inquired the priest.

But in such matters the doctor's word was preeminent. "What man can help it," Rendcombe had asked, "if a woman has lit a fire inside of him?"

Gwenbors nodded. "He was always a man, God save him, with an eye for the ladies."

"Surely no woman . . ." protested the priest.

"But she looks like the Duchess," said Ben Taynton, who had known the Duke all his life.

And that, for a time, settled everything.

Chapter Ten

ONCE, MRS. CURRAN THOUGHT, AND FELT ASHAMED
for remembering, she had been as thin as a willow stick,
with a fragile complexion and only enough bottom that
young men, passing her on the street, turned on their heels
and followed her along the meager row of the laborers'
cottages and into the shops. Now, because of the immensity
of her thighs and the greater roundness of her stomach, she
waddled as she went along the corridor. Her plump face
was pinched, her gray hair undone and her brow haggard.
Meeting her by the stairs, the little maids, lacking any flesh
of their own, scattered in alarm.

Elva stood against the kitchen wall, waiting. Without a
word to her, Mrs. Curran came in and pulled the skillet
from the hob. Mechanically, she cooked the first breakfast and, when she had finished, cast it into the flame.
Next she set out a saucepan and kettle. Out of the lock-
er came a platter of cold beef and from the cupboard a
box of curry and the hottest mustard pot. Still without a
word, she unraveled a pair of sharp yellow onions from

a knotted string above her head; but as she swung back, her hip struck the table edge smartly. All at once her heavy features slid, her iron resolve crumbled, and the tears, which she had been holding back, welled up in her eyes.

"We will stand against them!" cried Elva. Studying the big grieving face, she reached out and touched the old woman's neck. "Give him a day or two," she said bravely. "He'll soon be himself again."

Mrs. Curran patted her moist eyes with a napkin. "Tell me where they are," she said dismally.

"In the guest hall."

"No doubt yelling for their breakfast."

"And everything else," replied Elva. "Already they've sent the boy down twice."

"What word have you sent back?"

By then the boy was slouching again in the doorway.

"You've no call to serve them," Elva said to him. "No cause and no reason."

The boy, who was only a year younger than Elva, smoothed back his tousled hair and sneered. "I do for them what's master," he said and looked significantly at Mrs. Curran. "As others would if they knew what was good for them."

"Shut your gob," Mrs. Curran said sternly. Coming out from behind the stove, she began to announce the dozen items she needed fetched from the cellar, the wood cut and the kindling slivered and the armfuls of both brought in from the yard. "I'll tell you," she raged, "a thing or two about who is master."

"Just you remember what I said," the boy muttered and, not wanting to be dragged into any of her preparations, scurried off, whistling loudly.

The kitchen was filling with steam. As if exercising her authority over the heated air, Mrs. Curran continued to bluster. Her imagination jumping from one thing to another, she took down the plates and started arranging them noisily. But no pattern seemed to satisfy her, and soon, out of frustration, she abandoned everything in a jumble on the tray. Halfway through slicing the beef, she stopped and rubbed her thumb on the blade of the knife. Then, as if changing her mind, reaching into the cupboard, she began rummaging among the rows of small jars, each cryptically labeled in her strong, ruthless hand.

In the meantime Elva's thoughts had gone off on their own. "Do you think she's handsome?" she wondered.

"What she is," the cook said, "is plain enough."

The range door was open. The kitchen displayed none of its usual tidyness. There were unwashed tureens and pots in the sink and burnt crusts on the floor.

"Do you think she was a virgin?" the girl asked.

Mrs. Curran did not answer. Her mountainous shape bent over the table, obscuring the coffee service just for a moment.

The young woman stood by the hearth, trying to feel through the soles of her slippers the diminishing warmth that was left in the stone. There was a full wood box and plenty of kindling, but she had promised herself that once she had come to the great house she would never again raise even a finger.

"Someone must see to the fire," she said, catching sight of the cook squeezing though the door with the break-fast tray.

"Someone usually does," said Mrs. Curran.

"It must be done now!"

"That will do." the old woman chided, not looking at her but at Mrs. Curran who, her head resting solidly on three bulging chins, looked back darkly. Without dropping her eyes, the cook set the tray on the table and, removing the cups, began pouring.

"Will you have sugar, *Your Grace?*" she asked.

The two women studied one another.

"I do not remember you," said the woman in the chair.

"It has been a great many years. It is likely I still lived in the village."

"You would have hardly escaped my notice," the seated woman said. Aware of the silence, she had lifted her cup. "At the Saturday market or during haying. Or at the spring fair when His Grace was judging of the oxen." She sat for a moment, searching her mind. "Perhaps you won a ribbon?"

"There was a time when I might have made a man look twice."

"A man would have needed to."

"Once," Mrs. Curran began.

"Long ago?"

"Yes."

A pair of shriveled fingers tapped on the rim of the cup. "I have noticed," the more lightly built woman said, "that several important matters are not as they were."

Mrs. Curran adjusted her apron. "Would you have preferred tea?" she asked.

"No, this will be fine."

"I might bring you a loaf of barley bread."

"I assure you," said the other, "you will have to save a place for me among your most ardent admirers."

Mrs. Curran smiled. "Did you ever mean to tell him?" she asked.

For an extraordinary moment the smaller woman seemed to have lost her tongue.

"Yes," she said finally, in a low voice.

"But you haven't."

"I have discovered that like all men, he is blind."

"He is a man in some ways like others."

The old woman shook her head. "He *was* braver and, I always thought, more imaginative. He was . . ."

"And is," said Mrs. Curran with a touch of sadness, "still. Another man would have simply stopped . . . or, in time, gone on. He was young enough. There might have been other wives. Yet . . ."

"I find no comfort in his chastity."

Mrs. Curran smiled again. "He was not chaste."

"What do I care about that now?" said the other old woman. "What do I care about anything?" Raising the cup in both hands, she smelled it, sipped it and then took a great swallow. Her face, which was already withered, did not change.

Mrs. Curran watched her. "Your Grace?" she asked carefully.

"You have," said the other old woman, "a rather specialized knowledge."

"One of my husbands, God rest him, was an apothecary."

"I would have said a veterinarian."

A fine net of moisture glistened on Mrs. Curran's upper lip. "One might have done as well as another. In any event, I had thought it sufficient."

"For what?"

"To have stricken a bullock."

Cutting her off, the other extended her withered hand toward the plump, sweaty hand of the cook.

"In the future," she said, patting Mrs. Curran's thick fingers, "you might do me the courtesy of remembering I am already dead."

The young woman looked critically around the apartment, as if she had dreamt the bed and the bureau and was trying to determine whether either met expectations. It was not at all like the man's bedroom. That had been overpowering and she was glad to have left it. However, it was encouraging to know that she had been able to take everything to its essential conclusion. It was a strange business altogether. Yet, in fact, she had expected something rather stranger and, perhaps, more original. "I have no idea what I'm to do," she complained to the woman as they had waited beyond the door, making certain that there was no one in the corridor. "I know nothing," she had whispered. "Next to nothing."

"Then you must trust him," the old woman had told her. Still, the doctor could not have come at a better moment, releasing her from the leathery arms of the man who, even when he had finished, seemed restless and lonely and who, before he had sufficiently recovered his breath, had reached again for her desperately.

Elva turned once more to the mirror. She was wearing a new white winter gown, borrowed from the closet, which she did not quite fill. Because it was more elegant than any gown she had ever imagined, she did not mind that she had to stuff handkerchiefs into the bodice. Moving her shoulders, she examined her silhouette from one side, then the other.

She was conscious of the high color of her complexion and the exquisite line of her neck. But her hair was a nightmare. Too impatient to wait for the old woman's assistance, Elva took up a brush and, with the first stroke, pulled a snarl of black tangles away from the roots.

"Damn her," she thought aloud, blaming the old woman. Sitting on the edge of her chair, she stared into the mirror, held there by a kind of unresolvable urgency.

Now and then there were footsteps. The maids came and went. At intervals, she could hear them mounting or descending the stairs. She did not get up. The old woman did not come. Elva sat, determined not to pick up the brush again. Eventually, from the end of the corridor, the footsteps returned: a quick, short tread, hurrying.

"Come here this minute!" she called out.

The door latch clicked.

"See to my hair," she said sharply.

The Duke's daughter stared into the glass, watching herself and the other, seated in front of the mirror and gazing into it. She recognized the gown.

"By what right?" she asked from the doorway.

The girl in the mirror pushed the image of the brush aside. "I have an equal right here," she boasted.

"You have nothing."

The girl in the mirror did not bother to turn. She could see the other's face, and its reflected outrage was fascinating; she felt her own heart quickening. "He has asked me," she said proudly, "to share his life with him."

"We are his life!" the Duke's daughter shouted.

She meant herself and her brothers and the memory, however insubstantial, of the mother she had never seen. All their lives were one life. One implacable shell, broad as the house roof, shielded and protected them. It could never be breached, not from the outside and never by a wraith of a girl, with hair like an unruly thistle, wearing a pilfered gown.

"You will take off my dress!" she ordered.

"It is doubtful you would like me better without it."

"I do not plan to like you at all."

"It's not what you plan that matters."

"Still, I will have it."

The girl in the mirror never looked round. "But it's warmth I'll be needing then," she said slyly. "A man's big shoulders to keep mine from shivering."

"You wouldn't."

With a shrug, the girl in the mirror began to rid herself of the gown.

If it had been one of the barons or all of her brothers together, the Duke's daughter might have stood her ground, for she had learned to stand against men. She would have laughed at Gwenbors, screamed at Morgan Potent-Matthers and kicked poor Harry in the shins. But the only women in her experience were housewomen. For once, her nerve failing, she turned.

Meeting her on the stairs, Avle paused and looked after her. Thereafter the old woman took the steps more stiffly. At the top of the landing she lingered.

"You fought," the old woman protested when, finally, she had come through the door.

Elva did not shift her gaze from the glass.

Avle grimaced. Although she could not have said by what, she was puzzled. Moving discontentedly, she went to the window. As if in partial answer, Mrs. Curran appeared in the yard below, breaking a new path to the woodpile. Her movements were strong and, in spite of her ungainliness, tireless and economical, like the gait of a powerful old animal. Avle tilted her head and thought again that it was unlikely that in all the years before she had gone into the wood she had not met her.

"Something is wrong," she began.

But Elva had her own thoughts.

"We must be rid of them," she said.

Avle looked back from the snow and the sunlight. It was not a room with which she was particularly familiar. But then, there were so many rooms, a great many of them guest rooms and even more for the servants. "Which?" she asked.

"As many as I don't like," Elva answered, "but starting with the children."

Avle said nothing.

"Starting with the daughter," Elva continued, her voice even more determined than before.

Avle seemed uncertain.

"And then the three loutish sons."

"No," Avle whispered.

The young woman laughed. "I don't see who will miss them. They are not at all like the father. The oldest only stood in the corner. The youngest—"

"Not three!" cried Avle, horrified, remembering, in spite of her preoccupation with the man, the one trivial after-thought of her womb. "Never three!" she cried terribly. "Only Odlaw!"

Frightened, she turned again toward the window.

In the yard, the storm gone and the snow already stained by the urine of the dogboy and the bright streams of horses, a woman she did not recall but who had nevertheless tried to poison her came lumbering back with an armful of wood. Beyond her were the well house and the stables. Avle stared at the ice-covered walls, at the benches, now abandoned, where in summer the grooms sat cleaning their tack after hunting. Beyond the gate the branches of the enormous old mulberry held itself rigid against the first breath of the morning wind. Everything was the same; the differences scarcely mattered.

"Mother," Elva whispered, becoming alarmed.

The old woman did not answer. In the house below, a man who had never been her husband turned quizzically into the winter sunlight without waking.

Chapter Eleven

ELVA SHOVED HER CHAIR FROM THE TABLE, CRUMPLED her napkin and threw her fork in the general direction of Harry, who, in spite of what he was beginning to convince himself was his dignity, very nearly threw it back.

"I'll not be bullied," she announced loudly, hating everything.

"It's not bullying," said Arthur.

"Harry's not going to order me about," she continued to no one at all.

"But I'm oldest," said Harry.

Arthur, who had taken to wearing his father's watch and his smoking jacket, looked smugly from the top of the table. He smiled, making the blotches that covered his face seem all the more quarrelsome.

"One gets sick of your temper," he said.

"It's you that we're sick of!" cried Elva.

"Harry will decide," Arthur replied smoothly, "whether or not I'm in my place. It falls to him, since for the time being Da . . ."

His Grace, in fact, was in Devon, being measured by his tailor, buying rabbit nets and consulting with his solicitor about some tangle with Morgan Potent-Matthers. Unchastened as ever, he had risen from his bed before the end of the week, spent a quarter of an hour in the stables, visited by turns the fowl houses and toolsheds, eaten his regular breakfast and, without changing his boots, marched into the young woman's bedroom, where he had announced that he intended to make her his wife. It had been a day not unlike another thirty-odd years before when, walking out on his teachers at St. Berzelius, he had built a fire on the rector's lawn, using the pages of Aeschylus and Horace, and then gone off (still in his scholar's gown) on a day-long badger dig with young Rob Franklin. Now as before, those who had been pleased or offended, according to their own lights, felt much the same.

The Duke himself had not been in the least embarrassed to have acted so bluntly. He was not the sort of man to beg permission from his children. Certainly, there wasn't a man or a woman for twenty miles round who didn't know of his grief over the loss of his wife. Nor, to tell the truth, was there a tenant or neighbor in all of the villages and towns who was in the least surprised when word of the marriage came down to them. "There's to be a lady again in the great house," the women said among themselves, openly pleased by the restoration of order. "Let him have what he can get, God bless him," said the husbands, learning that the bride was no more than a girl.

"It falls . . ." Arthur repeated.

The sudden chill in the air made the candlelight shudder. The priest closed the door.

" . . . to God," he said, scraping his icy boots on the carpet.

"Good evening, Father," Harry said meekly.

In a glance the priest took in the maids' sour faces and the emptiness of the table. The bride-to-be and her mother were nowhere in sight.

"You dine early," he said, passing his cloak to the serving-boy.

"There was almost nothing to make," John answered truthfully. "Mrs. Curran wouldn't. And the b-boy . . ."

The old priest poked at the contents of a dish. There was little enough and nothing at all that he wanted. Nevertheless he pushed his chair a little nearer to Harry. "The blessings of heaven," he said in his pulpit voice, out of habit.

"Blessings to you," Harry said earnestly.

The boy went for another setting while, under the priest's nose, Arthur reached for the decanter. "To what?" he began churlishly.

"Guidance," said the priest. "Intervention when it's needed."

"Harry's of age."

The priest barely smiled. "In some respects," he said. "Though not spiritually. You wouldn't claim that, Harry? You wouldn't claim a primogeniture of spirit?"

Harrry seemed uncertain.

"No, of course not. You would suffer for it terribly."

"Leave him alone," Arthur demanded. His head was whirling with plans and experiments, and the last thing he wanted was the priest's coming, spoiling everything.

"Now I can hardly do that," said the priest. Leaning on the table, he touched Harry with the small of his yellow palm. "Dear friends," he said, "I have come out of regard for your father, God save him."

Elva made a noise in her throat.

"My poor child," the priest said, wishing to say something sympathetic. But he considered the young woman before him with a profound uneasiness. He did not care for young women generally. They were a snare. Not for himself—his temptations never lay in that direction; but they were no end of trouble for the young men of his parish. And this particular example of young womanhood, sharing as she did some of the worst traits of her father, was a sulfurous blot, a piece of unsavory hellfire and likely to burn everyone's fingers.

"We must try to be brave," he said, which was at least noncommital.

"I am brave," she answered.

Arthur smirked.

"I am braver than any of you!" she cried miserably.

"My dear child," the priest said, determined to shepherd them all safely to the inevitable conclusion. "We must strive to achieve understanding. And, if understanding fails, then at least love . . . which is God's gift . . ."

"But he doesn't!" cried Elva, her eyes aflame.

"That, surely, is a rather negative view of life."

"He doesn't! He can't! You don't dare make him!"

"He has made his decision," said the priest, mentally rolling up his sleeves, "and isn't likely to be chivvied out of it. Now that he's come around to it himself, not even those who care for him best could change him."

He could feel how much she hated this, and despised him.

"You might do better, my dear," he pressed on, barely controlling his irritation, "to remember that in the perhaps not too distant future you may yourself find the married life will, shall we say . . ."

Arthur laughed in his face.

"Shall we have a double wedding?" he exclaimed, shaking with glee. "Da and his woodwife and our little Elva and Hob Franklin!"

"The sacrament of marriage," the priest continued indomitably, "that holy protection against . . ."

John's cheeks had grown redder and redder. He had opened his mouth and shut it twice before he managed the words.

"P-please d-don't let him!" he pleaded.

"It's not him!" Elva exploded. "Can't you see he can't help himself? He's sweet and he's sad and all he wants is for everything to be like it was. But it isn't. And they just make it worse. They have nothing and they want to have everything. And they will! It won't take them a minute and they'll gobble up this house and the barns. And the pigstyes too!"

She turned fiercely, facing each of her brothers. She was splendidly angry and, as her head turned, the mass of her hair, caught in the shine of the candlelight, swung so disturbingly that Harry and John, unprepared for her beauty, although she was merely their sister, shifted uncomfortably in their chairs.

"And they mean to have you too!" she cried. "They'll squeeze you out. They'll take you one by one, if they must. Or, if they can, they'll have you all at once. And you won't do a thing. Not before it's too late."

Her lower lip trembled.

"Well, I'm going to do something!" she cried again, looking as though she were about to burst into tears.

Only she didn't. She stayed in her room, imagining tortures. In her thoughts she fed them to bears and to lions, watched with delight their burning like martyrs, their hanging like thieves. In her mind she pummeled and pierced them with javelins and arrows, and let the blood run. Meanwhile the women came down to breakfast and to tea. The old woman dressed herself in robes from the Duchess's wardrobe, the young woman in gowns from Elva's own closets, the maids sweeping into her bedroom and gathering armfuls of dresses without even a nod to her. Elva raged. She wept; until one bleak Sunday afternoon on the very eve of Christmas, vowing to make him choose between them, she stumped down the stairs at last and into the library where her father, a new fire roaring at his back, was puzzling over wrapping the presents he had gathered for every man, woman and child in the house.

His Grace had only just then come in himself, having walked the two miles uphill from the village, where he had drunk the health of the tenants and, after rather too much Christmas ale and the schoolmaster's Philosophical Punch, in the spirit of the season, made a gift of his mare to a small boy, whose name, at the moment, he could not, unfortunately, quite remember.

"Poor devil," he announced with terrible seriousness, when Elva flew in the door. "No sense of gratitude. Stuck out his tongue at me once. Can't remember the specifics. He was climbing a wall."

He looked terrible. His strong features were blurred, eroded by the ale, but enlivened by the gift of the mare.

"It's a thing he'll remember," he said.

She went across to him and sat down at his knee.

"Da," she began.

He grinned. "It's something, I hope, they will, every one of them, keep in their hearts, though it's foolish. And a damn fine horse too! I suppose I will have to send one of the grooms to make certain she's cared for."

His rough hands were filled with ribbons and he waved them in the air.

"These children," he said, "have no sense of what's fitting. I blame the fathers, of course." His Grace shrugged. "As I blame myself about the lot of you."

He was looking straight at her by then. His attention, in fact, had never flagged; but there was a curious lag in his consciousness, as though he could only manage to get around to the words some moments after his thoughts had gone elsewhere.

"I realize you object to her," he said.

"She's not . . ." Elva cried.

"I know," her father answered, "I've heard the talk. Whatever I had hoped, I was not deluded. I would have seen in an instant if she were your mother."

There was a twinkle in his blurred, blue eyes.

"I have found a cuckoo in the nest," he went on quietly, "by chance. At least I never looked to find her. And yet, one can't really blame her for being found. And it was all a mistake, of course. You know, I was sleeping. That, I imagine, was a shock to everyone. But the truly astounding thing, as it happens, is that she does not seem to mind!"

He noticed the fistful of ribbons in his hand.

"Christmas," he whispered.

For the first time she realized that he was very drunk.

"Da . . ." she began again.

"I've decided," he said, "there's to be a ball at the wedding, with all of the barons." He coughed and in his excitement muttered something she could not hear. "I can imagine what the priest will have to say to that. On St. Stephen's Day!"

In the firelight his long half-tormented face was swollen. He laughed suddenly and then fell silent. As suddenly he seemed about to wave her away when, prompted by some buzzing in his head, he added, "I'll tell you this honestly. I had put her out of my mind. Oh, I may have entertained a thought or two. But I dismissed them. And I never promised. When that old woman was swearing it was so, it never was. But, you know, it isn't the promise that matters."

He leaned down as though to tell her a secret.

"I would have thought long and hard about any promise that was asked of me. And the short of it is that I wouldn't."

She was already weeping then.

"In fact," he continued without noticing, "from the first, the whole business struck me as a little sinister. But, of course, that was the old woman's doing, not my own. I think, after all, I would have been content with what I had. This old house, for instance, and a bottle or two of old malmsey. You see, I'll be fifty next birthday and my digestion isn't what it was and my temper is quickly exhausted. It is no time to go lusting after new things. Only . . ."

There was a commotion outside in the corridor.

The Duke ignored it.

"So it's not the promise itself," he said and paused, although conviction had always come to him easily. "Not the actual promise, don't you see, but how one lives . . . afterward."

The disturbance in the corridor had grown louder.

"Not in this house!" a voice called out sharply. "Not even in the kitchen!"

With a bang, the library doors had burst open. The bride-to-be, her countenance wretched and unhappy, marched in wearing one of his daughter's sheerest gowns. The pale silk, brought suddenly into the light, gave the impression of nakedness.

"It doesn't listen!" she cried at him furiously. "Or it won't. But whatever it wants, I see no reason for it lurking by the stairs."

His thoughts were confused but he saw the danger in her face and rose so quickly that his daughter, resentful of the intrusion and grasping stoutly on to his arm, was dragged along with it.

"My sweet child!" he cried, when, as if drawn to the sound, the coarse ball of wood and ice and tarpaulin came tumbling in after her and, making a wet skid, came to rest in the middle of the carpet.

The Duke shook his head. Presented with the trail of muddy twigs and snow, the expression on his face softened.

"You mustn't mind," he said. "It's only Castleburry."

"It's a hedge."

"Surely . . ."

"It belongs in the yard."

He had known from the start that she was likely to be a handful. But her anger seemed to imbue her cheeks with a radiance. Aware of the wonder that had left him, he stared at the shining maze of her hair, at the bare white line of her shoulders, and felt with a certainty that for too long had eluded him that he had a share once again of the impossible glory of innocence. But to his daughter it appeared only that he wavered.

"Well, perhaps," he said shortly, looking faintly embarrassed, "If only just for this evening . . ."

His daughter went cold in astonishment.

The brollachan waited before her, its rough branches quaking. A noise like a door loose on its hinges welled up from within its old battered coat.

"What is wrong?" Elva shouted. "What do you want?"

"Myself!" the brollachan whispered.

"Myself! Myself!" it croaked twice more.

The Duke pulled at his moustache as though puzzled; and yet to Elva the vocabulary of the wet quaking hedge, which had always seemed inadequate, now suddenly had never been as clear.

The Christmas snow, like one of the priest's sermons, had no ending. Boundless and long as the service itself, it poured down majestically while Arthur waited impatiently for the usual climax—after Herod and the customary cold-heartedness of innkeepers—when the child of God's adultery, in a land of deserts where there was never snow, began piling up the tribute of lonely shepherds and star-blinded kings.

It was snowing hard and the tenants, arriving after the first carol, stood thawing apologetically in the back. While the priest read from each of the gospels, the choir, which consisted of three maids and the odd-job man, practiced under their breaths. Even the air smelled of Christmas. In the chapel, made over for the holiday, there were ropes of sweet-smelling hyssop and branches of evergreens. Candles smoked on the wall and on the altar there were large wreaths of bristling, green holly.

"What is the world coming to?" the priest grumbled, although everyone knew that in the end there would be pudding in the long room at the back of the hall.

The gentry sat in the front: Elva on one side of the Duke's pew, the bride-to-be on the other, with Harry, Arthur, John and George Gwenbors, slipped in as a buffer, packed in between. The old woman had a seat to herself, near but not quite at the same level as the wives of Morgan Potent-Matthers and Jack Bermoothes. In the spirit of Christmas, Ben Taynton, who no longer had a family of his own, made a point of passing her a hymnal.

"Though it will be a big snow," he said to her, doing his best to smile, "they've made it their business to come out. Not only for this . . . but to be here for the wedding."

"All the same, they must take it or leave it," the old woman snapped at him.

Elva looked straight ahead.

"Y-you all r-right?" asked John.

Elva squeezed his arm thankfully.

Harry was listening to the sermon.

"Ain't nobody seen him," the serving-boy whispered to one of his uncles who had come up from the village. "And that's funny, because all knows His Grace loves Christmas."

The uncle pulled at his socks. He was wet through, having followed the carriage ruts where he could until the snow, swept over the walls and into the lane, had filled them.

"Isn't everything he loves," he said with a wink and a snigger.

"We got most of the ewes into the hay," said a man in gum-boots still carrying his crook to no one in particular.

"I'll bet he's out thieving the pies," said one of the auxiliary cooks brought in by Mrs. Curran, pleased because she had chopped the mince herself. But Mrs. Curran, knowing him better, concluded he had found a bottle of malmsey.

"I must see to the roast," she declared with a sigh. But when she gathered her Christmas dress and trotted out through the door, instead of the kitchen, she turned toward the tower.

★   ★   ★

His Grace watched the snow. As frenzied as Methodists,
it came leapfrogging down the aisles of sky, one militant
gust chasing another across the night's swirling darkness
until, settling at last on the well house and the roofs of the
barns, everything blended and became part of one landscape
and seemed, he decided—sustaining himself with one more
swallow—all much the same.

Perched just outside the window ledge, he looked down
and waited for the congregation to be let out of the chapel.

It was the same ledge from which he had leapt with such
strange results. He wished to remind them of that. But the
bells were the reason he had wriggled onto the roof, the
strap of bells in one hand and the malmsey in the other:
when the doors of the chapel opened, he meant to stamp
on the tiles, shaking the roof beams, until by the size of
the commotion it seemed that Father Christmas himself
had brought his loaded sleigh to roost on the precarious
top of the Aviary.

And then he would ring the bells.

And then, through the whirling merry-go-round of
blackness and blowing snow, in the silence of her wonder,
he would go down to her.

He grinned at the darkness.

He remembered how, when he was a boy, the old Duke
had crawled along the ridge pole, the very same bells in
hand, and rung in Christmas. It had been so absurd, so
impossible, that he caught himself wondering. His father
had been sentimental and foolish, a man who kept owls
and kept Christmas too, long after his children understood
the presents were purchased in Devon, not lugged down
from the roof through the chimney by a saint in a sleigh.

And yet, here he was himself!

It was a delicious feeling.

Absurd, yes. Sentimental and foolish, but although he could feel his knee joints cracking in the cold, by God, he was glad of it. It was love, of course, and mischief and the delight of knowing that there were children in the house and that the young woman waiting in the chapel would soon be lying in his bed.

This thought pleased him so much that he made a resolution to be kinder to the priest. "He is not a man like I am," he thought, and yet, he reminded himself, "it is Christmas."

Such was his mood that, holding to the casement with one hand, he swung out nearer the edge to feel the snow falling. This meant that he had to put down the bells, but he held on to the malmsey. One foot planted on the tiles and one dangling in the air, with the snow pelting his eyes, he cocked his free arm and wondered whether, if he threw with all his might, he could heave the half-empty bottle beyond the pikestaffs of Mrs. Curran's laundry to the end of a paddock. Of course, it would be a shame to waste what remained, but the difficulty of the task (it was ninety yards if it was twenty) filled him with enthusiasm. He would have to throw high but not too high, judging the arc precisely so that the highest point was just short of the cow barn.

He was about to throw when he saw the brollachan standing below in the snow-filled yard, keeping a lonely watch on the tower. The Duke's heart knocked at his ribs. But then, as if his penitence had suddenly been made clear to him, contritely and woefully out of tune, he began to sing.

"*Hither page, and stand by me,*" he caroled, his sad baritone floating out softly over the slippery roof and the barns:

"If thou knowst it, telling
Yonder peasant, who is he?
Where and what . . ."

"Waldo!" exclaimed Mrs. Curran, coming in and finding the room empty and the window open, a drift of snow already piling on the floor.

But in a moment his flushed long face stared in at her.

"Bells," he explained, although it was not bells he was holding. "Just like the old gaffer."

"He's dead," the old woman told him. "They're all dead." She thrust out a fat arm to get hold of him. "She is dead most of all!"

Because he had been looking at darkness, His Grace blinked at the light. Patches of frost speckled his forehead. His tired, wise, beautiful face jutted out at her proudly.

"But I'm not!" he cried. "And I don't ever intend to be!"

On the afternoon of the Feast of Stephen, the great snow still falling, Rudyard Wenceslas, the Eighth Duke of West Redding, married the girl of the wood. Just after midnight, the sounds of the dancing competing with the shrillness of the wind, Dr. Rendcombe, at Mrs. Curran's suggestion, went through the house looking for Harry. Mrs. Curran herself, as she told everyone afterward, although she had gone methodically from room to room seeking Arthur and John, did not at first realize the extent of the calamity. But when finally they came together again in the hall, there could be little doubt that the heirs of the house had gone from it.

Ben Taynton found the tracks by the well house and,

although dressed for quadrilles and the saraband, followed them until he became hopelessly tangled at the edge of the Weald.

"They'll never be found west of the wood," he wept, when at last he had straggled back to His Grace.

And they never were.

"Except for John, of course," said the old woman, moving the child to a more comfortable place in her lap.

"What of the daughter?" complained the child. "What of Elva?" Impatiently, she brushed a switch of dark hair from her thin, troubled face. "Doesn't someone get to live happily ever after?"

"Well," said the old woman, "she marries."

"Is it better?"

"It depends on when the telling stops."

"No!" the child protested wisely. "When you go to the *very end* . . ."

The old woman did her best to straighten her apron.

"Different," she said with a jeery laugh. "Same as always. Though I suppose there's nowt for you, same as ever, but the telling."

Part II

The Promise

Does it really exist, time the destroyer?
—*Rainer Maria Rilke*
Sonnets to Orpheus 27

Chapter One

"AND SIX SOUR LOAVES AND A WHEEL OF RIPE Midland Stilton," said Mrs. Curran, tucking the bread and the cheese into the basket and the basket itself under the girl's bundled arm.

Elva was already wrapped in a greatcoat; her legs had been slipped into trousers that had been cut down, in secret, from a pair of Harry's discarded brown flannels. Her feet had been encased in wellingtons and on each hand she wore two sets of thick woolen mittens, both of which Mrs. Curran had sewn into the sleeves of the greatcoat with close double stitches.

The sewing and cutting had been done after midnight in the butler's back room, where the candlelight could not be seen from the hall, for the new Duchess, like an old wife, often wandered away from her bed. Like the pantry mice, the bride of no more than a week had the run of the house while His Grace, exhausted from seeking his sons among the farms and the hedgerows, was snoring. Hour after hour she counted the plates and the silver, marking the patterns and totals down on a fine piece of vellum, which every morning she locked in a drawer by the side of her bed. By the fourth night she had counted the bottles of claret in the cellar. By the fifth night she was numbering the lamps and the bric-a-brac, and the outside men were more than half certain that the farm cats and the foundation stones of the cow sheds were next.

Mrs. Curran tightened the scarf under the girl's chin. "Now you must hurry," the cook said severely, buttoning the last button. "Before she walks, you must be out on the hill."

Elva looked up apprehensively.

"But how will I find them?" she asked. "Da has gone out every day and he never . . ."

"All is seen to," said the cook, who, from the moment she had realized His Grace could not be deterred from the wedding, had begun planning.

She had found an excuse to go into the village, made one or two unnecessary purchases and then, as if by chance, met on a back lane a certain old gentleman long in the Duke's service, although now well into his retirement. She had collected Harry's old trousers and put aside mittens. She had taken the basket down from the shelf. Her only difficulty lay in convincing Arthur that it meant his life and those of his brothers unless they left the house at once. "They are merely women," the boy had smirked when she told him. "You have grown stupid and vengeful," he shouted and stormed down to dinner where he sat next to the young woman and helped her and himself deliberately to the wine. John, however, had believed Mrs. Curran at once. And Harry, relieved to be told what must be done, crept off without further bidding to the stables where, no matter how fantasic and foolhardy it all seemed, he ordered the grooms to have three horses ready.

"A few days, no longer," Mrs. Curran had lied to them.

Arthur, nevertheless, remained adamant. Left with no recourse, just before the wedding toast, she found his goblet and had it replaced with another.

"It's all right, Master Arthur," she had said afterward, her dimpled arm draped round his lean one and leading him away from the hall, "all you want is a bit of a lie-down, only the least bit of quiet until you feel better . . ."

Alf had been waiting by the stairs, his cap in one hand and a strong rope in the other.

At week's end, when Mrs. Curran and Elva came out onto the stoop, Alf was waiting again, his heavy cap pulled down snugly over his ears. He was rangy and sallow-faced like his father and had served the Eighth Duke as before him his father had served the Sixth and the Seventh.

"Whether he knows it or not, His Grace needs an hour more of your time," Mrs. Curran had said to him.

The snow had stopped and the first silver quarter of the moon was at last cutting through the darkness and the fast-flying clouds. By its light Elva could see the straggly shape of the man and the ewe he had brought with him.

"Together we'll take you east of the village, miss," he said. "She'll do the rest."

Elva huddled into her coat.

"Daughter of daughters, she is," explained Alf, who had a sheepman's appreciation for an obstinacy carried long in the blood, "back to your granddad's dam that my own dad lost and your da went after."

He paused and pulled on his cap.

"It's her your brothers followed, miss," he said proudly. "So I wouldn't fret. She'll lead you as good as they. And afterward have you home again."

But now that the night and the cold were in front of her, Elva fixed her stare at her boots. She fiddled with her mittens.

Mrs. Curran looked across to the stile where the cattle track lost itself in the darkness.

"As terrible as that wood is," she lied once more, "I would not send you into it, if you could not come back to me."

"It's not that I won't," Elva said, taking a breath. "Only . . ."

Mrs. Curran made a noise in her throat.

"Only . . . I've heard them whisper."

"Pay them no mind."

"Even Da says the Weald has but a single edge."

"And if it does?"

"And only one entrance."

"Same as ever," Mrs. Curran said curtly, "same as life." And she hugged the child twice and touched her cheek with her finger.

"You might tell Arthur I bear him no grudge," she said. "Hard as it seems, I was doing my duty as I saw it."

The girl nodded.

"And John," Mrs. Curran continued hastily. "Remind him to be brave. And Harry . . ." She stopped. For a moment she could no longer meet the eyes looking back at her.

"There'll be a fresh pot of tea waiting," she promised and then stopped once more. Unable to keep back her tears, the old cook stepped back into her kitchen and drew the bolt quickly.

★   ★   ★

There were still no lights in the house when the old man and the young woman set out over the hill. The ewe, its ears already whitened with frost, trotted ahead of them, picking its way daintily through the snow. The night was dark and from the beginning the basket heavy under her arm; but, although the man grudgingly offered, Elva told him she meant to carry it herself. It was less of a burden than her brothers were to her. Except for John, she did not love them very well, and it struck her as unfair that they had been sent away so quickly and that she, instead of one of the serving-boys, should have to provide for them. Surely, she thought, someone else could have been trusted. Nor could she understand why, if her brothers were in danger, she was not. Feeling a little sorry for herself, Elva poked about beyond the edge of the barn, lingering and hoping for a glimpse of Castleburry, who—banished, like her brothers, when the new women came—had been consigned to the cowman's shed and the kennels.

But the dog-runs were empty.

She tilted her head and waited for a minute, listening.

"Come, miss," Alf hurried her, knowing, if she did not, that in spite of the darkness, within the hour there would be some in the village peering out of their windows to have a look at the start of the day.

The ewe waddled through a break in the paddock wall and, crossing the unmarked field, set a course eastward as deftly as though she had a compass in her head. They followed to the bottom of the meadow, over a second wall, descending silently into the darkness. Soon the village lay to the right, moonlight and (with the clouds tearing) starlight glittering off the icy slabs of the roofs. They went swiftly now, without pausing; and yet, somehow, Elva felt a strangeness and wondered why she should be so vaguely troubled.

It was not that she didn't like walking out late in the snow. In truth she had been terribly jealous when her brothers, gathered up out of their beds by her father, went marching off with torches to spear eels in the river or, after the harvest, sat out all night at the oast fires with the fieldmen while she, the youngest and a girl, had been kept in her room with her books and her blankets, the maid coming in by ten-thirty to snuff out the lamp. Boys, it seemed to her, were treated like grownups even when, like Harry and John, they would never be. But then her father had never known what to do with a girl.

She supposed it would have been different if her mother had lived. That notwithstanding, the truth was that she was more like her father than any of her brothers. For several months, beginning when she was ten and without getting sick, she had smoked the pigman's big, ill-smelling briar behind the mews, and once, sneaking into the priest's room, she had pasted a picture of a devil cut from one of her father's books (Milton, with the Doré illustrations) into the bottom of the old cleric's chamber-pot. She was not as tall as the smallest of her brothers, but she was stronger than John and, even less like him, unwilling to sit at home staring stupidly into the fire. She loved commotion and, every bit as much as His Grace, a hard job well done. Just last spring, bribing the ploughboy with a look up under her skirts, she had walked behind the gray, opening two acres of her father's best barley field until the older men had seen her and chased her off. So it wasn't the dark or even the danger of being caught (as to the danger, what could be done to her?); and yet she was aware of a puzzling uncertainty.

They had come out of a fold of the hill and she was looking at the first snow-laden spires of the trees.

The tall old man beside her was silent. He too was gazing into the trees.

"This ain't the first time," he said softly.

"What isn't?"

"Your pardon, miss," he muttered, "I was thinking."

Her cheeks were white as mildew, and her hair, sticking out under her scarf, hoary and frozen. Yet he could see how she walked.

"It's one blood," he told himself, seeing how she went, her head held high and, in spite of the snow, her little hips swinging. He was not surprised. The wildness came, as it always had, from the wood.

It was not something much talked of. It was all so long ago. He had been a lad himself, trailing at his own mother's skirts, when the father of the present duke had married the woman out of the wood.

"There were always lots of girls," he said in a careful whisper, "in one of the big houses or another. And most of the big farms got bigger, matching farm to farm, as they did, more than man to maid. But your granddad never would. He had his own dreams. Never looked twice at any of them, though at dances and parties they was marched in for him to consider. But he never. So I'm thinking that it ain't that peculiar that your da, you see, leastways the second time . . ."

Elva trudged up in front of him and made him stop.

Alf smiled at her thinly.

"A trollwoman," he said. "Or so my old mother said."

The ewe, undeterred, went gingerly ahead of them.

"It's all happened before," he continued. "Your grand-dad married a wealdwife and, as maybe it must, paid the price for it."

Elva's eyes widened. She had never heard any of this. But in a house where her own mother was never mentioned, except in a whisper, perhaps it was not entirely strange.

"What price?" she asked.

"Forgive me, miss. I should not have said."

"I shouldn't mind."

Alf shook his head. "But I should have," he said apologetically. "It's not my place. Only coming out like this, I was struck by how things remain the same. And I thought . . ."

But now, more than ever, he was certain he should not have.

"What do you know!" she cried at him.

Above his nose-high muffler Alf squinted into the wind. He was an honest man, faithful to His Grace, and by nature not inquisitive. What he knew was sheep, not the lives in the great house. And although he had started the tale freely, with no more thought than a village gossip, now that he had half begun and saw the end, he was certain he should not finish. He took a step beyond her in his gum-boots.

The trees before him were white as wraiths.

"Summat about here, miss," he said dully, "I'll be turning."

Elva put down her basket in the snow.

"No," she said. "Not until I've heard."

The ewe had wandered back. As if joining the cause against him, she butted his legs.

"It's a pity, miss," he told her. "Not that I know it's true. Just something my old mother . . ."

She was scarcely more than a child, but the way she glared at him nearly broke his heart.

"Wild as a hare she was, your gran," he said, relenting. "Strange and wild and silent. Never said a word. Not even when they found her in her bed with the child beside her. The true heir. Before the first Arthur (not your brother) who died without sons of his own . . . before your father."

It was not his business, he thought, to be telling her, except that going out with the ewe had jogged his memory. And yet what did it matter?

There had been other sons, born to that same woman, born sound and then grown into manhood, as if the first had never happened. When the first Arthur died, the second son (the Seventh Duke, not Elva's brother), although he had died too soon himself (a fever taking him), he had died a man, not a babe in that mother's bed. But by then that mother was dead herself.

No scandal there. A death with sorrow and tears, like other deaths. A death hopeless and terrible but, unlike the first, without the stench of wickedness. But whatever it was, whatever it had seemed, was long since done with.

Only now, when it all should have been no more than an ancient story, the last and youngest son of that woman, had taken another woman from the wood so that he (Alf, son—without complications—of Alf), who in his old age wanted nothing more than a few last summers scrambling over the hillsides with his sheep, who was just a tired old man and no kin to them, was sent forth into the cold and snow to save a new batch of Arthurs and Harrys and Jacks. And this strong-willed girl.

He looked very hard at her.

"Your gran," he said. "His Grace's mother . . ."

Exasperation showed on Elva's face.

"Come from the wood," he said. "As now. And then soon to her childbed."

"And?"

"I do not know the truth of it," he admitted. "It is only something guessed at years ago."

"If you ever loved my father . . ."

"Blood on her mouth," he said. "Blood on her face and hands when they found her, the child's bloody bones fouling the sheets, as if she'd had a feast of it."

The ewe, its chin hairy as an old woman's, had turned again toward the wood.

"No one knew for certain," he said quietly. "She could not speak. Could not answer their questions. Robbers, it was said. Tinkers. Who is to say? The old Duke loved her. Later, there were two more sons."

She did not blink.

"Who else would remember?" she asked.

"Who else is as old?"

"Gwenbors?"

"Aye."

"The priest?"

Alf nodded. Forgetting for a moment whether he had served her good or ill by speaking, he wanted to rest his gloved hand comfortingly upon her shoulder. But she was so young. And she was the Duke's daughter.

"Aye," he said almost inaudibly. "He knew, if anyone."

He heard her mutter.

"Miss?" he asked.

"By God's balls!" she swore outright, dismissing him and the theories and petty gossip of men generally.

★   ★   ★

Before Elva entered the wood she looked back over her shoulder, staring after the old man, already grown small on the hillside. A crow circled steeply above him. Observing them both, she imagined. "It may be," she thought, "there is always someone watching." Sheepmen as much as priests. Watching and making up dreams. Caught up in her own life, it had never before occurred to her that in the village, as under the stairs, whatever was said and done in the big house was followed and remembered. And twisted too!

She chased the ewe under the low, sweeping branches.

"Wait!" she called, as if her chiding made a difference to the sheep, and hurried.

The path between the trees was narrow and dark. But it was not the first time. Her father had done this.

He had been no more than a boy, younger, in fact, than she was now. And he had been seeking the ewe, not trudging along after it. Still, it made her feel courageous. She could smell the oak boughs and the pines, sharp and resinous in her nostrils, and it helped.

From where she was, on its outer boundary, the wood was far from strange. Elva had been brought up within familiar sight of its trees. Its ragged towers were the background of her games. Although warned against it, she had played fox and hound in the hawthorn and, risking her neck, climbed into the lower boughs of maples and elms. While she had never gone in far or stayed long, she had been much more frightened of the vault under the house, where it was always dark, than the mist-threaded twilight under the trees. Yet the wood was cold; the closeness of the snow-burdened branches made it seem colder.

The crow, whose raucous cawing she had heard before she had turned and entered, had either left the field or else the wood drank up the sound. Even the wind, it seemed, had been trapped in the mat of heavy limbs and merely wheezed and sighed, all out of breath.

"Wait!" she called again, hearing the ewe crackling through the brush but unable to catch a glimpse of her.

Nonetheless, there was a kind of path or at least a narrow alley tunneling inward. The ewe kept to the left of it, as if preferring the bracken.

Which was all for the best, she thought. For the ewe would have been swifter on open ground, but delayed by the undergrowth, she never pulled too far ahead.

Elva clambered after her, reassured by the noisy snapping and switching of branches off in the darkness.

There was still enough of a moon to guide her. Here and there its cold light sparkled on the snow, laying out its own effortless path while she stumbled to the top of a rise and, although the drifts had grown deeper, started down the other side into the darkened bowl of a valley.

Far below there was the sound of water, distant and hollow, running hidden under ice. The moon had become tangled in the trees, guttering like a candle and, for minutes at a time, failing altogether. She wished then that she had brought a lantern. She wished as well that the little tunnel of a path wouldn't seem to be narrowing. And yet she took satisfaction in knowing that, while her brothers had gone three together, she had walked into the wood alone, with only the ewe for company.

"Harry would not have done this," she thought proudly. "Nor John."

There was a crunch of twigs, oddly, just at her back.

Increasing her pace, she asked, laughing, "Have you already grown weary?"

But the bleating that answered her came from up ahead. The other sound, which quickened, was behind her.

"Who . . ." she began, looking around.

"Thyself," something whispered close by her ear.

As if playing hide-and-seek, Elva smiled tentatively.

"Myself," something added. But now the hiss of its breath came from the darkness further down the slope.

"Arthur!" she cried out.

She had come back into the moonlight. The murky glow showed the ruin of a tree, not her brother. White and uprooted, with boughs like leprous arms, twigs like bone fingers, it lay cracked and twisted across her path. It did not move. It had never moved, she realized, from the place where, cleft by frost or lightning, it had fallen.

"M-myself," something else sputtered, far away from the path.

"John?"

A sudden gust swept through the branches, rattled the dry leaves and passed with a thin wail into silence. Afterward there was only the cold and the darkness.

Elva sniffed the sharp air and waited. "Harry," she called.

The ewe went on as before, invisible but clearly present, blundering through the blackthorn and brambles.

It was terrifying, of course. But years later, as a very old woman, she had to admit it was the easiest part of her journey. She had walked for what seemed forever in darkness and for longer under cold starlight which lit the branches in ways that made wind-tortured faces out of the clumped patches of dried leaves and bracken. She had heard voices that seemed to press near and then, vaguely, fluttered away harmlessly.

Sometimes she thought it was Castleburry and sometimes her brothers, mocking and then running off again. At first she had laughed. Then she had been angry. Finally she had begged whomever or whatever it was to stop. But she could listen only so long with nothing certain to hear; and in time she was left with as much a sense of absurdity as fear. It was a night she would always remember, a night filled with wonder and dread. Yet she would recall it with just a touch of gratefulness as well. All the rest that followed was so much worse.

The snow crunched underfoot. The voices cried, whispered and were gone, leaving her half wishing they might come back again.

She went on.

By first light she was walking out along a little causeway of stepping stones midway into the frozen river. The ewe, its cramped, stunted shadow tilted away from the sun, was already climbing the other bank. It seemed so small against the immensity of the hill. Even the new sun, peering above the trees on the opposite shore, seemed grublike, an unbright worm in a cumulus of unbright wool. And it wriggled. Or it may have been that her own thoughts were shaken.

But at least there was light! The darkness had shrunk by slow degrees into shadows, had hidden itself in the great branches, been broken into small, dark-stained puddles that reflected and winked. Elva blinked and stepped forward, still careful to keep her boots on the stones.

There were open patches in the ice. Around her she could see the racing current, white-frothed and streaked with brown. Her weary eye traveled over the course the ewe had taken. She did not want to go forward, but there was no way to go back.

When she went out onto the ice, there was a dull moan.

"Do not be afraid. Your step is light," said a voice from the water. "Lighter, dear sister, than mine."

Even before she looked, she knew it was Harry. Yet she did not feel the horror until she turned to gaze at him.

The square head floated just above the surface. His dark fingers, as though pleased with the river's coldness, did not reach for the edge of the ice.

"You must not stop here," he said, his low, unconcerned whisper one sound with the river's drifting sigh.

It seemed to her that he watched her from a great distance, his eyes blank, careless of what they saw or missed.

"So little of me is here," he said. "And what there is loves deep, brown stones and moving over them."

At once, pitying, she held out her hand.

Her brother shook his head. Water filled his lower jaw, and yet he did not gasp for air.

"I drift all day," he said remotely. "I float and wander. But in the evening I climb the hill and cross the hedge. If you do not lose your way, you will see a cottage deep in the glen."

It cannot be said that she believed what she beheld. It was less than broad daylight and he was mostly in shadow, and the whorls of the current, swirling over him, distorted her view.

When she squinted, she thought she saw the hacked trunk of a tree with armlike branches, torn from the bank and floating.

"You must save us," the hewed trunk whispered.

"Brother!" she cried to him.

But his lips were bark and could not smile or frown.

"You must be rid of my trousers," he said.

"Thank you very much," she said, shivering.

"Clothes are encumbrances," he said, peering up at her. Unable to smile or frown, he shifted his head. "You must know," he said, "that there is no better help for a desperate man."

She was not doing very well in understanding him.

"Than what?" she asked.

He was not being difficult. To him the matter was clear.

His sad eyes, turned inward in the time he had been drowned, slid over her with a terrible seriousness. "Than a young woman's nakedness," he said.

"I don't know what you're talking about."

Ripples frothed around his neck. Propped above the river, his immense chin dripped like the eaves of a horsebarn.

"It is as a woman," her brother sighed, "that you must save us."

"Harry!" she cried at him.

As he dove, the tangle of his hair glinted like wet, trailing ivy. She watched his twisted, straggling branches flowing back and then the pool, speckled and empty, in the bleak, first light of dawn.

When she looked again, there was nothing.

The wood looked brighter from the hill, perhaps because the clouds were racing from the sun or because, away from among the most massive trees, there was a clearing. The light had changed. Rocks and brambles stood out from the snow. Halfway up an oak, Arthur's matchstick legs were dangling.

"Go away," he said.

"It was hard work coming here," she answered, holding in her mind the look of him when there was more of him to hate. For, although she had no love for him, she had never wished for his death and felt certain she was dreaming.

It was all dreams, she thought, the voices and Harry drowned. Just dreams and nonsense, like the old sheepman's remembering blood on her grandmother's mouth. Only she could not, with her mittens, pinch her side to get herself to wake up. And so she was determined to go on. She had already turned. But the ewe, showing less enthusiasm for the underwood, waited beneath the tree.

When Arthur looked down, with a crack, the hard bones of his neck shifted.

The dry, stiff clink was clear enough. The light on the hillside was better and she could not help noticing.

"Are you really . . ." she asked, not trusting her eyes.

"I am not so engaged for my pleasure."

"I might cut you down," she suggested, although she had not actually decided if she would.

"I have little interest," he answered, "in rotting on the ground. Here, at least, the wind tips my head. Hanging for so long, I am half a tree myself. With the tips of my branches, I can feel the ice dripping. All day I watch the crows that come to peck at me."

"How do you see at all?"

"I give free rein to my thoughts."

"That is no answer."

If he were able, he would have smiled. "When I went wooden and blind," he said, "I learned to remember."

How she despised his claims of all-sufficiency!

"Where is John?" she asked defiantly.

"I have not yet begun to think of him."

She turned away. "Why can I never believe you?"

"As always, you will do what you like."

"You have not changed!" she cried.

His once sharp nose had been eaten away. His uneven breath rattled. "Only a fool," he said, "thinks to find a man improved by death."

Without glancing back, she snatched up the basket she had set down. The ewe had set out again before her. She took her first step, following.

"In the glen," he said, "there is a cottage."

She inhaled the cold air away from the stench of him.

"Before you go . . . ," he whispered.

She did not turn. Her face was pale. Her hair, escaping her scarf, fell over her forehead, concealing her eyes. In her greatcoat and with Harry's trousers, the rest of her was equally hidden.

Such a woman, Arthur feared, scarcely seeming a woman at all, would never save them. He was dead and, therefore, knew something of what must be. But lately he had been living, and he understood that only life came from life. And life seldom started clothed, looking like a man.

"Sister!" he cried to her.

She dug her heels into the snow to keep herself from falling. "It is merely the wind," she thought thankfully, scrambling into the drifts and out of the hollows along the side of the hill. "Only the blustery wind crying."

Soon the ewe would stop and there she would find her true brothers. And then she could go home again.

"I came alone," something continued desperately behind her, "with only a ewe to guide me. No choice I had.

Senseless, slumped over the mare, I was taken into the wood. Death took me stupidly."

She walked with her head down and the basket bumping against her.

"Elva!" something thundered.

But it was either the voice of the wind or the voice of the dead, and neither, Elva decided, was in the least worth listening to.

Chapter Two

"SOMEONE HAS A HARD-MOUTHED DOG!" THE Ninth Duke shouted. Tossing the badly eaten bird back to the game cart, he stumped off toward the house, leaving the beaters and loaders to see to the mess. The sporting men milled around for a moment and then followed along up to the guest hall for long pints and cider and the brawl that normally came after and which, as no one usually came to harm, they looked forward to just as eagerly. The damage, more often than not, was limited to a few bloody noses or a setting of crockery, out of regard for which the serving-boy never laid out anything except the third best; and the steward, expecting no more from His Grace than from his companions, kept back the better wine until last when goodwill had finally broken out again.

The countrymen and the footman walked around in the yard. With as little enthusiasm as they might have shown for the Mass, they tramped through the frozen dung and the slurry, not yet ready for home.

"Serves 'm right, I'd say," said Sam Maddox. "Who ever 'eard of going for birds in snow."

"Believe me, I believe you," agreed Tommy Chorlton. "The old Duke never would," he kept on, although when the present Duke sent him off into the spring mud or the bright autumn trees he complained just as bitterly.

"Ain't Odlaw, bless 'im," said Joe Gormley. "It's them young bloods the cause of it. Time is he was rid of them. Time, I'd say, he found hisself a wife."

The others, although they all had wives of their own, nodded.

Sam Maddox grinned.

"The wildness never lasts," he said, "once they're wedded."

Joe Gormley padded over to the cart. "Nothing does," he said sullenly. "Sure as life, it is," he said. "Sure as death." Picking up the greylag, he examined it closely. "Weren't a dog though," he announced.

"It's always dogs," said Sam.

Joe Gormley frowned.

"This one ain't."

He held it up for them to look at.

"One of the bitches brought it out," he said. "That's clear and that's certain. But none of them young bloods shot it. Take someone braver than that lot. Take someone to go where they won't."

The hen was fleshless and he held it gingerly and shook it so they could hear the bones rattling.

"Not one of today's," he said contemptuously. "Come from the wood, me lads. Been dead since forever."

The wood seemed hushed, waiting. It was quiet, remote, almost as secret as her dreams. The path ran crookedly, rising between evergreens and clumps of indestructible ivy, its leaves and tendrils unpolished and spotted, more baleful and blighted than green. Elva stumbled on north or east, edging through a gap of stones. But in the next moment, unexpectedly, a tall hedge, threaded with sharp sticks and brambles, was before her.

It was as much a wall as a hedge and not, she discovered quickly enough, where any sort of obstruction was wanted. At least as wide as it was high, it was compounded of hawthorn and dense, old cypress. At her first meeting, she drew back. She did not think she could pull her way through. She walked first down one side of the ridge and then back up the other and, with neither end visible, soon felt herself trapped in the middle.

The ewe had stopped. Scratching her rump on the thorns, she seemed without interest in proceeding.

"So much for your help," said Elva, feeling the cold and half wishing, in the quiet, that the ewe might answer.

"I expected more than this," she explained to the air, needing a witness. "I plan to live to a great age. And . . ."

Improvising, she took her mittened hand and ran it over her face.

It was not a plain face. Indeed, many of the young men coming into her father's hall had found her beautiful. (One of the housewomen, listening where she should not, had overheard a baronet talking and had repeated to her, word for word, what had been said.) Encouraged, Elva drew her hand further down until she could feel the fullness of one of her breasts pressing back through the coat's heavy padding.

"I have given the matter some thought. . . ." she said.

In the solitude, not even the wind sighed.

Elva closed her eyes, imagining, as she always did, worlds of strangeness and wonder.

She took a deep breath.

On her sixteenth birthday, which, unlike her brothers', was never celebrated (because it was the anniversary as well of death) she had awakened quite frightened in her bed. "Nothing will ever happen to me," she had told herself while still wrapped in the blanket. "Not here. Not with Da so sad and unable to forget."

"He relies on me too much," she had thought. "He watches me, and although he never says a word, he thinks of her." And so, from her first memory, she had determined to get away.

"If I don't take care"—she had been certain, watching night after night her father sitting with his bottle of malmsey—"I'll become dull as a head of kale, and nothing, ever, will happen."

But in the world beyond!

Wanting is the beginning of getting, she had thought.

"Always, always," she whispered, "the getting starts in dreams."

"Give me a push," she said suddenly, with a laugh, to any of several young men who were not there.

She wasn't sure which of them took hold of her shoulders. But as they toppled together through the bracken, she understood she was about to be kissed. And not the chaste, dry birthday peck of Mrs. Curran, sorry because under the circumstances no greater fuss would be made.

In response she felt her flesh prickle.

Trusting to hope and chance, she bent forward, smiling.

She tripped once. Then, without drama or difficulty, as easily as wriggling through the border of rosemary barberry at the bottom of her own garden, she stepped away from the hedge.

The other side was utterly commonplace.

Elva gazed out on an uninspiring spectacle of trees. The sky, which had not noticeably changed, was still cloudy.

And she was still cold.

Below her she saw a tilted chimney stack. Except for where it was, screened by firs and rowans, the cottage under it might have belonged to any of her father's tenants.

"Y-you'll have to c-come in," John said to her. "T-there's n-nowhere else."

But she hesitated.

There was ruin everywhere. The wind blew in through the broken patch of the window as much as through the door. The smudge of a fire in the grate wasn't enough to melt the tracks of snow on the floor. The room's one cot was unmade, the two bundles of blankets tucked into opposite corners in a jumble. A collection of pots and dirty bowls lay upended on the table.

"It's awful," John said. "B-but Arthur d-doesn't care and Harry won't. So it's l-left to me."

Tears were running down his face and his thin shoulders were heaving. He put his head in his hands.

"I c-can't b-bear it," he cried.

But it wasn't until she had knelt before him and pressed his hand to her check that she understood he was dead.

"How . . ." she began.

"I d-don't know. I've f-forgotten."

Nevertheless there was less denying it than if he had been stretched out on a board with a sheet over him and the priest reading Latin out of his book. There was no practical explanation. He wasn't cold, and in much the same way as ever, he blubbered and was afraid. It was only that she was certain that if she stopped believing he was there, if only for a moment, he would be gone.

"I've seen Harry," she told him.

John went on sitting in his chair.

Later she built up the fire. When she looked, she found tears still clinging to his chin.

She took the broom and swept the floor. She cleaned the pots and, holding fast his image in her mind, went out into the yard to replenish the water from the well.

"Do you hear me?" she asked when she came back.

"Sometimes I think you are the wind," he said.

In the evening, as she was eating her dinner from the basket, her two older brothers came to the door.

"Where is the ewe?" Arthur said.

"Gone back," she answered, not realizing he had not asked her.

"Who found her then?" he continued.

She had half opened her mouth.

"Myself," said Harry.

"Myself," echoed John.

Harry came in and crouched down by the hearth and began picking the weed from the wet thicket of his hair. Arthur went to the table and looked in the basket. He found a rind of cheese but left it.

"What do you hope to do here?" he asked.

"I was sent to feed you."

"W-wait for our s-sister," said John. "S-someone must w-wait."

Harry lifted his head. "She will come by the river," he said proudly. "I shall be the first to see her and shall climb onto the ice and tell her what she must do to save us."

Arthur spat into the fire. "You will drift among the stones," he laughed, "and she will pass above you none the wiser."

"You are blind," Harry reminded him, "and, like all the wood, your heart is the heart of dry rot."

"Ah, but it is a high tree," Arthur answered. "From such an outpost I shall hear her footsteps the moment she comes into the Weald and then I shall call to her."

"And if she d-does not c-come?" asked John.

Arthur sneered. "She will," he said stubbornly. "She is our sister."

"And we were her b-brothers," John said, remembering a sadness older than their deaths.

While they were arguing, Elva rose and bolted the door. She took off her coat and combed her long hair. She removed her great boots and put them into the hob-holes and hung her stockings on pegs by the hearth. Before she wrapped herself in a blanket, she pushed a fresh log and more kindling into the fire, but the wood was damp and the flame sputtered and soon forgot how to burn. In time Arthur went off to the cot. Harry crawled into a corner.

Elva wriggled out of her blanket and blew on the coals.

Barefooted on the dirt floor, she reached into the hearth and retrieved a branch. Blowing urgently, she made a bright tongue of flame.

In its light, she looked straight at Arthur and, lifting the brand, if not out of simple justice, at least out of anger and pain, prepared to drop it against his cheek, until Harry, turning in his sleep, called out to her.

"Elva," Arthur echoed, although he was no more aware than the other of her presence.

When they were both snoring again, John opened his eyes apprehensively and looked for her.

"I g-grieve for you," he said to the darkness.

"Why?"

"B-because of how you m-must s-save us," he said.

"I have not agreed to that."

"S-still you m-must."

The last pinkish glow of the branch had faded and the cottage was as black as the wood. For him she was no more than the sound of her breath.

"You m-must p-promise," he said.

"What?"

"N-never to s-speak more . . ."

"No."

" . . . than C-castle . . . b-burry . . ." he stammered on.

"I will not."

" . . . until n-next w-winter's snow," he said.

She lay still, feeling neither wonder nor horror and in their place simply the dull ache of uncertainty.

If she had met her brothers stone dead in the wood, she might have wept.

The deaths she had seen as a child—a stillborn calf limp-necked in the stalls, a hare frozen in the stubble—had filled her with terror.

Once, even in Mrs. Curran's kitchen, finding a pigeon senseless and cold on the shelf, she had fled weeping into the hall. But those dead had the hopeless look of empty immobility, derelict and abandoned, reminding her that her own life, like her mother's, could be snatched away.

Here, her brothers lurked in and out of shadows, one moment distant and the next as blunt and self-absorbed as they had been in life.

She plucked up the corner of her blanket she had dragged with her and, putting it to her face, inhaled the heavy scent of smoky wool.

John hugged her then, unexpectedly, with both arms.

She had not heard him leave his chair. But when he pulled her head against him, all at once she felt his matted hair against her cheek and his flesh that was neither cold nor warm. Something trickled down her face.

He drew his hand between them, feeling what it was.

"Are these your t-tears, my s-sister," he asked, "or are they m-mine?"

When she woke, John was sitting and Arthur and Harry were gone. She had awakened slowly, floating upward out of her sleep until she recognized his impassive face, pale and yet untroubled, as if the night had emptied all his thoughts. The room, which she had cleaned and tidied, had returned to disorder. The fire was out.

There was a cold branch, where she had dropped it, in the middle of the floor.

"Why do you stay here?" she asked.

"It is easier to sit than stand."

"When I go," she said tentatively, "you might come with me."

"When you came," something that was no longer quite her brother answered, "you gave up any hope of leaving."

Her mouth was tightly drawn. "I shall never . . ." she began but, hearing her father's voice at the back of her own, she stopped.

At the edge of her hearing, she noticed the whispered assault of sleet on the window, the dilatory beat of the wind at the door.

"You must not allow the course of your life to be determined by hope," the thing in the chair was saying. "Hope is the mother of illusion. The wise . . ."

"It is death," she thought angrily, *not John.*

"I will never . . . ," she said aloud.

She was crying when she woke.

Somewhere off in the wood guns were firing.

"The D-duke is out early," a thing that barely spoke had stuttered.

Elva thought she saw a movement with the tail of her eye. But when she turned to the hearth, there was an empty chair. She climbed out of the blanket and pulled her stockings from the pegs and her boots from the hob-holes.

"I am going home," she thought, stumbling clumsily into her wellingtons and drawing her coat over her shoulders and the sleeves into her arms.

At the door she heard the guns again.

She looked back once and did not see him.

"John!" she almost cried out. Instead, although she had never promised that she would, she held her tongue.

Chapter Three

Before dawn, having awakened the sporting men by choice and not a few of the tenantry by accident, His Grace, the Ninth Duke, left the stable yard and the village and was riding his strawberry roan down the very center of the willow-girt meadow. Behind him his fieldmen, more reluctant than any of the young gentlemen to have been roused from their beds, were dragging the game cart and swearing. The sky was still dark, and the snow, even where the horses had trampled it, was slick from a mist that was too mild for a sleet, not warm enough for rain and too little of either to keep His Grace at home.

"Ach, laddie," Sam Maddox growled, his toes and hands freezing, "I dinna wish to be going. But if going we must, it would better be dusk as dawn."

Tommy Chorlton, whose job it was to agree with the senior man, nodded. His forehead was hot from exertion and cold from the damp, and he pushed the cart grudgingly out of one rut into the next.

"Don't hear no gabbling," he admitted.

"And won't," muttered Sam. "Fool waste of shot. Not even the old squire went for white-fronts or greylags at this unholy hour. And never with horses."

"Nowt that I heard of," Tommy Chorlton said solemnly.

"Never as long as he lived, I can tell you."

Tommy Chorlton's bleary eyes, looking ahead, searched the pocked plough land as apprehensively as if he were reconnoitering the shadowed craters on the moon.

"Certain," he added, "we've got a bit of a job on our hands."

"Bloody fool waste!" Sam Maddox shouted again, in case the point had been missed.

Joe Gormley gave up listening and blew on his nails.

Whether there would be geese in the winter-sown fields or geese on the ponds or out under the trees was none of his business. Their business, being fieldmen and beaters, was birds.

His was not.

He was an indoors man. And indoors was indoors, even if, more often than he liked, he carried His Grace's twelve-bore over his arm and His Grace's breakfast in a satchel instead of, as was more fitting, on a plate. Still, Joe Gormley was what he was, however unsuitable the place or the hour. In his pockets he always kept one good silver dining fork and, preserving a few crumbs of comfort against want, a container of gentleman's relish.

"Indoors is indoors, me lads," he would say if any looked at him oddly, "whether indoors or out."

He straightened his tie and scraped along behind the fieldmen.

By now they had left the meadow and were turning toward the first solitary clump of trees, a mile from the house as the crow flies, which, of course, in this weather it didn't. A ragged mist blew in their faces, making any determination of location difficult.

They tramped over the hill like a small routed battalion, lost and defeated in a country not their own. In the dampness the steaming rumps of the horses rose and fell ahead of them, seeming less the undulations of flesh and blood than a procession of spirits.

Nonetheless, Joe Gormley stepped around an unmistakable reminder of their mortality.

"Them horses is for the wood," he said loudly, for Sam to hear.

"Horses won't," Sam protested.

"Whether horses will or horses won't, is the reason."

The game cart lurched sideways, but Tommy Chorlton, struggling, got it right again.

"Don't prove that means the wood," Sam said.

Joe Gormley smiled. "Explain to I the coming trees," he said, pointing.

"Explain nothin' I will," said Sam, who, in fact, was troubled by the wall of pine and beech before them.

"Horses," Joe Gormley said.

"No sense in that and no goose besides."

The footman went on smiling.

"Crack-brained as hares," Sam muttered.

"So they was ever," said Joe Gormley, who living all his days in the big house knew firsthand, both fathers and sons, the waywardness of the Dukes of Redding.

"Nary none of them," he said, "but allus lived in dreams and folly."

He shook his gray head. "And dreams it is. And so . . ."

"Like his sad old granddad," Sam said unhappily.

Joe Gormley gave an affirmative shrug of his shoulders.

"So there you are," he said, watching the young Duke up at the front of his companions, urging them on. "Certain as death. And same as ever."

"What of the goose then?" asked Tommy Chorlton.

"Damn you, lad, keep the cart straight!" Sam shouted, tramping on through the puddled snow and leaving the boy none the wiser.

When His Grace rode under the trees, only George Grass and Rob Milton stayed beside him. Even with his back turned, riding ahead of them, they could feel his great irritation. But in the shade of the dripping branches, with just three horses walking in the waist-deep snow, there was silence.

"God's balls," His Grace cried all at once. Reining the roan, he turned sharply and trotted back.

At the edge of the wood he dismounted and waited for the cart to catch up. The other horsemen milled up and down, trying to avoid looking at him.

"Don't want those beasts of yours winded?" he asked.

"There'll be nothing in there," one of the men answered.

"You can be damned sure of that," said another, supportively indignant.

Although bitterly, His Grace grinned.

"What a nuisance," the first man said, unwilling to smile.

"It's my hunt and over my land," His Grace answered. "I choose the place."

"You might have said."

"Would you have come?"

The man looked hurt.

"Oh I say—really," he snorted and jerked up the head of his bay.

His Grace laughed openly.

Odlaw Wenceslas was about twenty, very much his father's son and therefore, by turns, both courtly and impatient and something of a contrary in a world that expected things to stay, as much as possible, as they were.

He was also long-legged and long-shouldered, with a mane of reddish brown hair that fell into blue eyes that squinted as much when he looked into shadows as into sunlight.

As a lad he had broken his nose in a fight with a blacksmith and once again with a baronet and each time over the reputation of one of the land girls he barely knew but whose good name he said, since her mother's cottage was within a day's walk of his farm, was one with his own.

Like his father, he was poorly read and ill-schooled, but he had a fondness for anyone who could teach him how a thing was mended or made. And although he went for woodcocks with the sons of the barons, he generally preferred an evening of darts in the village with the beaters and the men of the town. With some of the same men he picked sprouts in the mud and the cold until his hams ached and his hands cracked and had never complained. But when the old Duke fell from the tower, he had fled alone to the cattle barn and wept like a boy of seven.

By then the cart had come up to the trees.

"I'll have the gun," His Grace said, his hard voice—not directed toward his man—like a blow in the face, "and the cartridges."

The horsemen drew back their mounts.

"Will you be wanting me?" Joe Gormley couldn't help saying.

"And a half dozen more like you," His Grace answered, speaking not to him but over his head to the rest.

Settling his boots again in the stirrups, His Grace hoisted the gun to his shoulder.

Yet in spite of his disdain, only Joe Gormley, looking nervously over his shoulder, followed along into the bracken.

It was only a short walk, but to the footman it seemed forever. After only a few yards, Joe Gormley felt he had plunged into a jungle of nettles.

"I may as well have been a pincushion," he thought, pulling the briars and spinneys from his arms. And when the thorns cleared, there were tier after tier of bent old sycamores and tall pines, crowding in with low branches and dripping with cold winter rain.

Joe Gormley shuffled along in his gum-boots wondering how the horses could manage. He was weary and cold and felt more like a man at the end of the day than at the start of it.

His horror of the wood was frank and open and, in his mind, not associated with any sort of shame. He was not a foolish man and therefore not prepared to give up his life to darkness without a struggle.

And the wood was death. Of that he was certain, as certain, he thought and never tired of saying, as . . .

He had already lost track of His Grace and was speculating whether he was lost himself when he heard Rob Milton call out, "Come back alone, have you?"

"Only my man."

"You should have told them."

"Shouldn't have thought I needed to."

"Wouldn't have mattered. I daresay I'm not at all certain why *I've* come."

"Ghosts."

"A touching story. And a lie more than likely."

"But enough," His Grace said, "to bring you out in the rain."

"Mornings are long enough when you are awakened early," said George Grass. "Besides, cards before lunch is immoral."

Joe Gormley pulled himself blinking into their sight.

"Isn't it birds then, Your Grace?" he asked, doing his best to simulate innocence.

His Grace lowered his gun to his lap.

"Are you brave, Joe?" he asked.

"Not so I've noticed."

"Well, neither am I. Only curious."

The man's dark eyes followed His Grace carefully.

With his thick squashed-together features the old foot-man looked somewhat doglike, a clever dog that offers absolute obedience only in its master's clear line of sight.

"You seen 'im, Your Grace?" he asked.

The young Duke looked off into the trees. The snow had grown heavy on the branches, bending the boughs and making a damp tunnel that dripped like the vaults and cellars under the house.

"A month back and in the middle of a hedge," His Grace answered. "Only he wasn't . . . was someone else, in fact."

"Yet he looked like your father," said Joe Gormley, whose mind was made up about devils.

"Only different . . ." His Grace struggled. "Turned . . ."

" 'is insides out," Joe Gormley offered. "The devil's part showing."

"No," His Grace laughed. "Still a man."

Joe Gormley shook his old head with a bachelor's abhor-rence, the scratch of a woman's bush and the tearing of thorns seeming much the same to him.

"Nay, if he's been through the hedge," he said firmly. "Worse that is . . . ," he started, then stopped.

The others were silent. It was Rob Milton, not His Grace, who first directed the head of his mare toward the tunnel's dark mouth.

"It's not as near as it sounds," Elva told herself the next time she heard the guns. (She could not know that it was only George Grass shooting stupidly at shadows.) She had been walking at the river's edge, trying to cross, but because of the thaw, the ice was soft.

The river bubbled and sighed; and although she hated it, she had been thinking of Harry.

It was not, she knew, that he had ever meant ill, only that he was always uncertain. But life, she was convinced, although she suspected the conviction came from her father, needed a firm hand. Even if bullheaded and wrong, a man must believe something. She was half a child and therefore still expected, as only the very old return to think, that the business of living must remain wedded to truth.

Like all rivers, the water's only intention was slapping its cold waves vaguely against stones.

It was hard to believe that on the day before she had crossed easily. She was not exactly disheartened, but her flannels were soaked through and on the still air the sound of the shots had been startling. With the next volley she looked for a place to hide. But the bushes were wet, and knocking the branches caused the snow to fall in huge lumps that went down her neck.

A moment later she heard the nickering of horses, followed by the shouts of men. The cries seemed to come from several directions at once.

Caught in a panic, she considered the possibility that she

would be trapped between the wood and the water and a target before she could make herself known.

It was Joe Gormley who saw the last bit of the boot disappearing into the branches.

He had heard only a scuffling and, since the crooked boughs and the late-clinging leaves were twined with rainy shadows and mist, saw nothing more.

He craned his neck.

"Copped something, have you?" said Rob Milton, coming first out of the bracken.

The others were scattered, their horses picking their courses clumsily along the flooded bank.

"Summat, perhaps," Joe Gormley whispered, "though what exactly there's no telling."

"Two-legged or four-legged?"

"Boots, sir."

"Ah well, never a ghost then," Rob Milton said. "Although whatever it is isn't to be trusted. Wouldn't be an honest bugger hiding himself."

"Don't ghosts have boots?" the footman asked.

Rob Milton grinned. "Wear them backwards."

George Grass came out of the trees, his mare sloshing through the muck. The two under the oak stood stock-still, each frozen and both more uneasy than either would have cared to admit.

George Grass set aside his slippery reins and climbed down.

"What on earth?" he asked, seeing their faces.

"Treed summat," Joe Gormley said.

"What?"

"Has boots."

"What has?"

"Dunno."

"Ask it."

George Grass pushed his way forward, and now all three were standing under the lichen-covered trunk, great cold drops falling down on their upturned faces.

"Nice and quiet and warm up there?" George Grass shouted.

Nothing seemed eager to answer him.

"Doubt it's very warm, sir," Joe Gormley said.

"Could be made to be," George Grass said, fingering the lock on his gun. "I could warm its trousers."

"Might be a poacher," Rob Milton suggested.

"I shouldn't hope it," Joe said stoutly. "Nothin', if you'll pardon me saying so, poaches on the dead."

"You living or dead?" George Grass shouted, but as nothing answered he began to wonder if he were being a bloody lunatic talking to trees.

"Dash it, man," he said. "Are you certain?"

"Boots, sir." Joe Gormley was adamant.

"Then, by Christ, I'll have some proof of it," George Grass announced, loading the cartridge and pointing the gun indiscriminately.

"Boots!" he shouted, letting off a thundering shot.

Far up, after the pellets had torn through the nest of disheveled leaves, something shifted. After another long moment, a pair of muddy wellingtons suddenly plopped down at their feet.

"I'll be damned," Rob Milton said, looking about disconcertedly.

George Grass grinned. "Trousers!" he called out.

When nothing happened, he raised his gun again to his shoulder.

They waited in silence and after a little while a pair of wet brown flannels came tumbling down on them.

"Stockings!" George Grass cried cheerfully, seeing the effect.

Balled to keep them from catching the branches, the stockings dropped in front of Joe Gormley, who bent to examine them.

"Beg pardon, sir," he began.

"Coat! And dickey!" George Grass shouted, enjoying himself. "Braces!"

"Bloomers, more probably," said Joe Gormley, unraveling the stockings.

"What?"

"Wouldn't bother asking more for gentleman's clothing," Joe Gormley said. He held up the small stockings. "No point, if you see what I mean."

"Well, I never," Rob Milton said in true admiration.

As he was making his way between the clumps of hawthorn and dog rose, His Grace heard the last burst of shooting and turned back toward the sound. On the premise that most things, even the oddest, repeat themselves, he had hoped to rediscover his father's double near the tangle of hedges where he had first found him. But there was no ignoring the guns.

Rob Milton saw him coming.

"Look into the tree!" he cried.

But His Grace was staring at Joe Gormley holding a pair of damp stockings and at the dirty flannels and wellingtons on the ground.

"It be a woman," Joe Gormley said.

"What is she doing there?" His Grace asked.

"Undressing, I'm afraid," George Grass answered somewhat shamefacedly. He had put down his gun. "Joe here said it was boots and I . . ."

His Grace steadied the roan beneath the tree. "You all right?" he called up at the branches.

Nothing answered.

"I'm certain she's not hit," George Grass added. "No question of that. Kept throwing things down." He shook his head apologetically. "Rather more, I suspect, than she should have."

His Grace reached for a branch. Pulling up his legs, he balanced himself on the saddle.

He made the first great limb easily and managed the next. But there was only a blur of dead leaves ahead of him. Long snaking branches twisted and curled into invisibility. There was no wind. Just for a moment, he hung in the silence, enjoying the unexpected excitement of anticipation.

But what he liked best had never been standing wonderingly but plunging headlong into you-never-knew-what. For it was never the wondering on the brink that drew him, not the "what" or even the "what if," but the simple, unembarrassed delight of tumbling ahead unknowingly.

He stretched out his hand.

Like a wren, she was perched on the smallest branch that would hold her, as high and as far as she could get from the men with guns.

From underneath, he could see her bare legs and more than was decent.

She had a sudden glimpse of his square head, the shock of his red matted hair fallen in his startled blue eyes.

"Who are you?" he asked.

It was the first time in her life she had ever been tested.

He asked her again.

There was almost no sound, only the harshness of his breath, the prattle of a few leaves, the cough of a crow circling somewhere in the gray sky above her.

She tried to close her legs but it would have been impossible to keep from falling if she did. When she had come into the wood, she was only a child, but now under his gaze, sharp as the flame of a new candle wick, a flush that began in her legs blazed all through her.

He too had climbed as far as he could.

"Until yesterday I lived in my father's house," she thought. "Until today a man never looked at me so."

A third time he asked her.

"Tell me who you are," he said.

"Myself," she said, finally.

Thinking that she had begun at long last to answer him, His Grace, the Ninth Duke, smiled.

Chapter Four

"WHERE DO YOU COME FROM?" HE ASKED WHEN he had got her on the ground and then up beside him.

The roan was a bit flashy, more a steeplechaser than a hunter and wrong for the wood and the weather, but the young man held it skillfully. Elva locked her arms about his waist, holding on for all she was worth as the roan bolted away from the bank, heading she couldn't guess where.

Bewildered and perturbed and excited, she watched the back of his neck. The young man smelled of the damp and the oak. With an authority which reminded her of her father, he had half pulled and half carried her from the treetop down through the branches to the melting snow at the bottom and accomplished the feat with no more consequence to her than a single bruise and a scratch that began at her knee and bled only just a little.

At the base of the tree, she huddled behind him, concealing her nakedness as well as she could. For an instant the other burly young men, in their gigantic wool coats and with their long black double-barreled guns on their shoulders, seemed to her as fearsome as giants. But, as though out of courtesy, each looked away. One had even unbelted his trousers and, since her own were hopelessly muddied, handed them across to her.

The rough green tweeds, however, were much too big. She felt nearly as naked inside of them, and she was glad that her young man, concentrating on his mount's footing, did not turn his head. Nevertheless, when the roan made a leap to the top of the bank, she had grabbed him in alarm.

It was then, with the horse trotting more easily away from the river, that he asked her once more. Her earlier reluctance he had reasoned was the result of her shyness among so many. But now George Grass, abashed and riding uncomfortably in his hose, and Rob Milton, laughing until his sides ached, had gone well ahead, and his footman was walking behind, muttering.

When she did not answer, His Grace asked her in school-boy French and then, even more haltingly, in German.

She shook her head but he was keeping the branches from switching their eyes and so was not watching.

Out in the open field, the roan raced; and, with each jolt, she felt herself shaken. Uncorseted under her shift, the awkward heaviness of her breasts rose and fell. The center of her legs came down hard on the back of the roan.

"What are you doing?" she thought.

"Lady," he started again.

She had not realized it would be so appalling. Although she could see that she would have to do something to save her brothers, she had never agreed to what John said must be done. She had never actually promised anything. Indeed, she did her best not to think of them.

"Thyself and myself . . . until next year's snow," she thought, remembering instead the dear, sweet, pitiable thing that was more than a hedge and yet less than a man. She could hear it croaking and sighing its two plain words over and over pathetically.

"Lady," he said.

"Turn your head!" she thought, blushing till her face was red to the black roots of her hair. "Stop and look at me!"

"Lady," he repeated. "Is something wrong with you?"

"Thyself!" she screamed at him like a demon.

" 'Tis hard as death," Joe Gormley maintained when, last and on foot, he straggled into the meadow where the two fieldmen—although it could not be said they were waiting—were at least still dragging the game cart up the rutted slope in the rain.

His Grace and the young woman had already left the lower field. They could be seen in the distance, with the rest of the horsemen about them, recrossing the willow-girt meadow on their way to the house.

In spite of the work and the water, Sam Maddox waved his fat hand. In the cart were the young woman's boots and her trousers.

"Have you seen such ever?" he laughed.

"Isn't a joke," Joe Gormley muttered.

" 'Tis awe-inspiring rather," Sam went on laughing. "We heard it told. A girl such as that disrobing in a tree. And George Grass galloping away in his knickers!"

"I were there and you wasn't," Joe Gormley said darkly.

"We seen it," Tommy Chorlton protested.

"Seen 'er come out was all," Joe Gormley answered and wouldn't say more but only trudged on, complaining under his breath. He had no intention of speaking and only meant to go to the chapel and pray. But when he came to the house where the maids were rushing about with fresh linen for the young woman's bed and building up the fire for her comfort, he told all and sundry, upstairs and down, that they and their laughter could every one of them go to blazes.

His, however, was not the general opinion.

"Don't it just lift the spirit?" asked the maid who was assigned to watch outside the young woman's door. She smiled with a cheerful acceptance, finding delight in the discovery of the handsome young woman and the assumption, shared by the house, save only his footman, that her recovery from the wood, as in a tale of wonder and daring, meant a blessing and good fortune for His Grace.

She kept the door open a crack, to satisfy her curiosity and to see if anything were actually needed. But the young woman only sat on the sofa, with towels all around her, combing out her hair. As a precaution the doctor had been sent for. But the weather being what it was, the maid knew it would be some hours before the courtly old physician drove his chaise up the cattle track and into the yard.

Fog smudged the windows. The fields were blurred with a mist which swallowed up the barns and contracted the afternoon until it seemed almost night. There was scarcely any noise. In spite of their excitement, the servingwomen went about on tiptoe. Although usually ready at any excuse to kick up a row, His Grace's companions sat glumly in the guest hall, gazing unsteadily into their glasses and growing increasingly ill-tempered. The Duke should have told them, they thought, that he had some other intention, not birds at all, when he rode into the wood. Sam Maddox and Tommy Chorlton, both with a story to tell, had gone home to their wives. Joseph Gormley, however, returned to the tack room where he set to cleaning His Grace's boots and, although urged on by his conscience, refused to speak to the grooms.

By then the Duke had visited the kitchen. He did not look about himself and was unaware that the house was watching and listening. Carrying the bowl of warm broth, he climbed the stairs. Dismissing the maid, he shouldered his way through the doors of the young woman's bedroom.

"The weather is devilish," he said, finding her staring at the window into the fog. She had her back to him, and when she turned suddenly to look, her waist-long hair, now mostly dried by the fire, surged in several directions at once like something with a life of its own.

"How lovely!" he thought, more pleased with himself than before for having brought her into the house.

He set the bowl on the table. "Here is something to warm you," he said.

She smiled at him gravely.

"You could have something else, if you like."

Again her mouth twitched up at the corners, but she shook her head.

He put his hands into his pockets, took them out, her shyness making him uncharacteristically uncertain. "Are you feeling better?" he asked.

"Thyself?" she replied.

"Fine," he said, relieved to have had an answer. "Quite wonderful, to tell the truth, now that I found you. It is extraordinary, you know. The wood is so dreadfully huge, so endless and strange. No one knows how to find one's way about in it. And no one will ever go in. I only dared try myself once before." He paused, putting his big hands again into his pockets, but staring her full in the face.

Beneath the smoothness of her complexion, he noticed something dark and uneasy, just the slightest knot of fear, which, because it gave him an advantage, he found very encouraging.

"Now," he said, no longer embarrassed, "you must tell me who you are. And what it is you were doing there. And whether there is anything I can do to help."

She peered at him so oddly that he did not realize at first she had no intention of answering.

"You do have a name?" he said finally.

She unwrinkled her nose.

"Oh hell, yes," he laughed. "Everyone's got a name."

His skin was pulled taut over his cheekbones and his striking blue eyes, which when he laughed retained a certain hardness, looked straight into hers and made her so nervous that had she been willing to speak she might have found herself babbling. She tried to put herself at ease by thinking. Whenever she was flummoxed and uneasy, the best thing, she had always found, was tugging the bloody nuisance into pieces and reassembling it from a jumble. The solution, more often than not, was chucking out one way of looking and seeing the same obstinate mess differently.

The fire was behind her, the bed on one side and the dressing table on the other. She ran her eyes over both, searching. Stepping back, she walked up and down. As he watched, she went through the shelves of the closet, pulling out one thing and another and putting them back. It wasn't until she was seated at the dressing table, rummaging through the drawers, that she glanced across at him shrewdly.

The pencil had been far to the back, the paper the loose plain wrapping on an ointment jar.

Begging his patience with another smile, she wrote quickly in a small firm hand, covering the scrap of paper to its edges.

"You must forgive me," she wrote, "but for reasons I do not in the least understand, I must not speak more than you have already heard. You have been kind. Still, you must do me the added kindness not to ask me. To do otherwise would betray my brothers who are lost in the same wood. My name is Elva."

When she had finished, she handed him the paper.

He took a very long time studying it. Twice he looked up, seeking some explanation in her eager face.

But although he saw there were words and sentences, their meaning eluded him utterly.

He laughed aloud all at once. "Never before," he said, leaning over her as if letting her in on a secret, "have I ever wished I had stayed on at St. Berzelius or paid better attention to that bloody damn fool of a language master."

"Romanian, perhaps," His Grace explained to Rob Milton.

"You ever see it written?" Rob Milton asked.

"Or badger, for all I know," His Grace said. "Or tree writing. Or gibberish. Who is to say?"

"You might show it to the priest."

"I might climb to the roof like my da," His Grace said coldly.

There was an awkward little pause. In spite of the mystery of the woman, the guest hall was nearly empty. Although the weather was no better, the majority of His Grace's companions, finding the Duke preoccupied, had gone into the village and some even further on into Devon. The platters of roast guinea-fowl lay undisturbed on the table. Ignoring his plate, George Grass poured out a third glass of port and drank it without feeling happier.

"Why don't she come down?" he asked.

"Invited her," His Grace said. "No telling though, if she understood a word of it."

"She isn't ill, do you think?" Rob Milton asked.

"Not that I expect." His Grace turned impatiently toward the windows. "Rendcombe, damn him, if he ever comes, may know better."

"It's the fog," George Grass said, examining the inside of his glass.

"Queer, strange weather, there's no denying," His Grace admitted.

"January thaw."

"Still, we'll need a fire for the damp."

"And covers after midnight."

"But a pump for the basement."

"Aye, when I look ahead, it's storm."

"Mark me," someone said, "by Sunday there'll be snow again."

There was the gentlest of taps on the window, as much dark drizzling mist as rain.

"Do you imagine anyone has told the old woman?" Rob Franklin asked.

"My great gran," His Grace corrected him, although the point was much debated, and opinions, both in the house and in the village, were openly divided.

"If you choose to believe her."

His Grace reached for one of the birds. "Someone must."

"Your father wouldn't have."

Without taking offense, His Grace smiled. The tales and stories were older than his memory and unflattering.

Sticking his fork deeply into the breast, he said, "Everyone knows, George, we are a great disaster of a family."

On her own business, far from the house, a woman, padding softly as an aged cat, crept from under the trees. Straightening her rheumaticky back, she went across the willow-girt meadow through the wet grass, half expecting to find frog-spawn in the ditches and cowslips poking up their heads at the bottom of the lane. She was used to quirks in the weather. In her vague, unnumbered years she had come to see the oddities of nature not as disturbing extravagances but the simple recurrence of a longer, slower pattern. Very little was actually impossible, only rare. She had seen snow in August, heard thunder at the turning of the year. Neither amounted to much. And there were stranger things. But there was a quality of this fog that had left her with a premonitory disquiet and had put her on her guard.

When she climbed what she thought was the hill behind the house, (as though the world were no better than a stage set changed between scenes), she had found herself instead outside the tack room.

Joe Gormley was sitting on the bench, bent over His Grace's boots.

"Madam," he said curtly, not bothering to look at her.

"Out and about, was he?" the old woman said.

"Come back."

"No birds, I gather."

Joe Gormley chose another brush. "Summat though," he said, aggrieved. "Treed. Brought down and carried off. Took by his hand into the house. And there to keep, I shouldn't wonder, till it's all done again."

"A girl?"

He put down his brush.

She needed no answer.

Knowing the yard, now that she had found the stable, even blind and in spite of the pains and penalties of the stairs, her crooked fingers found the latch. Inside the warm kitchen she could see again.

"Bag full of squirrels and jays?" the cook asked cruelly, watching the old woman remove her patched cloth sack from her shoulder.

"Crows and weasels, Nanny?"

"Fox piss," the old woman hissed at her. "Will make you beautiful."

"Use it yourself then," said the cook.

"Which room?" the old woman asked.

"She's to be let be," the cook said sharply. "Only His Grace until Rendcombe sees her."

The old woman took up her bag again.

"As pretty as that," she said reflectively and went past the chimney corner by the hearth which, before this cook and perhaps before others, had been her favorite seat.

"You durst not!" the cook called after her.

In the hallway the old woman could hear the men gossiping and ignored them. She found the stairs. It was not the walking that troubled her. In her eighties she had been seen along every field path and beside every gate from the houseland down into the village. Once, when the old Duke lived, the local fire brigade had recovered her from Stephen's Well, ambling along with Gypsyish folk, keeping up with their wagons. But she hated stairs (or at least a certain high bedroom) and would not go up to the other stories unless provoked.

At the first landing she rested for a moment.

"You mustn't," the little pinch-faced maid said when she saw her.

"I do what I like in my own house," the old woman answered, and while the maid was considering what she might do to stop her, the old woman pushed her way past and locked the door.

Elva brushed back her hair off her forehead. The young Duke had come and gone, leaving her bewildered but not distressed. Whatever he wanted and whatever would happen, it was pleasant to be dry again. The borrowed trousers and what remained of her underclothing had been discarded in a heap on the floor. She had found a robe in the closet, a soft robe of rich, green velvet; and, although it pulled at her breasts and caught at the armholes, it was pretty and it was warm.

All the rest was a great embarrassment, of course: the horsemen and the tree, the young man who had seen rather more of her than anyone had except Mrs. Curran. By rights, she supposed, she should be in agony; in fact, now that she had been left to herself, she could hear her heart beating. But the truly extraordinary thing, blowing everything else violently before it, was that she had crossed from her side of the wood to the other.

Elva sat at the dressing table, only just beginning to realize how profoundly—without being different—her life had changed. She held her breath, remembering how in the murk, coming out of the trees among the helter-skelter of horses and fieldmen, she had seen the unmistakable shape of the tower that, except that it was turned, seemed the replica of her father's.

The cattle track had been neither shorter nor longer. Neither the mews nor the barns, nor even the formidable appearance of the great house itself, with its long chilly porches and many gables, its grizzled winter gardens, well house and drains (except that in profile all its pieces and appurtenances had been hauled out of the earth where they truly belonged and set down otherwise) were as she remembered. Even the enormous old mulberry in the yard, except, of course . . .

"Which are you?" someone muttered behind her.

She did not move.

"Which?"

"Myself," Elva said at last wearily, already growing tired of the promise.

Someone laughed. "No, no, child. You must do better than that."

She looked around.

A toothless mouth smiled at her.

"Cecily?" the old woman asked. "Olivia?"

Elva shook her head.

"Violet? Pru? Elizabeth?"

Elva looked down.

"Good," the old woman said. "But I had to ask. Curse of the family Wenceslas. Trial by a thousand questions, even when the answer's certain. Now," she said, coming nearer. She stretched out her withered hand, not as a gesture of comfort, but almost as an act of bravado.

The hand was like a claw.

"Just nod," the old woman said.

The two women eyed one another.

"Is it Elva?" the old woman chuckled. "Often is from that side, as it's Avle on this. Not that we do the naming, mind you. That's for our husbands and we haven't the practice. Never speak, you know, when the first child comes. And yet we don't lack for cleverness. If we wanted, I am convinced we could, even without a word, persuade them of anything we wished."

Elva pressed her lips very close together. She was afraid she was going to scream.

Grabbing hold of the old woman, she pulled her roughly to the dressing table. Certain now that all was saved, she pointed to the scrap of paper excitedly.

The old woman stared at it for a moment. Then her eyes drifted up to the mirror.

Before Elva quite understood, the old woman snatched the paper from the table.

"No," she said without pity, "not if you care in the least for your brothers."

Hobbling toward the hearth, the old woman tossed the scrap into the flames and, as though with great satisfaction, watched the curling edges of Elva's one hope begin to darken and burn.

Chapter Five

THE FIRST KISS WAS APPARENTLY AN ACCIDENT. HIS Grace had been in the kitchen by chance and his thoughts were on other matters. His footman, as it happened, had forgotten to return his boots and His Grace had gone off in his stocking feet through the servants' wing to reclaim them. He went swearing through the halls. Without any reason, he yelled at the dogboy who had come in from the kennels for bread and porridge. The kitchen was merely partway between one place and the other. His Grace had never expected to find the young woman's breakfast only just then come from the oven. At that moment the cook had set it down on the table and the maid, except that His Grace had rushed in so suddenly, had all but lifted it to her arm.

"I'll take it up to her," he had offered.

Arguably, this was no more than a gentle reaffirmation of his original injunction that no one but himself was to be permitted to intrude on her until Rendcombe had delivered his opinion. But the physician, who had not come

194

by nightfall, even now had failed to put in an appearance; and, if the women were curious about the new house guest, they were also understandably concerned that she was being neglected.

"Give it here," His Grace had said, his voice edged ever so slightly.

The newly laundered shirt and fresh collar he had drawn on was for no purpose other than he had worn the last, being involved with the hunt, for several days running. That he had noticed his reflection was, in much the same way, unavoidable, since the mirror, set at the bottom of the stairs, was directly in his path. This was not cant. He had never been disposed to plan unnecessarily. Joy, he would almost certainly have said if, in so many words he had tried to explain it, was slow to come to any who overly prepared for it.

Nevertheless, he might have knocked; only he had been holding the tray in one hand and had to work the latch with the other.

It was not that she was entirely naked. She had just finished wrapping a blanket over her shoulders. She was not even facing him, but staring out of the window into a morning that was still more mist than light. But her thoughts raced.

A large bump, the result of climbing out of the covers into the wall, darkened on her forehead. At the moment of waking she had swung out her legs into a little space, not knowing it was so small, and, as she had pulled herself up, thrust herself into an obstacle that had she been in her own bed would have been on the other side.

"Everything's moved around," she thought, remembering the paper the old woman had burned.

There could be no question. Everything was inverted,

not only the house and the bed, but her very own words on the paper.

"I should introduce myself," His Grace was saying.

"And yet she read them," she thought, surprised, and although some part of her was aware of the white shirt peeking out between the worn lapels of his coat, she returned to the mirror.

"Wenceslas," His Grace was telling her, "like in the old carol. He was real, you know. Not a king at all, of course, but a duke in Bohemia, a martyr, murdered by his own mother. It's rather a sad story. But then, all the stories that get remembered are sad. Happiness, it seems, never outlasts those who experience it."

He stopped.

"I know it's ridiculous," he continued. "At least it sounds so conventional. But I sometimes think that all that ever interests us is one another's pain."

It was a long thought for His Grace and, it may be as well, that he gave words to it because he believed she did not understand him.

As though made uncomfortable by speaking, his white teeth caught the corner of his lip.

Until that moment she had been kissed three times. Once by her father and twice, when she was eleven, by Harry, who was experimenting but, as usual, had been too frightened to consider anyone else, even though the between-maid had sometimes sat beside him for a quarter hour with no good reason.

"Odlaw," he went on.

She had missed the parts between.

It was not that she had never longed for a young man. She had waited all her life for just such a moment. Sitting as a child among the women in her father's hall, she had watched the young men at the dances, young men but older than herself, feeling, even as she sat on the stiff-backed chair among the plump, unwanted women, hands that were not holding her creep experimentally along her shoulders toward forbidden places. In truth, the moment, standing naked under a blanket in the presence of a young man who had rescued her, was grander than she had ever allowed herself to think might actually happen. It had simply never occurred to her that it would come at the very instant she discovered the duplicity of the universe.

"The old woman knew!" she thought. "Knew everything! The writing and who I was and why I dared not speak!"

Her face at that instant went brick red and her hand, which she had all but forgotten, loosened its grip on the blanket so that the covering, together with her descending blush, dropped down on her shoulders.

When he reached out to save her from what had seemed to him the likelihood of an even deeper embarrassment, she was still only partially aware of him.

Even then, with both temptations staring him equally in the face, he had felt an obligation to protect her modesty. To his credit, it must be said that afterward he never made the excuse of his honorable first intentions. What he told Rob Milton later was that she did not seem to mind.

His initial reach was clumsy. But when the blanket slipped, she did not lower her eyes. It was then, with a humorous acceptance of what appeared no more or less than the inevitable, he drew her into his arms. And it was then that Rendcombe came through the door and discovered her, quite as naked as the day she was born, her mouth pressed, for that one time entirely innocently, against His Grace's.

*　　*　　*

So the kiss was first; the courting came in the long days that followed. The difficulty of Rendcombe's finding them, however, was gotten around rather quickly. The old physician, who had been young himself, handled everything beautifully. He dismissed His Grace at once and, under the pretext of needing one or two items he had neglected in his chaise, removed himself for ten minutes. When he returned, very properly, with one of the housewomen to wait by the door, Elva was dressed and seated in a chair.

The day was beginning to clear and a pale light was climbing in shyly at the windows. Elva, looking hunted, was peering out, watching a pair of fallow deer which had wandered onto the lawn.

"What's the excitement?" he asked, pretending not to see either animal.

Elva made a desperate gesture toward the lawn, her white fingers trembling.

Rendcombe laughed kindly. In ten minutes below the stairs he had learned as much as anyone knew about the young woman. "Escaped from the wood," he said. "Bold as brass sometimes. They get bolder every year."

He began looking through his bag. "Must know they can't come to harm here," he added, and he gave her such a generous grin that, although her thoughts had been in an uproar, she smiled back at him gratefully.

After a moment, he drew a chair up next to her. "Now I've been told," he said, "you don't speak."

In a half hour he had come down again to his Grace.

"Won't," Rendcombe declared finally and stopped as if no more needed to be added; but he had not lost his grin.

He had, however, taken the liberty of closing the door against the women.

The library was dark and, in some corners, still smelled of the old Duke's pipe. His Grace had already seen to the fire and a lamp. Feeling younger than he liked, he waited while Rendcombe fumbled in his pockets. Before the second wick caught, the match seemed in danger of burning the old man's fingers.

"Many's the night, Your Grace," Rendcombe said, at last settling himself comfortably, "I sat here after dinner, solving the country's problems. You don't know how your da and I enjoyed ourselves! Politics, bless us all, and ethics too!" He made a point of not looking up. "Arguing the right and wrong of things into the small hours."

Under the shadowed rows of unread books, His Grace frowned.

"It was a mistake," he said. "I know that."

"Not by half," Rendcombe said, "or there'd be no cause for me to mention it."

"I know it now."

"Try to see it stays learned," Rendcombe told him flatly. "The women and the priest, God help us, are likely to make a fuss otherwise." He slipped the box of matches back into his pocket. "Fortunately," he said, "the young woman doesn't seem inclined to mention it."

His Grace squinted, uncertain if the old man was making fun of him.

"Because she cannot?" he asked.

"Because she doesn't seem inclined to."

"Because . . ."

"Because she won't," Rendcombe repeated, "whatever the reason. Healthy as a horse. Talks too much, if anything. Will 'thyself' and 'myself' you to death, if you ask her."

"Pretty, though," he said, more to himself and a shade resentfully, as if remembering and then putting aside something he thought best avoided, at least for the moment.

He did not look up.

Between the shelves above him there were prints of gentlemen dressed for hunting in the style of eighty and a hundred years before. He knew the faces without looking. It was curious, he couldn't help thinking, how the look of certain men and women went out-of-date as swiftly as the cut of their coats, while there were others, like the young woman, who even years and years ago . . .

Rendcombe stood.

"She looks seventeen or eighteen," he said, "although she could be younger. What is clear is that she hasn't any relatives, not on this side. And we can't send her back. But as much as you should let Rob Milton take her along to his mother, given what you and I know, since all the rest of the world doesn't, it would only seem worse."

He was a very old man, with his skin loose on his cheekbones and fallen into a sack on his neck. But although his tone had turned grave, His Grace wondered, for a disturbing second, whether Rendcombe was still making fun of him.

"I'm sorry to disappoint you," he said stiffly.

"You never have," Rendcombe said. "It was brave to bring her out of the wood. Braver to keep her. Only I caution you to remember, even though you are a lad yourself, you stand, Your Grace, as a father . . ."

"I stand," said Odlaw Wenceslas, "to walk you to your chaise."

They went through the house without speaking.

The cook, with two of the servingwomen peering out over her ample shoulders, watched from the kitchen as His Grace waved Rendcombe silently into his carriage.

"What on earth can be wrong with them?" asked one of the women.

"Advice," said the cook, knowing men well enough, and these two in particular. "No man ever took it gratefully. And never a man, young as he is, with six thousand acres."

Puzzling over her face in the glass, Elva wound a switch of her hair on to the top of her head. She had already tried it with a knot and with pins. She took up the brush and in exasperation put it back, letting her hair fall as it liked.

Neither the extraordinary young man nor the kindly old one had come back. The next time the door opened it was a maid with the folded pile of her clothing, now cleaned and pressed. Elva shook her head, trying to show at once that she was grateful, but that, grateful or not, since she was no longer trekking through snow and brambles, she hadn't the least intention of returning her legs to her brother's cut-down trousers, that, after all, what would they think of her if she did? The maid, who, in fact, along with the rest of the house, hadn't been altogether certain what to think of her, looked relieved. Nonetheless, there was another awkward silence, as though the maid, bewildered as to how one spoke to someone who didn't, was trying to fashion some alternate communication from blinks and squints.

At last Elva poked her finger in the middle of the maid's bony chest.

"Thyself?" she said firmly.

There was a final uncomfortable silence.

Then the maid, realizing that she had been a fool, gave a sudden agreeable little snort.

"Your pardon, miss," she said, almost in her normal voice. "It's Em. Short for Emily."

Emily scooped up the trousers. "I'll just put these away," she said. "Told Mrs. Curran I didn't think they'd do. 'Well, they're hers,' she says. And so you should have them. And so you do. But anyone could see they're for snow and for walking out in bogs and bushes and who knows where. I'd be frit myself, though. Nobody I know ever did. Not in such wilds and rambles and whatnot."

Emily, having found a place for the trousers, had come back to the center of the room. "How long you been there?" she asked.

Elva raised one finger.

Emily smiled. "Days I hope that means," she said. "Weeks would . . ."

Elva shook her head.

"Well, I wouldn't an hour. Still, you don't seem no worse for it," Emily continued, giving her a quick glance-over, now that she dared look. "That's his mother's dress," she said. "Her room, of course, with her clothes in it. The old Duke wouldn't change it and His Grace left it too. But she, if you don't mind me saying, miss, was something smaller."

They met each other's eyes, both thinking, curiously, the same thing.

"Might take a minute," Emily told her. "There's rooms and rooms. But they're all sentimental. Being men, if you know what I mean. Not just the husbands. The sons and grandsons too. Won't throw out anything. So the dresses are liable to be a bit musty."

Emily paused at the door as she went out. "But you

know that," she said, having heard something of the tales.

Elva's head whirled.

She knew and yet she didn't. Wenceslas, but it was Odlaw. Rendcombe, but his flesh was gray not pink. Even Mrs. Curran (for the maid had said the name), but Elva knew that it wouldn't be. Had both cooks been the same woman, this other one would have been up to this bedroom as quickly as her fat old legs could have carried her. But she hadn't and therefore there could be no question of their being, even remotely, the same. And then too, Elva knew, she was only herself, had been herself on the other side, was herself now. "Which can only mean," Elva thought, not finding much help and getting lost again, "that everyone here must as well . . .

"Yet if," she started again, "I am, no matter where, myself, then I am for certain and everyone else can only be . . ."

But they were real and not shadows. That was clear.

Elva threw herself down on the sofa.

Astonished and still dismayed, she tried instead to think of her brothers. The problem, however, she was beginning to realize, although more horrifying, was exactly the same. They were dead. Yet they persisted. They were lost because they had gone into the wood. Nevertheless, because she had entered under the trees herself, she could save them.

But then, if the first was true, the second couldn't be.

Except, the second was just as true.

"Then there has to be a third!" it had suddenly occurred to her when, with a scratch at the door, Emily reentered with an armful of dresses.

For a moment, each seemed surprised, as though in the intervening minutes both had begun to wonder a little whether the other might not have gone up in smoke.

Then Emily giggled and a sense of absurdity, like a breeze through the window, blew away Elva's fear.

"Can't say I know what it's like where you're from," Emily laughed, "but here ladies is expected to dress for lunch."

Wriggling out of what she was wearing, Elva began to look over the mounds of white crinoline and four colors of satin. In the presence of the maid she was quite unconsciously naked when, out of the corner of her eye, she saw her two brown nipples bobbing up and down in the mirror and, without fully keeping track of where her thoughts went, found herself puzzling over what one said to a young man who had already kissed her once and twice seen about as much of her as there was to look at.

Chapter Six

Elva, of course, said nothing, but Rob Milton, accepting a cup of tea, leaned toward her as though speaking confidentially.

"I'm certain His Grace wishes you would forgive him," he said. "He has had to go into the village quite suddenly. Some matter, it would seem, over which, frankly, he had no choice."

Because His Grace was away and because it was only luncheon, Mrs. Curran, having brought out the dishes herself, had remained at the back of the table where she could hear every word.

She was a large woman but not, Elva had already discovered, quite as large as her own Mrs. Curran. Although her nose was of a great size, and the span of her shoulders nearly as broad as a whisky barrel, her breasts, unlike her mountainous double's, were small and so misplaced as to be indistinguishable within her general roundness and lumpishness. She walked slowly, flat-heeled and unhurried, and this, as with the rest of her movements and demeanor, called to mind something intractable and rude, rather more like something that had its proper place in the paddock instead of at the center of the house with the afternoon china. Elva resolved to have as little to do with her as possible, an attitude which, whenever their eyes met, Elva was quite certain was reciprocated.

"It's Gormley," George Grass said abruptly, to the other man, with a tone in his voice that implied both that it was a matter of some wickedness and not worth the trouble.

Elva smiled uncomprehendingly.

"It's quite a nice salad," Rob Milton tempted her.

In fact it was slivers of cold goose and a kind of wild berry she had had once on the other side but whose name she didn't remember. However, it was more than acceptable, although she doubted it went equally well with Rob Milton's tea and George Grass's champagne or the teaspoonfuls of brown mustard with which the smaller man smothered his goose and his bread.

She had begun to sort them out. Each had introduced himself, Rob Milton gently, saying his name once clearly without embarrassment.

"I am George Grass," the other had announced three times over, as if she were deaf. He had made his way across the highly polished floor when she had first come into the room and shaken her hand until Rob Milton had stopped him. But then, she imagined he was uneasy about depriving her of Harry's trousers.

She was wearing the red satin, which her own Mrs. Curran would have thought better for evening or, more probably, best not at all. The Duke, however, was absent.

"Found the man in the Royal Charles," George Grass whispered, as though she couldn't hear him.

"Not the same since the old Duke," Mrs. Curran said to herself, although everyone could.

"Drunk as a lord," George Grass added.

Rob Milton stared at them both.

"Would you try an apricot?" he suggested to Elva, his plain bony face doing its best to distract her from any consideration of unpleasantness.

Elva smiled radiantly. She had inherited her mother's shining gray eyes and a splendid mass of black hair that, forever escaping from its pins, was her glory. But she had her father's combativeness and in the big houses on the other side, especially when she had been goaded by Arthur, her cleverness had often muddled her success with young men. But here and much to her surprise, her silence had the effect of charm.

"A damn sight better than crows and possum, I imagine," George Grass said to her, unable to think on what else in the terrible, unholy wood a young woman might dine.

Elva smiled again, practicing.

But the young Duke's absence was as tangible as a hole gaping in the well-polished flooring just under the table legs. She had to hold herself protectively, as though, if she forgot, she would tumble over the edge, down into, well, she couldn't say where, but tumble head-over-heels, her gown and petticoats flying over her head, her own bare legs kicking and scissoring and in full view of either gentlemen.

She wasn't exactly ashamed of her thoughts, but she would have been grateful for her own kitchen and the presence of her own Mrs. Curran and the chance, just this once, pressing into her, to cry out, for joy or dread.

Like a baby, Joe Gormley cradled his head in his arms, but the head was so heavy he was soon compelled to pause for breath. Indeed, the head hurt so much that he was glad that from time to time it did not seem quite to belong to him. To keep it from spinning away, he had wedged it against his belly and supported it under his arm. But it was hard work, and less than a mile from the Royal Charles, he gave the head a fatherly pat and sat down with it by the stile to rest them both.

It was not, in any event, he decided, a good day for walking. He had slipped a few too many times because of the mud, and the head huffed and whizzed. Winded, it seemed to him, not from the road—since what did a head suffer from walking?—but from having so much to say to the barman and the two or three other gents hunched in grave silence over their porter and pints through the last of the night and the start of the morning.

"What come up backwards, come out wrong!" the head had tolderolled suddenly late into the evening. Until that point it had merely sat quietly side by side with Joe Gormley, as if there wasn't a half penny's difference between them. But after that it had been certain that all the while the head had been brooding independently, simply awaiting its chance.

"Thaw in January mean rot in May," the head had announced sternly and, once it had started, had gone a deep plum color and, as full of fiery indignation as if it were the priest himself, called down damnation on nearly everyone from Devon to Stephen's Well, starting with Sam Maddox and Tommy Chorlton and proceeding through the sporting men and on to the housewomen but ending with His Grace.

"He's a lad," the head sputtered bitterly. "All the same, he's no right to put us in the way of such harm. Has he, I asks you?"

No one had seen fit to answer.

"Had I been holdin' his gun," it declared wildly, "hadn't I already give it him, certain as I am of heaven, I would have blasted 'er back to twigs and leaves."

It may have been that until the girl they hadn't much paid attention.

The discussions that evening had run in the usual circle from the hunting of rats and the likelihood of angels, to the wiliness of spaniels and whose black mare or spindle-legged gray had the surest chance at the spring fair in Carrick. But the other conversations had stopped then, although it wasn't until after closing, with the windows shuttered against the local sergeant, that they had stitched enough of the ragtag pieces together to follow and knew, as once long ago they had heard whispered, that once again a woman who would say very little had come from the wood to marry the young Duke of Redding.

For the next hour everyone talked except the one who had started it. The barman said it was lies, since it was only lies, he confessed, although it pained him to say so, that anyone uttered under his roof. "Eats their children, I heared," said the oldest of the company, but he was the slowest as well, and as he said nothing more, all had another round and ignored him. Nevertheless, there were morning sparrows and finches (although where they came from was a mystery) chirping in the eaves and the outside bushes when the barman, because he could not remember such a rare night, made breakfast and, when the bacon was grilled and the frizzled fat eaten, lovingly applied his hand to the pump and filled all the glasses one last time.

"How do you know?" someone had asked, a hint of skepticism waking with the finches.

"Saw her nethers," the head answered. "Saw 'er as she

was when His Grace brought 'er to ground."

"They's all the same underneath," the same one snig-
gered.

"Not this 'un's, damn you!" the head tolderolled again,
puffing and snorting, as though ready to begin again. "I
seen it, if no one else. I dinna turn."

"What? Saw what?" the barman drawled wearily, ready
for bed.

"Twigs and branches," the lolling head answered. "Same
as she was a tree or a hedge."

It was about the same time that Rendcombe, having
come down from the house and seeing the lantern through
the shutters, halloed at the door. And it was Rendcombe
who, after he had been let in and having heard a little, sent
word back up the hill to His Grace. Still, had he listened
to everything, he would have gone himself.

The head saw the legs of His Grace's roan, but the head
wasn't much troubled by them. Joe Gormley's own legs,
however, beginning to have a better sense of what was
fitting, tried to stand.

For a moment His Grace disappeared behind the legs of
the roan. Amused at the peekaboo, the head beamed like
an infant, its puffy eyes crinkling.

"Iss gone," the head giggled, rolling back, its laughter
bubbling over and undermining its defenses.

"Wouldn't bother," His Grace said.

"Bother what?" the head asked.

"Trying to stand."

The head considered that. "Could, if I wanted . . . ," it
began.

"I'd recommend different," His Grace replied critically.
"Save you the effort of getting up twice."

★   ★   ★

The second time, looking for the outside door, Elva turned left at the kitchen. The difficulty was in learning to distrust her expectations. It was as if her nerves, not her brain, had always been in charge of her comings and goings. She had had to teach herself to think instead. But if thinking was sometimes useful, sometimes it wasn't. As in her own house, there were too many doors down too many corridors. Looking for what would have been John's room, although here it wouldn't be, she had found George Grass, by himself, playing at billiards. She had blundered into the library and the laundry without looking for either. And yet it all should have been rather simple: whatever you expect to do, do the other. Only the differences here were more subtle and insinuating, not exactly a duplicate but a refraction.

The main stairs, thankfully, were at the center, and she could, whenever it seemed she would never find her way, return there and start again. In the middle of the afternoon, holding on to the banister at the bottom of the stairs and trying to think where she would try next, she had met Emily coming from the first floor landing.

Without being asked, Emily had shown her once more to her room. Left to herself for ten minutes, Elva tried on a pair of riding boots from the closet and, when they nearly fit, a long skirt, an underblouse and a sweater. When she was dressed, on only the second try she found her way past the kitchen before Mrs. Curran, who almost certainly would have stopped her, had noticed and was out the back door.

Because of all the rain that had fallen the day before, the hill that led down to the wood was a morass of small lakes and puddles. But although the weather was warmer than

winter should have been, the air had grown cooler and
the dark mud was frozen and the small lakes were armored
thinly with shields of cobwebby ice. For the most part,
the regular workmen were indoors, the grooms with their
horses, the cowman in his barn. The horseman, coming
slowly out of the village, was so distant that he scarcely
seemed there at all and her eyes, improving on the shape,
imagined two heads and a double set of arms. But then
everything, she was discovering, that wasn't wrong altogether was at best out of true. She did not wait for this
wayward smudge to become one again, which, because it
was His Grace and his footman, even when it was closer, it
never would. The path behind the well house wound left
instead of right. But beyond the long meadow, the rough
line of trees still rose up gloomily. There was simply no
helping it that, contrary to her experience, it was west.

Nonetheless, she had expected that returning to the
wood would have been easier.

The meadow was just difficult. As often as the ice shat-
tered, the mud held, so that half the time she was mucking
through water. The rest of the time she was hobbling. The
heel of one boot then the other stuck in frost heaves and
furrows, threatening her balance. And where the ground
was less broken, there were flints.

The wood, however, when she had finally managed to
stumble against its broad edge, was impossible. It did not
seem to matter that the Duke, with three men following,
had gone in and ridden out again, with herself slung up,
like a captive, beside him.

They must, she thought, have ridden in and come out
at some other place. The old trees rose up taller than the
house. Their huge black trunks, each set as closely together
as by gardeners for a windbreak, were threaded with wild

interwoven branches. She walked unhappily beside them. Inside, the afternoon sunlight slid between crevices too thin for a child, even the incorporeal ghost of a boy, to wriggle through. In her thoughts she could almost hear John crying out to her. And although she was certain that he would never be so near the danger of an open field, that his crying was only in her memory, she did not wish to leave him.

"God save his soul," she whispered to herself. "God save mine."

She looked up at the leafless boughs, her gaze searching. "I can walk here for a quarter of an hour," she thought, "but shall I ever leave this place? Or shall I die here?"

Beyond the determination that she should do something, she had had no clear plan when she had left the house. Yet, for a little while at least she had no need to worry about the expression on her face. In the house, even for as short a time as she had been there, she knew they watched each bewildered flicker of her startled eyes. She had watched herself, rising in the middle of the night and lighting a candle in front of the mirror. If she had spoken, little by little they would have stopped paying attention. But silent she was a mystery—even to herself. "For how can I know what I truly think," she had wondered, "until I've said it?"

She remembered the promise that had been asked of her and shivered. She had never answered. Then was she bound? And yet she knew, the truth shaming her in the instant she had discovered it, that to declare it outright and openly was to break her word.

She walked within a yard of the wood's edge. Although she could not see it, she felt the sun sinking. Unseen as well, somewhere among the trees, things were scurrying. Weasels and stoats, she thought. Or wrens, with hearts as panicked and pattering as the hearts of mice. But not even a hare broke into the clearing.

She was not frightened. She was in the very midst of strangeness, but the slowness of her movements was mirrored in the slowness of her thoughts. The cold was not enough to clear her head. The stirrings in the wood were merely echoes. She would have liked something bolder and less enigmatic. As straightforward as her father leaping from the roof. As unambiguous as the young Duke's arms, clutching her across the smallness of her shoulders, the chaste, protective blanket falling to her feet.

Perhaps the wind changed.

She was awakened from her reverie by voices in the wood. She couldn't make out completely what was being said, but after a while she understood that one of the voices was Harry's.

"I was taken too soon," he said. "Before I was ready."

"Hush," said the other. "Don't talk so loudly."

"Hush?" he said, displeased by the reprimand. "Hush?" he asked. "Surely, something more is due me."

"Duke's son or king's son or the son of a butcher," answered the other, "living or dead, few are satisfied."

"Jesus, what do I care of philosophy? I would speak with her."

"Death is silence."

"I am cold."

"From the cold I can give no help."

"Then, I would have what you carry in your sack."

"If you have you a liking for weasels and crows," said the other, "put in your finger."

"It has the feel of a child's head!" exclaimed the Duke's son.

The other laughed. "You may not eat without saving your sister's share."

Elva's warmed face turned.

The wind had changed again.

She listened but there was nothing to hear.

When she reached the cattle track, Elva paused to look around. From the back, she recognized the old woman, toiling up the hill before her, a patched brown sack on her shoulder. Elva stared across the furrows.

Although the light was failing, she was nearly certain she could see a sprig of hedge leaves caught in the hoary extravagance of the woman's wild, tangled hair.

That evening there were two sour soups and one sweet one; a cold pheasant pie; hot roasted pork loin and a tile-fish cut into pieces like flowers; two curries, and a salad with apples and walnuts brought up from the cellar. There were four side dishes and six kinds of bread. When His Grace saw what had been done, he asked Mrs. Curran to join them at the bottom of the table.

"Kind of you to ask," Mrs. Curran answered, "but, even if some doesn't, I know my place."

However, in spite of the splendor of the table, most of the places remained empty. None of the sporting men had come back; and George Grass, having no objection to staying over when there was a day's shooting, had left by late afternoon when it had become clear that His Grace had lost interest.

"We had six days straight in October," he had complained when he met His Grace in the yard. One of the grooms, who had run out to claim the roan, had stopped in his tracks, and George Grass had stopped with him, staring at the footman.

Everyone, George Grass concluded, now and then had trouble with servants, but although discipline was often necessary and a knock or two common practice, privately he considered it less than sporting.

"He had a few more words to say than was fitting," His Grace had said. He was looking calm and fit and stayed mounted, unlike Joe Gormley, who, pale and bleeding from one ear, climbed down at once from behind His Grace and limped away as quickly as he could.

"Well, it's his business," George Grass had thought, and the rest of the house, knowing that the footman had been acting oddly, thought the same. What the 'few words' were wouldn't reach indoors for some time and by then, because His Grace and his bride-to-be were the wonder of Redding, it was largely disregarded.

The men rose when Elva came in. There was a general movement. Rob Milton pulled out a chair for her. The priest, who after His Grace was the only other man present, stepped back as well, so she could sit beside him instead.

"It is a kind of sport," he announced dryly, "but given that I hold the threat of damnation, I am certain of victory."

"If you win so, what will she think of us?" Rob Milton asked.

"We shan't know, I believe," said the priest, since he already had been told what to expect. "Although one shouldn't despair. We are taught, are we not, that the hearts of young women find their most generous expression in silence?"

"Like children?" Rob Milton asked.

"Like God," His Grace whispered close to her ear, although he seldom gave himself to speculation. Grinning, he pulled out a chair for her himself.

Guided by his arm, Elva sat contentedly beside him and smiled while His Grace introduced them, first the priest and

next Rob Milton, for until then it had never been done
formally.

"And this is Nanny," His Grace said last, gesturing to
the old woman sitting below them, where one of the
servingwomen could stand easily beside her to cut the
roast into pieces.

"A Wenceslas, same as him," the old woman muttered,
as though concerned by the slight and showing no sign that
they had met.

Elva went on smiling.

She was wearing a white silk with a low neck, or rather
no neck at all, which showed all of her shoulders and the
tops of her breasts.

"That looks like my grandmother's dress," His Grace said
admiringly.

"Older," croaked the old woman. "It was mine."

"For my sake, you might build up the fire," interrupted
the priest, without shivering.

Elva could see that he hated her. His smile, she had
noticed, was pulled as wide as her own. Apart from that,
he was motionless. Even his breath, in spite of his age,
was soundless. He reminded her not only of her own
priest but old Tommy Chorlton, her father's odd-job man,
who, whenever she had met him out on the hill, nodded
and tipped his hat to her and smiled too without, for
all this activity, taking as much as single breath. There
were, she knew—as everyone did—nets and pegs in his
pockets and a knife behind his back. But such was the
power of his stillness that, when in the dark the rabbits
kicked and were about to scream, he conjured them to
silence.

"Your pardon, Your Grace," said the boy, taking their
words for fact. "I should have lit the fire earlier."

"This house," Rob Milton said, "is not as cold as my own. But if anything, this weather . . ."

"Will be worse," sneered the old woman. "I've looked about. Will be hard again and soon, for there are hips and haws aplenty still. So birds will have something, if men will not."

"Sweet Christ!" the priest exclaimed. "Have you not kept her from the wood?"

Rob Milton did his best to laugh.

"So my ploughman shouts," he said hastily, "when he turns his team. 'Hip' for right, I gather. 'Haw' for . . ."

"*Viburnum prunifolium,*" said the old woman.

Even the priest stopped then, his mouth souring. For his Latin was no more than he spoke in the Mass.

But Rob Milton pressed on about his ploughman, launching into the unresolvable argument as to which was best, a good straight furrow or short French gores when the headlands narrow, distracting the others, he hoped, from the more vexatious topic of what the old woman knew which often led—as he was certain it would now—to who she was and what rights, other than Odlaw's whim, she had at his table.

"Or long double curving rows," he was saying.

"Who told you that?" demanded the priest.

"My granddad told my da, and he told me."

"You remember his old granddad?" the priest asked, turning slyly to the old woman.

"This is my house," His Grace reminded him coldly.

But before the old woman herself had answered, Mrs. Curran, driving the servingwomen before her, came through the door and, when the wine came, the guests turned at last to their dinners.

The roast was rare. The priest, Elva noticed, watched her as she lifted her fork.

"You have a drop of blood on your chin, my dear," he said and, although there was no need of it, he passed her his own white napkin, his soft hands moving with deliberate ceremony, as if the fingers remembered that they were accustomed to wipe the cup of Christ.

He had not been invited beforehand, she decided, but had come, as her priest would, at a time that made the invitation unavoidable. She had hoped that she would see Rendcombe. She would not have minded having George Grass as well, for all his fumbling, since it was strange to dine with so few men. On the other side she had always had her brothers and, as often as not, poor Ben Taynton, because his own house was empty.

For a fleeting moment, as if he had seen her gaze droop, she felt the Duke's hand pressed comfortingly at her back. Then, as if it were no more than her wishing, interrupted by the persistence of the priest's questioning, it was gone.

"I might ask . . ." he began.

"Only if she wishes," His Grace amended.

But it would be fine, she thought, nodding, since His Grace was there to protect her.

"It may seem indelicate," the priest continued, with a look that told her that he granted himself a far greater liberty.

Still, she nodded once more, trusting His Grace.

By then the fire had blazed up and, perhaps because of its heat warming one side of her, she felt instead that the room had grown colder. There was a cozy glow to the lamps, and looking into the shooting flames in the hearth made her think of how the room must look from outside on the hill. It seemed to her that she was watching from a distance in the dark, observing herself with an unfamiliar objectivity, a sensation which made her catch her breath with excitement, as though all the while she were waiting for something to happen.

"Our Lord," said the priest, "teaches us to be careful. The world is full of snares. A man who walks outside his door must learn to tread cautiously."

Rob Milton grinned. "Beware the poacher devil, is it? Shun the net-and-peg man!" He laughed, staring at the priest's sharp profile and trying to decide whether a man, given to such platitudes, could be serious.

"It's a wise man that knows his enemy is often not what he appears."

"We'll have an example," said His Grace, smiling himself.

"Lazarus."

"Ha!" His Grace shouted. "Have you there. Dead as clay, because he was. So the world's proved honest. Even the gory dead don't sham. Your lord would have been a fool to raise him otherwise."

The Duke had placed his hand openly on Elva's shoulder.

She let it rest there, pressing against her, unwilling to fault him even though she realized that in his enthusiasm he had got it wrong.

"There were two," the priest said quietly. "I meant the leprous beggar. Luke if you will, not John. The point is, no matter the world's opinion, what a man is truly . . ."

But the point seemed lost and, while His Grace remained convinced he hadn't lost a thing, Rob Milton was relieved, at first, that the conversation had gone on to the pudding wheeled out on the cart by Mrs. Curran.

"I take a different view," His Grace was saying, inspired by the presence of the girl. "The greatest pudding," he said, burying his spoon in the dish, "is never made by following some tired and ancient recipe."

He had lifted a heavy spoonful to his chin.

"It's inspiration that counts for most, and inspiration, I've always thought, comes upon one sudden."

He hadn't understood a word of what he said. He had merely taken the contrary view. Still, he looked across at Elva, expecting her approval.

Distracted, she did not at first hear the priest's repeated question.

"My dear?" the priest asked her again.

She stared at him.

"My dear," he continued, "are you dead?"

Elva's chair fell backward when she fled.

His Grace caught her in the hall. Bewildered but sensing the opportunity, he took her in his arms. His mouth found hers.

Yet this time, although he tasted of Mrs. Curran's mullein and quince, because she desperately needed holding, she kissed him back.

Chapter Seven

ELVA HAD BEEN CERTAIN SHE WOULD DREAM OF HIM, but to her dismay it had been Harry. Awake again in the darkness, she had pulled the blanket disappointedly over her head; but before she had buried herself, wondering if His Grace might be down by the stables, she had peered out. She had not dared to think that he could, just as easily, have been climbing the stairs or that he might have stopped, if only for an instant, outside her door. And if, perhaps, she had such thoughts?

But she had been dreaming of Harry!

Frightened by the priest, she had come away before the maid had turned down the coverlet or brought in the warming pan. Crawling between the great, icy sheets had been so like plunging into a stream that the blood from every extremity contracted toward her heart and she had nearly forgotten and cried out.

It could only be the cold that had reawakened the memory of Harry, his large, vague, frightful head bobbing listlessly in the river at the heart of the wood.

Elva sat up in the bed.

"It should have been *his* face," she thought, for even now she could feel her own mouth pressed against the young Duke's greedily.

"How dare anyone say that I am dead!" her thoughts cried out, his phantom presence goading her beyond endurance.

She turned again to the window and found a sharp half moon staring back. Below, on the narrow bank above the well house, she saw the old woman, in a scarf and mackintosh, clasping a length of rope in one hand and a bundle of wooden pegs in the other. Because of the moonlight, Elva could see the rope and the pegs clearly. Over the course of the next few moments it became equally obvious that the old woman, turning onto the cattle track and then leaving it, was headed toward the trees.

Her spine stiff against the headboard, Elva watched until the figure grew smaller and smaller against the hill. Perhaps her breath came more deeply as she watched. She did not remember if the figure vanished or if she had closed her eyes.

When the hand, that must have been waiting, reached up and took hold of her, her own hand dropped. Twice she grasped at the knuckles. Twice instead, she felt the bark's deep-grooved roughness.

"Do you love me?" he asked.

She would not answer.

"I had wished for someone else," she thought.

"You came to the wood."

Her silence contained the germ of irritation.

"I went only to see where I was," she told herself, knowing that he was in the wood or the river and that she was in her bed.

Slowly, he floated upward till she recognized his chin. The hair all around his head was gray moss and tangles.

"You are cold and snobbish," he said, "and you lack a sense of fellowship."

"When have you ever cared what I lack?"

Uninvited, a tendril of waxy leaves curled near her breast.

"I am your sister!" her thoughts rebelled.

"It is upon that . . . ," a voice she knew whispered.

She dug her face into the pillow, feeling dags and twigs instead of down. To protect herself, she put out her hand and the bracken, cross with her for delaying, caught at her.

At the wood edge, the chalky field rattled with the stalks of thistles. The sound preceded her into the darkness, the hanging oaks parting, the drowsy wood stirring, beckoning her within.

It was not yet light when, the coverlet thrown aside so that nothing hidden could find her, Elva noticed the old woman was standing by her bed.

"I have done what I could for them," she was in the act of saying. "I have bound them, as fast as I was able, so they would not wander away from one another, for the wood is endless and the poor dead are forgetful and drift off by themselves. But it is not enough. Without their flesh, they feel the cold. It is sad to see them shivering and yet my fingers have lost the skill to stitch and sew. Knowing that, they have asked me if, out of pity, you would make coats for them."

Elva drew the coverlet over her head.

Nonetheless, the question stayed in the air.

Opposite her, at a convenient height from the headboard, there was a small square window through which Elva could watch the notched, eaten moon. It was a clear night but it was colder. In time, out in the yard over which she was looking, the old woman emerged from beyond the well house and, intent on her own concerns, hobbled away down the hill. Her bent figure grew smaller until it had almost gone out of sight.

Elva breathed deeply.

When she opened her eyes again, a pale light was slipping gently over the windowsill. The door to the room was closing. At the bottom of the bed, heavy on her feet, were a pair of shears, a spool of coarse thread, and several yards of stiff, folded tarpaulin.

"She wants a needle," Emily announced in the morning at the servants' breakfast.

Joe Gormley, his right ear bandaged, sat frowning at the head of the table. There were still twenty minutes before he must go in to His Grace in the big room where the high and the mighty had their toast and tea and all the rest, on heavy silver platters and under crystal. Hours before, while Mrs. Curran was still in her bed, he had filled the kettle and coaxed the cold black stove back into warmth and then, with a cup set steaming beside him, seen to the boots until they had seemed to shine with cleanliness and a fine, high polish, except for a clot of dung beneath one heel, which he had left quite deliberately. It was only then that he went out the back door to the privy. There was frost on the ground, and, in spite of the new light, the air had turned bitter. Too late, he wished he had thought to draw on something more above his livery.

What with the cold and because his bladder ached painfully, he had stopped in the grass and let out a smoking stream just where he was. He was not half done when he saw the old woman, halted at the far end of the yard, watching him.

"Going out or coming in?" he had called across to her in a harsh whisper, letting himself finish and more troubled by the stinging in his lowers and the darkening in his water, which because of where His Grace had kicked him, he was nearly certain must be blood.

The old woman had continued on to the house, without answering.

His anger unabated, Joe Gormley pushed his empty plate into the center of the table.

"What is it she wants with needles?" he muttered. "Mark me, whatever is, the old woman's behind it. She's up to summat. Always was."

Mrs. Curran gave another poke to the fire and sat back down again.

"There's my sewing basket in the pantry, Em," she said.

"It's her trousseau she'll want making," the between-maid said, who at the end of the evening had come upon His Grace and the young woman in the hall. "I seen a little. He had his hand. Well, almost . . ."

Then she blushed.

"What you seen," Mrs. Curran admonished her, "you didn't."

"I seen," Joe Gormley started, who, disregarding all that was in his own best interest, knew perfectly well what he had looked at in the wood.

But all the house was still ignoring him.

His Grace was not at breakfast, although Elva had special-ly dressed for it. She knew he had the farm to run. None-theless, she felt she had some right to expect more of his attention. Taking the yards of tarpaulin and the shears into the front room, she sat under the windows where the light was better and she could look out over the yard.

She could get up, she knew. She could walk among the barns or down to the wood, only there was no telling when he might return to the house. She was trapped, but it was a trap of her own making. She kept herself prisoner, convinced, without quite knowing when or how, he would come to free her.

In the meantime, although it was not the sort of business she knew, she set herself to the coat.

The work was difficult because her hands were unaccustomed to the shears. After a short time she had raised a blister and a soft deep bruise in the ball of her palm which went on aching long after she had set everything aside. In fact, on the first day she made little progress. She had no pattern and had to try to remember the shapes of all the pieces. Just how she was to guess the sizes had seemed an even greater problem until, when she had spread the tarpaulin on the floor, she discovered there was material for one coat only and at that, not enough for Harry, and perhaps a bit over much for John. Yet she assumed the old woman would supply whatever else was needed when the first—Arthur's, it seemed now unavoidably—was done.

Darkness was falling when she and Rob Milton went alone in to dinner.

He sat in his usual place and she sat opposite him before the fire in a long, flowing dress borrowed from the closet. Her hair had been scooped up and pinned.

Mrs. Curran and the servingwomen came and went, leaving them by themselves.

"Lumbering in Badger's Wood, I think," he explained to her when he saw her look of disappointment. "He didn't say actually. But it must be something like that. At any rate, something that needed doing quickly while the weather holds."

He had looked in on her once or twice already through the day and had seen her with the cloth on her lap and the shears in her hands and so he did not remark on the rawness of her fingers.

He did not say either, although he knew the truth of it, that the Head Keeper in Badger's Wood had a daughter.

Like most good men, he owed at least some measure of the finer aspects of his character to simple innocence. While by now the maids talked of little else, he had not understood what had passed unspoken between this young woman and His Grace and had refrained from mentioning the Head Keeper's wench, not out of particular regard for tender feelings, but from general courtesy. Then too, he was perhaps not altogether unfamiliar with the path up to the Head Keeper's cottage or unmindful that the poor man's responsibilities kept him away when the moon's brightness made easy work of walking abroad in the evening. It was this same courtesy that, on the very first night he had noticed His Grace's roan tied outside the door, had made him ride, with much greater trouble, into Devon.

"So it's lumbering, I think," he was saying, although the light had long since gone.

He could see he was no company for her.

Although not a man of a great many words, he did his best to hold up a one-sided conversation. But she had little interest in seed potatoes and less in oast houses, and until he brought up His Grace, she had merely tried not to yawn.

"He's a born moralist," he told her, relieved by the effect. "Always had a great sense of justice. Nearly killed a blacksmith and a baronet because of it. Might have made a judge, possibly, if he wasn't a duke. Pity he couldn't settle down to a book. But strength and nerve. You do see it? That's what's important. And that, well . . . Still, I see we both wish he were here."

As a postscript, he had refilled her cup.

Because her smile had improved so, he continued.

"Known him all my life, actually. Our families in the same circle. Were together at school, you know. At least as long as either of us lasted."

She kept her eye on the door.

"Can't be helped," he told her again, at the very last, as he bid her good night and pleasant dreams.

Instead of going straight to bed, Elva sent Emily to draw a bath. But the maid, determined to see for herself whether His Grace, better late than never, would march in over the tiles, twice laid out the towels. Three times she adjusted her cap. In the end, Elva threw the soap at her.

Unsatisfied, but at least without the maid's company, Elva wriggled out of her petticoats. It was a big tub, wide and steamy as the jungles of Burma, and the warm, deep water rose to her neck. In the damp heat her black hair flattened unbecomingly on her head.

Still, all the rest of her, she saw well enough, was inviting. She let her hands play, poking and nibbling, pretending to be snub-nosed fish. She made water spouts and, at last out of boredom, washed her back. She took a cloth between her toes. As chaste as in the booth of the confessional, as carefully as if Mrs. Curran were watching, she scrubbed behind her ears. Yet in time the bath became nearly as cold as the river. Prepared now to despise him, she stood.

She abandoned the towel. She neglected the robe on its rack. Goosefleshed, and just as obstinate as she had come from the bath, she padded off down the full length of the long corridor, daring any servingman she might meet there to stare at her.

No one did.

In the silence of her bed she could hear her heart beating.

The next morning, in the front room before the great windows, Elva finished the cutting and began to stitch.

"Wishing is a sin against Providence," she thought. "I must do something useful."

She did her best not to look over the hill.

Yet, it needed no weather wizard to see the storm coming. Rob Milton, looking in on her one last time after chapel, went down the cattle track with the priest, meaning to get back to his mother's house before the worst began. Elva watched them. She had closed a sleeve when, with the wind coming up and the blindness starting on the hill, the Duke, like one of his beaters, white-smocked by the snow, emerged out of the paddock, only his broad, wide-brimmed hat marking him as one who, instead of listening, must be listened to.

The snow was still clinging to his shoulders when he came in the room. His boots dripped on the carpet. Seeing her sewing, he had a maid called and everything gathered up and taken out.

He was in high spirits, notwithstanding his long ride in the cold, and kissed her good-humoredly on the cheek, by way of greeting, as he might have kissed any of George Grass's sisters, although only one might have been called half pretty and the rest were plain.

"Haven't I women enough for that sort of drudgery?" he said with a laugh.

He had worked his way slowly westward, spending some hours in and out of several beaters' cottages on the way back

from Badger's Wood and the rest of the morning at the
Royal Charles. He had banged on the bolted door, making
the barman open. And then, although every chair but his
own was up on the tables, he borrowed a pipe, and while
he had sipped at his pint and sucked at the stem, blowing
out quantities of thick, maggoty smoke, he discoursed at
length about the virtues of eager blonde women over black
leaf and bitter brown ale.

"Nonetheless," he announced with a wink, while the
weather was worsening, "it must be admitted that the three
of them bite."

The barman had gone on with his reading.

"You know something of women?" His Grace asked,
wanting to be asked an obvious question.

"You've had some success," said the barman, deciding
that it was to be the same sort of conversation as might be
had with any gentleman with a gamebag on his shoulder.

The barman marked his place but left the book open.

"Made a kill, then, Your Grace?" he asked.

It was snow that made the marriage. By midnight there
was a foot and two more by morning. Before lunch the
cowman and four others were sent out to shovel the roofs
of the barns, for those beams were the oldest, having been
raised a hundred years before. But by evening, the men
were onto the house. The drifts were then rising noticeably
in the yard, still haphazard and random, leaving almost a
bare spot by the kennels but beginning to overrun the
carriage shed. When the sills of the first floor windows
started to be buried, His Grace went up himself with a
straw broom, sweeping the slates over the gun room down
to the cutters. The young women lit torches and positioned
themselves outside so the men would have light and the

older women, kept indoors, stoked the fires so that the heat, escaping into the rafters, would melt what it could.

On the afternoon of the second day it was still snowing. His Grace had not slept at all, but he let his men rest in shifts of four hours. Although he was too unsteady himself to go back on the roofs, he went frequently into the yard, wading out at a distance, so he could watch the progress and yell up to the men, directing them from the washhouse to the roof of the library. Only one man fell and then it was from the kitchen gable, which was only one story, and, at that point, only a harmless drop to the drift alongside the basement door.

"We haven't a hope," chided the big, ugly woman as she passed His Grace in the hall. "We're destroyed."

His Grace ambled out toward the door.

"Only prayer," the fat cook called after him. "Only prayer will save us now."

"There is better hope in our backs," His Grace said. "More hope in shovels."

Caring for nothing but the blowing storm, he slammed the door. He bolted it against the wind.

On the morning of the third day, with the sky clearing, Joe Gormley, having spent his morning and evenings warming cider by the hob because of his infirmities, declared to the women that the undriven snow was as tall as His Grace with George Grass on his shoulders. The women, who could see for themselves that the snow covered the windows, went on ignoring him while the men, any one of who would have disputed the measure, adding or subtracting the depth of one hand or the width of some fingers, were in their beds.

It took another day, with every man and woman up and working again, to dig paths to the hay and the barns. Elva had dragged on Harry's trousers and put herself into her wellingtons. Going out to the fowl houses, with the piled snow to either side of her above her head, was, she thought, like daring the tunneling mazes in the hedge gardens at Stephen's Well where she had been taken once to visit by her father. It seemed to her so precisely the right image that she found herself wanting to describe it to His Grace. Even more, after she had begun to think again, she wanted to find the old woman and ask about her brothers. But the old woman had gone off and all the others were dressing. Joe Gormley gave an hour to his own cracked boots. Weary as they were, the maids explored the locked rooms and closets of duchesses who had gone before and Mrs. Curran, having left some minor final matters to the undercook, because no one's dresses fit her but her own, took off her apron.

His Grace had invited every one of them into the big room. He had the plain benches brought out from the kitchen. He had shaved and put on a clean shirt and even fastened his collar. It was obvious to anyone watching him giving instructions, carving the joint himself and sending the steward into the cellar for a case of the old Duke's best claret, that he was enjoying himself. His glance along the table told them that any doubts they might have harbored about his youth, about his skill and firmness, when it came to the test, might now be safely set aside. He stood by the chair that had been his father's, with the household about him as they gathered only at Christmas. Above their heads he saw the shining windows reflecting back their faces and the fires. It would be weeks, he knew, before the roads were open to the nearest farm.

"My thanks," he said quite loudly. "We've done right well. Done splendidly."

Someone cheered.

"We've had a bad time," he said. "I don't remember worse. But the men worked hard. And all the women, of course, were wonderful."

Mrs. Curran, taking this as a straightfoward reference to herself, settled her head smugly in her chins.

"Still," His Grace continued, "there're days ahead and a few more than I like to think, before we can get out much beyond the barns. I shall count on your high spirits. Yet, you'll be pleased to know . . . At least Mrs. Curran assures me that nothing will get truly disagreeable. We shan't, I'm quite certain, have to turn into cannibals."

It had been clear only to those nearest him that he had been drinking, but it was easy enough to forgive the common vices. Yet, when he sat, the applause was no more than polite.

"Cannibals, indeed," the cowman thought.

His Grace would have been surprised to learn that the men and women in the hall considered his last remark a lapse in judgment. They knew what they had done, and it was just, they felt, to praise them for it. But generally speaking, a man, they thought, should stick to praise. If he wanted to joke of cannibals, he had his sporting men.

But he hadn't. Every man he knew and trusted had gone off to his own house and lands. Now, when he was disposed to talk, he found himself with no one but a mute girl beside him. On such an evening, except for the snow, he would have ridden into the village. At the Royal Charles there were men who only now and then took his wages and, being independent, were less inclined to take offense. But in his house his moods and deeds became larger, as if they watched him through a magnifying glass. When, once, some months before, on his way to his bath, he had pinched one of the upstairs women, half the household twittered, and when, as had just happened, he had set his hand on Joe Gormley, it was a drama followed by one and all.

Although His Grace didn't know what, something had entered the air. It had been breathed in generally.

The sun had already gone and the fires in the chimneys roared. Shadows filled the alcoves and crevices of the room around them. Their reflections glittered and were distorted and shrunken in the goblets and silver.

"They were all quite magnificent, don't you think?" he said to Elva defensively.

"Thyself," she answered.

He could not guess whether she meant to praise or question him and, while he stayed to drink another glass, before too long he rose and, thanking them all again, went to his bed.

He blamed himself, although he was uncertain as to the fault. It was a little thing, not worth his unhappiness. Yet he did not see what could have been done to alter anything.

When he dreamed that night, it was not of the young woman who had sat beside him or even the Head Keeper's daughter, whose chief virtue was that she cried out loudly from the moment he entered her, but of the beggar Lazarus.

In his dream His Grace was dead and lying in a lake of fire. In his torment, he was startled to hear the sound of rounds being sung, it seemed, out of the highest heaven. He looked up, and at the top of an enormous tree, saw God, with Lazarus holding the hymnal, practicing for the Sunday choir. Only Lazarus had Joe Gormley's frown. But it was not until His Grace saw the man's bleeding ear that he recognized him.

"Father," His Grace cried out, "have mercy, and send my footman, that he may dip the tip of his finger in water and cool my tongue."

"Have you considered a butt of fine malmsey?" God asked, as if wishing for a more ingenious conversation.

"Had I known I had a choice, I should have asked for ale."

"They all asks for that," said God, who more and more was beginning to resemble the barman at the Royal Charles. "Myself, I have a fondness for bottles of gooseberry and rhubarb."

"I would taste a little," admitted His Grace, noticing that the joints of the branches were stacked with casks and bottles, piled hundreds deep.

"Son," the barman said apologetically, "remember that while you lived you had all that you wanted and your footman had only pain. But now he is comforted."

"I would repent something," His Grace began.

The barman shook his head. "There is the matter of delivery," he said solemnly. "Between us and you there is a wood . . ."

His Grace was not a monster, it must be remembered, although there are accounts of what came later that found him so. As Duke he was more than magistrate but judge and jury and, if it came to it, hangman too. The beating he had given Joe Gormley was given honestly, for cause and with provocation and, he believed profoundly, as a matter of honor. He did not love her then, any more than, as a lad, he had loved the land girl over whose reputation he had fought both a blacksmith and a baronet. It may be that the pursuit of justice, like the chase of love, is a kind of intoxication. At the very least, it can be said that there are worse gods than an able barman and far too many gods less willing to hear the outpouring of a tormented soul. It might be said as well, that neither gods nor men are made quite fierce enough to match the best moments of their good intentions.

Being silent, Elva did not laugh or sing. She did not engage him with praise. Once or twice her cheeks and her neck deepened to a dark wine color. She had kissed him and been kissed. She wore his mother's and his great grandmother's gowns. She was the handsomest woman he had ever seen. All of these counted for something. But what mattered most, more than her beauty or the strangeness of her finding, was that she was there when the roads were closed not only to Devon and into Stephen's Well, but to a certain rude cottage at some distance from the village in Badger's Wood.

She was at breakfast, one day to the next, and, with Rob Milton gone, His Grace's only company. And if his duties sometimes kept him away at noon, she was there, always, in the evening, the table set for only the two of them. Now, understanding that they bewildered him, she seldom spoke the two words she could. In the beginning he said little. There was no outside work to explain to her, no fresh tales of dogs or the hunt or society with which he could entertain her.

His days, inside, were now spent mostly with the Estate Book and on such matters as were usually left to winter when there was time to unravel the jumble of accounts that piled up quickly and out of order during the rest of the year. But gradually, with nothing pressing to concern him in the present, he let his thoughts wander. With the fire banked and the candles gently fluttering, he began to talk of himself, of his childhood (wonderful among the fields and barns until he was seven), his terrifying school days at St. Berzelius, his father living, his father dead.

He had never had a better audience or, as the days went, been more scrupulously honest about his private hopes and fears. It may be that half of love is no more complicated than the unimpeded opportunity for confession. Certainly, before another week had come and gone, with breakfast lingering at the table and hours, after dinner, sitting on into the evening by the fire, His Grace was half in love with her.

Elva began sewing the coat again in the front room, having with patience and with pantomine convinced His Grace to reverse his order. Sometimes, when the accounts made his head ache, he even sat with her while she worked, finding in the tilt of her head and the endless small movements of her fingers a picture of reassuring domesticity. His mother toward the end, when she was dying, had worked on a small sampler, but with a tiny needle and many colored threads.

"Who are you making that great thing for?" he asked her one evening.

He had not expected an answer. But Elva looked up pleadingly.

"Myself," she cried, so mournfully that, although he seldom did, he found himself trying to imagine what she thought and felt.

He walked over and stood beside her. One of his large hands slipped down on her shoulder.

If life had been like any of the stories she had read in her bedroom on the other side (after the maid had gone and Elva had lit the lamp once more), His Grace would have lifted her in his arms at that very moment and carried her to the top of the stairs. But it ended briefly with a kiss.

Afterward His Grace had taken his chair again.

For a very long time he had stared out at the snow and the darkness, as if he were no more able than herself to say a word.

It was not until late the next evening that Elva heard the soft knock at her door.

Confused by sleep, she thought at first it was the maid come to pester her for reading Miss Streets's *The Recluse of the Apennines.*

Chapter Eight

IT MUST NOT BE FORGOTTEN THAT HER SOUL WAS
stirred. Although weighed down beneath the surprising
thickness of his legs and arms, for a time his breath faded
and she was caught up and carried beyond his reach. Her
own heart thundered distantly. Free of him, she quivered
into supernatural life. And yet it was not like flying. Whatever imagination gave the existence beyond this existence
"wings," still clung to its mortality. For if, in a sense, she
was lifted, it was not above him.

She existed for herself alone, on a plateau of unself-
conscious pleasure, which whirled and tumbled, drawing
her further and further away. Once more she felt that
she was dreaming, that neither she nor the man was real.
Yet, when the moment vanished, what was left on her
reawakening senses was only the vaguest impression. When
he seized her again, suddenly, she was in her bed.

He had not said he loved her.

She did not smile.

"Look," he said. "I don't know what happened to either
of us."

She turned her back, believing that his arms must follow, or—as if both their bodies had been struck from one good mold—that his hips must pull against hers, the one fitting into the other like spoons on a cupboard shelf. Instead he slept and, although after he woke again, he did not hurry from her, yet it seemed to her, when at last he had thrown off the coverlet, that he went too soon.

In the morning she hid the sheets in a corner of the closet and ran down to breakfast.

"Looking for someone?" Mrs. Curran asked.

Elva shook her head.

She applied herself dully to a muffin. But the pleasure of eating was not pleasure enough.

"Out in the barns," Mrs. Curran answered what she had not asked. "Some mystery, no doubt. But we shall have it presently. His face, my dear, shows everything."

Elva left the table shortly, looking tired.

It was not until she had gone back to her sewing that one of her fingers, roughened by the stiffness of the tarpaulin, cracked below the nail and began to bleed. Seeing the tiny spot of crimson, Elva's eyes flashed in despair.

Because of her sobbing, as Elva's gaze shifted, the old woman's shape was blurred.

"Well, it's started then," she croaked. "All I can say is that it's about time. In my own case it was not so long. But then I was not so young and his great grand-dad was not half so squeamish about his honor or my own."

Elva wiped her eyes.

"There, there," the old woman said, and kissed her. "You do your part and I'll do mine."

In her crippled hands there was a double pile of thick wool cloth. At first Elva thought they were blankets.

"Everything goes quickly now," the old woman said. "I'm sorry to tell you that. The best seems over before it's started. But it will not wait."

The old woman set the wool down on a chair and immediately assumed a serious expression.

"Poor Harry's cold," she whispered and left the room.

There were fresh sheets on the bed that night. Elva couldn't imagine what she had been thinking, the stupidity of leaving the bare mattress suddenly becoming clear to her. On the following morning, after His Grace had gone, she brought the first stained sheets from the closet and left them out for Emily. It seemed unnecessarily foolish to hide them—like a book she had been reading on the other side—when the whole house knew. On the next evening they met by the stairs.

By the time Rob Milton was seen riding up the cattle track, they were sleeping openly in the great bedroom, where each of the dukes of Redding had slept since the Third Duke had the land and built the house, moving it from its old foundations, nearer the wood.

"But will you?" Rob Milton asked.

They had made their way to the top of the hill and sat looking over the paddock.

"Yes," said His Grace awkwardly, "I'm fairly certain."

Rob Milton considered that. "You could think. I might still bring her to my mother's house."

"She was under my roof," His Grace said. "It might have been different if from the start she were somewhere else and I had gone off quietly to visit her. If, like . . . But she was here."

"Then you love her?" Rob Milton said.

His Grace's eyes shifted, looking toward the wood.

"God's balls!" he laughed. "Just imagine, I found her naked in a tree!"

The footpaths were still closed but the better roads, though mired, were finally open. Knowing that he had been away too long already, the priest had himself driven up by Rendcombe in his chaise. Ordinarily, nothing short of a fatality would have set him stirring in the mud. (The hill farms, all admitted, were unreachable this time of year.) But having heard the worst from George Grass's drayman, who had it from the old loafer who looked after the game for Rob Milton, the priest would have walked, if it had come to that.

There were already spikes of new grass in some of the meadows. But if the roads were rivers, the sky for three days running had been blue as hedge-sparrow eggs. After two hours on the jolting seat beside Rendcombe, the priest's bald head was bright scarlet from the sun. But it was self-righteous fury that gave the purple to his face.

"I'll not permit it," he had declared loudly, striking his soft hands more sharply than Rendcombe applied the whip.

But he had to wait for the medical opinion, until after they reached the house and Rendcombe had gone in alone to the young woman.

His Grace, however, would have none of it.

"Whether she will see you or not is her business," he said curtly, having met them on the front porch. "But the verdict doesn't matter. As far as I'm concerned, it's as good as done."

"Corruption," hissed the priest.

His Grace stamped away, unwilling to be troubled. There were more pressing matters, rats in the corn crib and grooms that needed talking to about a mare they had let go lame.

While the priest waited, Mrs. Curran brought out tea. As soon as she had poured his cup and vanished into the kitchen, the priest sent Joe Gormley for two bumpers of whisky.

"Don't water it," he whispered. "I shall need my strength."

The footman lingered with the glasses, wanting a word or two.

"I'll be here again on Saturday for confession," said the priest, dismissing him impatiently.

After that he sat alone, less a stranger here, in this room, and in the house generally, than the young Duke himself.

Unlike most priests who were sent scurrying from one parish to another, he had never traveled further afield than a few hours' ride by train into New Awanux, to the seat of the bishop. He had been born in a cottage not six miles over the hill. His father, a man as sharp-faced and tiny as himself, had married a Devon girl who spoke his speech and thought his thoughts and who had never, any more than her son, walked or been carried beyond a half a day's journey to the north or south. Before St. Berzelius and the year in the seminary, he had learned to lay a proper Redding hedge and to pile stone along an embankment in the local fashion. He knew every culvert and subsidence in the greatest and the smallest farms. And after the better part of a century he had not forgotten which men, now dead, sold ill-kept cider or why the cooper's wife's unlucky child bore the smith's long nose. It was not just prophets who are without praise at home. While every man had his particular reason, for the greatest part, it was because he was their own, they hated him.

When Rendcombe slipped back through the door, he was smiling.

"There's no point in your protesting," he said.

"I'd say you hadn't the skill to judge as soon as this."

Rendcombe studied the familiar thrust of the priest's small chin. He had known the man, good and ill, for a lifetime, back to the long years before the century's turning.

"Perhaps," Rendcombe said dryly. "Yet there was never much difficulty starting life. And if I'm wrong, in a few more days they'd only prove me right again."

"I won't perform the service."

Rendcombe grinned. "They may live, I shouldn't wonder, without it."

"In sin."

"In and out of it, like most of the young." Rendcombe began to pack up his bag. "Of course, the child will be born a bastard then and grow up beyond a priest's comfort, outside the church."

"I've thought of that."

"And given your blessing?"

"It's a complication."

"Just one more to be considered?"

"No," said the priest with bitter annoyance. "If it's what I think, then before its christening, like the others . . ."

"Once," Rendcombe almost shouted in disbelief.

The priest shook his head. "The Enemy repeats himself."

"I thought that was life."

"Don't try to teach me my business," said the priest.

"Once," Rendcombe continued, "and that long ago and . . ."

"There was blood on her mouth."

" . . . and none of it certain," Rendcombe finished. "We were no more than boys ourselves, after all, and the old woman pretty enough then to stir even a priest's cold heart. Your first death, professionally, as I remember. Your maiden 'though I walk through the valley,' although you hadn't even the bones to put in the box."

"The child was dead," said the priest, "because it came from the dead."

Rendcombe took up the whisky that had been sitting there. It would be tempting, he thought, to remind the priest that Adam, although promised little more than death for his inheritance, went on to have sons.

"Babies," Rendcombe said instead.

"What?" barked the priest.

"It is something to bear in mind."

"I have no idea what you're talking about."

It was in the middle of the day, but Rendcombe took a long swallow. "Life . . . ," he began, unable to think of the young woman without smiling and unable to smile without recalling the old woman when she too was young, before all the troubles. But troubles, he thought, couldn't be stopped from coming, any more than a priest could stop His Grace from climbing the stairs or the young woman from waiting with her door unlocked.

"So you won't . . . ," Rendcombe started again.

"Won't isn't half strong enough!" cried the priest, the growing malignity preying on his mind.

But if the priest had God's ear, the bishop had a short but unequivocal letter from Odlaw Wenceslas. While the bishop had never met the young Duke, he had known the older generation of all the great families. Like them, he believed that land in oats and barley was the backbone of the country, and, not incidentally, the mainstay and treasury of the church. That he was a bishop in the first place was not unrelated to the few thousand acres his mother's uncles farmed with considerable profit south of Stephen's Well. The bishop was a thick-set, heavy man, who through the winter, out of honest appreciation, kept a manure shovel by the side of his bed. He was a farmer sprung from farmers and had always been a little disappointed that his Savior had called forth Peter to be a fisherman. "But God," the bishop often complained to the canons, "when He started, before He thought of complications, gave man a hoe."

He considered His Grace's letter for less than ten minutes and before vespers, wrote the reply himself.

There was no question of disobedience. Even before the priest broke open the great seal, he knew he would be given no chance of squirming out from under.

"I'm to be turned out, unless . . . ," he said to his housekeeper when the letter lay open before him.

"To think they can do such things," said the woman, although it was clear to her as it was to everyone the wedding would go on, with or without him.

The orders had already been sent out to the village for what could be found close at hand and Mrs. Curran, although it had meant installing her in a hay wagon in order to get a seat that was broad enough, had been driven into Devon by Joe Gormley.

Clerks and shopgirls flocked about the immense cook like excited finches, and boys bearing boxes and satchels followed her from one shop to the next. In the house, Emily and the seamstress worked on the gown. After he was finished in the barns, the cowman spread straw over half the yard to protect the boots of the guests from the mud. From Wednesday to Saturday everyone was always

in a hurry, rushing off down the corridors, airing the linen
and making up rooms. The tables in the kitchen were
piled with marrows and sprouts, the lockers emptied of
the hanging birds, the back stoop swept three times of
feathers. The butcher from the town was given a room
in the attic so he could wield his hacking knife long after
dark and start again before morning. Rob Milton lent
His Grace four of his mother's women; two more, as
reinforcements, were sent by George Grass before Saturday noon.

Like truant schoolboys, the fieldmen walked up and
down on the hill, trying to look inconspicuous.

"Even the fiercest dog fears his own master," Sam
Maddox said, when toward the end of the day he saw
the priest, his best robe in a bag at his feet, driving
up the cattle track toward the house with Rendcombe
beside him.

It was not quite dark. In the failing light Rendcombe
could see the women going in and out of the chapel with
sheaves of wheat and boughs of evergreens to be hung on
the pews and the altar.

"It is fitting," the priest muttered, holding his nose.
"Married with the field and the wood."

"It is too soon for flowers," Rendcombe said.

The priest frowned. "The stench of the dunghill," he
thought, watching the cowman spreading new straw over
the ruts and hoofprints in the mud.

Rendcombe took a deep, appreciative breath.

"You'd think it ambrosia," Emily said, describing the
kitchen, as she pinned up the outer hem of the gown.

Elva stood as still as she could but it seemed she had been
standing for hours. There were six petticoats on the bed and

on the floor a dozen satin slippers, ordered by Odlaw from New Awanux, in half sizes from small to medium just to be certain, although Elva had traced each foot on a piece of stiff paper. There were two colors of beige and three of cream. Elva could see them all, the gown, the petticoats and slippers, reflected back at her in the mirror. But it was her own face she watched, wondering if somehow she could manage to look truly extraordinary or would merely seem frivolous.

For this night she had moved back to her first bedroom, away from him. She had been cautioned not to peek through the door. She could not have even a glimpse and must not herself be seen. And when she was taken down the backstairs to confession, Emily warned, as an assurance of invisibility, she must wear a cloak and a hood.

"It's his revenge," said Emily, who had had it from one of George Grass's maids, who had spoken to the priest's housekeeper. "Shame on him, I says," she added, "for there isn't no cause for it, only his pique for the bishop made him do what he wouldn't. And what, I wants to know, does he think you will tell him?"

Thinking of the confessional, Emily began to laugh, dropping the first of a mouthful of pins. "Of course, His Grace, miss, might . . . But you can see how men are. But it's us besides, you know. Mrs. Curran and all the maids and the outside men. And the serving-boys too! Can you imagine how they are squirming this minute, with all their impure thoughts rattling inside of them?"

By then every pin was lost on the floor.

"Bless me, Father," Emily cried gleefully, "I have taken a fancy to our Mary's knickers that I have seen flapping on the drying line."

★   ★   ★

"Are you stricken?" asked the priest, taking the silence for the bride. But it was only a boy. For a while he ceased listening. Beyond the booth he could hear other feet shuffling and imagined the line of country men and maids, invisible in the chapel that was already made over for the joining of male and female. Their footsteps, because of his presence, were resentful and unwilling. Increasingly over the years he had felt their coolness to him, their stubborn refusal to examine their souls. They were not analytical; they talked only of trifles. He did not wait until the boy had finished.

"You will surely burn," he said, unsure of the reason, but knowing that the boy expected it.

"Gluttony," he said to Mrs. Curran. He could hear the sad wheeze of her breath as the immense woman labored to extract herself from the booth.

"Bless me Father, although I haven't . . ."

"You were seen drunk at the Royal Charles."

"Beat I was for that."

"The danger," the priest said, "is not earthly punishment."

"I dinna dispute it," Joe Gormley answered with quiet dignity. " 'Tis heaven I'm fearin', things wild and supernatrul. Things watched that I shouldn't, like what the poet Shakespeare warned of when I was at school. Two years I was and no fool either then or now. A great poet, so they says, and I believe 'em too. For what he wrote I saw."

"Are you sober?" the priest asked grimly.

There was an offended silence on the other side.

"I knowed somethin'," Joe Gormley said at last. "Knowed it when I seen her nethers. And seen it meant trouble although I couldna' told you what. But I have it now. Plain as the day, Father. For they's out in the tidy fields already, as the poet said would be. Come against him and us besides, I shouldna' think. And worse! All a man need do is listen. Squeak they do and mew and whisper, although Shakespeare never . . ."

"What on earth!" the priest cried.

"On the hill," Joe Gormley said. "Behind the cow barn. Planted beside the well house, where never anything before was put since we tramps back and forth there. Just three so far. Slipped through the hedge-gap and crawled up. Just three but, mark me, Father, more to come until . . ."

The old priest shook his head invisibly.

"Great Birnam wood," Joe Gormley continued unreservedly, "to high Dunsinane hill shall . . ."

"And three Our Fathers," He finished as the man went out. "When the head is sick," he thought, convinced this was the young Duke's fault, "all the lesser parts are cursed." The priest took little notice when the next came in. He pulled the slat back automatically. The silence went on for a long time.

"Child," he said finally, a word that would do for man or woman, young or old.

"Harry? John?" he thought, picking the names of the serving-boys at random.

There was no sound.

"Violet? Pru? Elizabeth?" he thought, thinking of as many maids as he remembered.

Unaccountably, he found himself noticing the blossoming smell of the new boughs that had been tied to the altar. The chapel breathed with the sharp sweet smell of budding leaves, the musty twig and root smell of a dug hedge.

"What grieves your soul?" the priest asked, running out of patience.

"Myself!" Elva cried joyfully.

She did not sleep. What bride has ever slept on the eve of her wedding? She dreamed, with her wide eyes open, of two young rams butting each other playfully on the lawn on the other side of the wood. She dreamed of the mother she had never seen going to her father's bed. She dreamed of Odlaw, as if she had never slept with him, napping naked in the sun in the front room while, as the housewomen hovered without useful occupation, she dutifully stitched up his trousers. It was funny, she thought, how her dreams were always filled with crowds of people while her waking life was mostly solitary. She dreamed of herself without a stitch of clothing, wading through the barley fields at harvest. The women binding the stalks were largely from the other side. The men sweeping with their scythes were anonymous. The stacks rose about her. It was the heaviest yield she had ever seen. Caught up in their work, no one noticed the great sack of her belly or the hardness and swelling of her breasts.

The old woman woke her long after breakfast. The yard was full of birds, the mulberry tree alive with the cheerful bickering of thrushes and sparrows.

"Why have you not finished Harry's coat?" she asked.

But Emily came close behind her, bearing a tray of biscuits and tea.

"The guests are arriving," she said.

As in her dream, Elva came naked from the bed and looked out the window at barons and their mothers and wives being helped down from their carriages by Joe Gormley.

"Come away," Emily said, hoping she had not been seen.

But she wouldn't. Elva watched the grand, handsome women stepping onto the carpets that had been put out to protect their shoes and their dresses.

"The youngest daughter of Lord Washbothem," Emily explained, raising her eyebrows and pointing. "It was almost a match. She would and so would her father. But His Grace . . . There were some hard feelings, it was said. Still, it was more than a year ago."

Grizel Washbothem did not look up.

The next carriage emptied.

"Cicely Potent-Matthers," Emily went on warily. "A widow, although she is not yet twenty. If she pulls you away during the dancing, remember that whatever she tells you is lies."

The widow Potent-Matthers passed quickly into the house, escorted by two of the young men Elva had seen on horseback when she had come out of the wood.

She pointed to a woman with an older man walking up the cattle track into the yard.

"No need to worry your pretty head," said Emily. "Just them for the servants' ball."

As she approached the porch, the woman stopped where she was and looked up at the window. In her loose bodice, seen from above, she seemed almost as naked as Elva. Their eyes caught, appraising one another. The day was springlike but not enough so for either of them to be as they were.

Coming from behind, the Head Keeper of Badger's Wood drove his handsome, blonde daughter before him, away from the front steps and toward the kitchen.

* ★ ★ ★

Odlaw had gone ahead to the chapel. Elva crossed the yard alone, on the length of mahogany carpet. Mrs. Curran, who had gone back and forth a half-dozen times, having some final matters to see to, pushed her out.

"I ain't your father," she had said firmly. "You'll go yourself."

Elva lifted her gown away from the mud. With everyone waiting inside, the farm seemed empty and still.

As she turned the corner of the house and came out into the wind, she shivered. A magpie hopped ahead of her, pecking the straw. By the well house a bush no bigger than a man made a queer, awkward movement. It was nothing, only the smallest of gestures, tugged by the wind.

"Be wary, my sister," something whispered.

The wind chirped. A door to one of the sheds banged on its hinges.

But even if it was no one, it was not what she needed to hear. Her mind was already riddled with doubts. Did she love him? Did Odlaw love her? He was brave now and she believed he was kind, but what would he be at forty? Would he grow in generosity and gentleness? Or, like her father's barons, would he simply coarsen, his only humor the tiresome jocularity of boys who have grown older but never learned to be men? And when he himself became a father?

In the clear morning, with her eyes bright and unclouded, she could see the line of sons that would spring from her, straight and tall as the patch of elm-hedge by the barn. Her mind wandered, imagining. All at once, the magpie, which had been busy at her feet, flew up before her.

Elva stopped, listening to the timid sound of its wings.

"If it flies to the wood, I shall flee with it," she told herself and then wished she had not.

The magpie circled the yard.

At the same moment the old woman, an empty sack in her arms, hobbled from behind the barn.

"Stay still!" Elva's heart cried. "Do not frighten it!"

The old woman paused, aware of Elva, aware of the magpie and something beyond the sight or hearing of either.

"How will you change it now?" her look seemed to ask, her withered lips soundless.

Emily had come out onto the steps of the chapel.

"Miss!" she cried aloud impatiently. "Inside all are waiting."

Odlaw was standing by the altar rail, shifting his weight from one foot to the other, like a boy of eleven, wanting to be off. Elva was halfway down the aisle before she saw the old woman slip into a pew in front of her. Faces, most of which she didn't know, turned to watch. Women in wide feathered hats, their piled hair glittering with tortoiseshell and diamonds, peered back at her like a roost of judicial owls. Young men, brown as wrens, old men, black as jackdaws, nodded. Rob Milton winked. But it was the priest's countenance that held her. Plain as a scraped bone, he stood in the middle of everything, as if this were more his business than her own.

Her stride, which from the beginning had been wrong, shortened as she approached the stranger who was to be her husband. She was used to walking in cow boots and found the gown and the slippers that had been bought for her such an inconvenience that she almost wished she could have been married barefoot in Harry's cutdown trousers.

There was a rustling around her. It was a small, familiar sound. By itself it may have had little meaning, but it was part of a pattern. Feathers were shaken, legs crossed and wings returned to their more customary positions. Elva could not have said at which moment the congregation detached itself from the evidence of her senses.

Again she felt that what she was doing wasn't real and yet, she knew as well, that she couldn't stop doing it.

She walked slowly forward. Lowering her head, she did not look at Odlaw directly, but she saw his yellow feet, their sharp talons clutching the topmost rail.

She stopped, terrified by the frantic, heavy, desperate beat of his wings. Caught in the updraft, a single leaf, blown from the rafters, circled irresolutely in front of her.

At intervals, of course, she knew where she was. The fragile blood in her brain was merely heated. Nonetheless, she confused the smell of the evergreens with the smell of the tower where her father worked gluing feathers onto a wooden frame. It was, she recognized, the smell of impossible longing. How different men are from us, she thought solemnly.

But by then the priest's old man's voice had begun rolling over the pews.

"Dearly beloved . . . ," he recited.

She had been thinking of her father, and it was not until then that she realized that the terrible old woman on the other side, coming out of the wood, could only have been Odlaw's mother.

Odlaw, his hands stiff at his sides, glanced at her.

"Who gives this woman?" the priest asked, no doubt delighting in the difficulty of its answer.

Elva waited for someone to help her.

The sunlight streaming in through the chapel windows did not cry out.

"How can I want him so?" she thought. They had never talked. She had never whispered her love to him. "I should have written him letters," she told herself. "We should have danced out of my father's hall, down the long corridors and onto the porches under the stars."

Her eyes enormous after the long silence, she looked back over the congregation. The fine-boned heads seemed almost skeletal. They were all very still. But they were men and women. It was her fever that had jumbled things. And fear. Elva turned again to the priest.

"Myself," she said hoarsely, thinking not of him but of the witch of a woman on the other side.

The priest looked disappointed.

"Do you, Odlaw Riding Wenceslas . . . ," he continued.

"Yes . . ."

"Do you . . ." The priest stopped, almost gleefully.

"Elva," the sharp voice of the old woman rang out clearly.

Odlaw kissed her before she was ready. Elva saw his big moustache come at her. Pressed close, his skin was sallower, his nose thinner and longer, his eyes flat and the eyelids turned down at the corners. When he turned quickly to go up the aisle, it was almost without her.

The congregation smiled. Such was the way of grooms, whether they were lords or country men.

Finally, his back straightened, his pace slowed. His gloved hand rested on her arm.

"Odlaw!" someone cheered.

"Elva!" another began hesitantly, for the name was new. But then everyone stood and pressed toward the aisle.

"Odlaw and Elva!" they cried over and over.

As the bride and groom passed, the eager congregation crowded behind them.

Joe Gormley, whose place had been at the back, stationed himself on the chapel steps when they came out. There was a knot by the door, and because of the number His Grace did not notice him.

"Aye," the footman announced loudly. " 'Tis a wonder!"

He was standing beside George Grass, who did not answer.

" 'Tis a miracle," Joe Gormley went on boldly. "And to think, not five minutes married."

"What the devil?" George Grass asked, feeling the man pushing into him.

Joe Gormley was pointing.

"Stop your wickedness," George Grass ordered, upset by the manner in which the man talked to him. His eyes flashed from one side to another, trying to find a way past. It was then that he saw the straw man which had been hoisted to the top of the well house. A straw bride had been lifted beside it, the pair of their makeshift hands groping with the imprecision of manikins.

"Good God," he thought. And yet when he noticed the hedge by the barn wearing a coat of stiff tarpaulin, he dismissed it as more of the same.

Joe Gormley shook his head darkly. "Aye, as I told ee," he said. " 'er babe it iss, sir. And where there be one of 'er wood children, sure as death, there be more."

Chapter Nine

EMILY HUFFED AND BLEW OUT HER CHEEKS INDIG-
nantly when she heard the between-maid tell Mrs. Curran
during the dancing.

"Elva's children, indeed!" she cried, and had Joe Gormley
been in her sight, she would have boxed his ears then and
there, even with everyone watching.

"How incredibly stupid!" she complained to the women
peeking out from the kitchen.

But the sporting men grinned. Cooling off on the porches
after a few too many turns on the floor, the men eyed the
hedge. Although short of breath, they had been long at
glasses of one thing or another and so found the conceit,
which otherwise might have been beneath their notice,
wonderfully apt.

Beyond them, in the shadow of the barn, the little hedge
trembled.

"I suppose it pleases its mother," said the baronet. "Marriage, you know. The comfort of legality. That sort of
thing."

"Every brat needs a father," agreed Oliver Thwaite.

"What a lad needs is discipline," laughed John Stamp, his good humor, which had been rather shaken by a young woman who wouldn't accompany him into the library, quite restored by standing with his fellows by the railing.

"How do you know it's a lad?" asked the baronet.

"I am prepared to look under its coat," Oliver Thwaite announced with a smirk and, straightening his trousers, started to go off into the yard.

John Stamp gave a thick snort of a laugh.

"I'm with you," he cried, eagerly joining the other on the steps.

The hedge, however, seemed to have uprooted itself. After another few moments, cheated of their entertainment, the sporting men drifted again into the hall.

"It is all quite ridiculous," said Emily, refusing to smile.

"It's very well for you to dismiss it," said Mrs. Curran. "But you saw as well as me her making its clothing."

"Proves nothing."

"Of course, if you think so," drawled Mrs. Curran and turned to tell the undercook.

The cowman heard it from Violet Fortescue, who because of the champagne and the queue of ladies in the back corridor, had wandered rather adventurously into the men's privy.

In due course the footman's slander was known to the servingboys and even the grooms in the barns.

One of the fiddlers, sitting out, played softly a chorus or two of "O Tannenbaum."

"Shall you let the gardeners inside?"

"I don't think so," said His Grace, puzzled.

"Well, I hope you will now consider it."

His Grace turned Grizel Washbothem slowly under his arm and caught, for a moment, a look in her sparkling blue eyes that made answering even more difficult than the strangeness of her question.

"Now, Odlaw darling," she continued when they met at the bottom of the set. "Don't you think it would be cruel to require her to do her own pruning?"

All around him the dancers were smiling.

"God's balls, Grizzy," His Grace whispered uncertainly. Without another word they slid and turned along the floor. But His Grace remained restless.

"I've had the oddest conversation," he complained to the young men about him after the fiddlers had put down their bows. "Wants gardeners in the nursery."

"Nurserymen," someone suggested.

Rob Milton nodded dismissively to Oliver Thwaite and George Grass. He put his arm around the Duke's shoulder.

"I'd best have a word with you, Odlaw," he said quietly.

The lamps were burning low. The guests who were staying had gone to their rooms. The other carriages had long since rattled down the hill. With the house at last quiet, Mrs. Curran sat upright, surrounded by mountains of dishes and platters, and snored. The cowman slept in the barn, dreaming of the thin white legs of Violet Fortescue. Joe Gormley, awake and contemplating the boots of a half-dozen gentlemen, lifted a bottle of His Grace's best malmsey to his lips.

" 'Tis truth I gave them," he muttered to himself. "What blame I for giving them such as that?"

The mysterious stumblings and hissings of truth still racing in his mind, His Grace's hands moved down her sides, slowly, controlling himself. He felt his wife go limp and knew, whatever was thought in the hall, that he had conquered her. He drew her undershift about her breasts. Tearing it, he pulled it to her waist. She helped him, smiling at his impatience. Climbing out of her petticoats, Elva lay on the white coverlet, waiting.

They had returned to his room. Or rather his father's room, the bedroom of the husbands and their women who, lifted above the rest, even above the priest, gave the law from Devon down to Stephen's Well.

"I have always held my head high," he said.

She drew him closer and stroked his long shoulder.

"But you!" he cried aloud, "have shamed me!"

And then he beat her.

That night she did not leave his bed. In the darkness she listened, waiting. But, when he slept, his hands and his knees pressed into her back, craving her. She did not move, fearing that, in love or anger, he would wake again. What did it matter which? she thought. She could feel the stiffness on her face where her tears had dried. On the left side of her head she could feel the knotted blood hardening. But in the tips of her ears the thin hot blood was running, a scorching rush roaring into her so that it seemed that her hair and even the pillow beneath it might burst into flame.

For a time, in the darkness, she remembered fires. In her thoughts smoke coiled from braziers and open pits. It reddened the black stove in Mrs. Curran's kitchen, blazing like the murderous poker Harry had pulled from the hearth.

For a terrible instant everything seemed to stop.

Then, out of her memory, a sickening substance was

descending on the backs and arms of her brothers. Clots
of fibrous soot fell on the bed where her husband slept.

"Poor Castleburry," her heart cried. "Poor, valiant . . ."

Her husband stirred.

When his breath slowed and deepened, she tallied all she
had seen and learned about men. It was then that she recognized the truth: it was the fear of laughter that drove them.
More than death, greater than the fear of ruin. Killing every
natural impulse and making them prey to every argument
and nonsense. As it had driven Harry, because he did not
trust himself and was afraid of whispering. As it had driven
her father, although in his case he had tried to outlaugh his
priest and the barons, shouting them down with a greater
laughter of his own.

Nonetheless, it was all the same.

Elva ground her teeth, pressing hard as if pressing would
expel the unconscious groping of a hand on her breast.

She awoke within an hour of daylight, hating him less
for the beating than for the indisputable fact that she had
given her life to a man no better than Harry.

When Elva came into the kitchen much too early, the
look Mrs. Curran gave her was frightening. "You're not
wanted here," she warned sharply. "Get back to his bed."

But Emily gathered the bride to her arms.

" 'Tis only natural," she said. " 'Tis a hard time for a
girl. Why I remember . . ."

But when she saw the bruises, she stopped.

"A duchess," she said quickly, pulling a rag of torn
cloth over Elva's blackened shoulder, "is never seen in
her dressing gown. Just you come with me a minute."

Emily pushed her into the butler's pantry and out again
through the back.

"Sweet Christ," she whispered and hurled Elva ahead of her, toward the stairs.

Oliver Thwaite, his braces still unfastened, appeared at his door, surveying the unsettled carpet and wondering whether he could navigate the distance to the end of the hall.

"Ladies," he said, unable to distinguish one from another.

All the same, at breakfast, out of friendly regard for the younger man, he thought it his duty to counsel His Grace about the management of his household.

"Maids," he said frankly, "must be well-schooled, I should think."

"Latin?" someone asked.

"French," said the baronet. "All maids must be French, isn't it?" He laughed, since there were only men at the table. His Grace had let it be known in the evening that the mothers and wives should be left to rest while the men spent a pleasant hour or two at targets on the hill.

"Clothing," Oliver Thwaite said thickly, disliking the baronet's grin. "No matter the time of day."

"What?" someone asked.

"All I'm saying," he continued unhappily, "is that they shouldn't be allowed, you know, to run bloody damn naked through the halls."

George Grass laughed.

"Quite right," Rob Milton said in a rallying tone, trying to soothe the man's feelings. "We musn't, you know, encourage the nakedness of woman." But his own words had tripped him, and in spite of himself, he spilled helplessly into laughter.

His Grace put down his cup. He had been so quiet that they had almost forgotten him.

"The husband rises!" someone cried.

"You might find your guns, gentlemen," he said softly, avoiding their eyes.

"Husbands," said Cicely Potent-Matthers succinctly.

"How loathsome," said Grizel Washbothem.

"Exactly," Lady Milton nodded. "Every one of them. Even my Robby—if out of kindness one of you would have him—would scarcely be an improvement."

At the women's breakfast there was a round of smiles.

"Guns," they agreed.

"And dogs."

"And daily walks in the mud."

"And forays, once a month, into Badger's Wood."

Lady Milton pushed a wedge of toast to the side of her plate. "Of course, it's our fault mostly."

"We permit it," Cicely Potent-Matthers acknowledged.

"Ye-es."

"Encourage it."

Lady Milton chuckled. "I did at every chance. Otherwise . . ." She turned toward Elva. "Your servants, my dear, ought to have a standing order not to let His Grace in the door without a pair of netted rabbits."

"A moorcock," Cecily Potent-Matthers thought.

"Or a wood duck," someone said.

"At any event," Lady Milton went on explicitly, "something dead. One hates to admit it, my dear. But unless there are certain outlets, they forget themselves."

Not one of them had directly looked at the marks on her neck.

"A woman, alone . . . ," Lady Milton continued, "without . . ."

"Relatives," Cecily Potent-Matthers added.

"Brothers . . ."

No one was quite certain who had spoken that.

But the conversation, having risen almost above its banks, swept again quickly into its usual channel, returning to certain persons—not, thankfully, in attendance—who, while adored by their children, cheated on their husbands although all, one could be certain, were . . . of the highest quality . . . green with envy . . . enslaved by two gentlemen from Devon . . . lovely . . . wicked . . . ruined.

"You wouldn't think, would you?"

"Certainly not."

"Except that one likes one's husband to believe it."

"You sew coats for no one at all," said Grizel Washbothem finally, having heard it from her maid. "I do wish I had thought of that. I have spent two of the dreariest months possible working a pillow case for my uncle's niece."

Lady Milton took Elva's hand.

"Quite right you are!" she cried enthusiastically. "If one is to have any hope of peace, one must start with rebellion!"

The guns boomed for two hours. Afterward the boys were sent into the grass and the waist-high bracken with baskets to clean up the targets. But there was nothing dead. The dogs, left in the kennels, whimpered as if puzzled. The men came back with nothing better than wet shoes.

Passing by in the hall, His Grace looked in at the women. He stood at the door, watching in silence, then, hearing the others behind him, went on to the library and closed the door.

One by one the men joined him. It was midafternoon, not late enough to have recovered from the evening's revels and too soon to begin again. They sat, with their stiff collars fastened. As a concession to comfort, Oliver Thwaite, who was too big for a chair, was allowed to occupy the better part of a dark leather sofa. Rob Milton stood by the bookcase leafing through a leather-bound volume, although it is doubtful he would have been able to recall whether its contents were letters to a young shooter or a short history of the Balkans.

"Quite a nice day," George Grass said at last.

There were grunts of lukewarm agreement. His Grace drew up his long legs on the ottoman and stared at the ceiling.

"Did you learn anything new?" someone asked him.

It was such an indelicate question that each man, privately, was glad he had not asked it. Rob Milton was about to protest but His Grace answered:

"No. Nothing." He did not seek out the eyes of his questioner. "She was the same, before and after. Women generally are, I think."

"Even after her w-wood ba-ba-babies?" someone stammered, although none of them did.

"Christ, I could do with some whisky," Rob Milton said tartly, ignoring the peculiar odor of twigs that had somehow crept into the room.

But if the husbands and brothers didn't know when to go home, the wives and mothers suffered from no uncertainty. Lady Milton had her son's bag pulled together and sat with it on the front steps until her waiting wore him out. Cecily Potent-Matthers sent word by her footman that, with the weather so pleasant, she would be more than happy to walk alone into Stephen's Well. Grizel Washbothem simply knocked on the door. After that the others went quickly.

From the old bedroom Elva watched the last of the carriages disappear down the hill. She crouched back against the cushions on the bed, knowing that the life that only yesterday had seemed so full of promise was ruined. The desire for him that, almost unbearably, had swirled through every atom of her being had turned to rot. The thought of his cold hands, the harsh smell of his breath, his hair, his back, his chin, everything about him that made him himself was sickening. She closed her eyes to shut out the sight of the marks on her arms.

Like spots of sunlight dancing against her eyelids, she could see the faces of women, and not only Emily and the maids, but the grand women from their great houses, their gentle, not unsympathetic looks recalling, as the faces of some women always did, the ancient helplessness of her kind.

They knew.

Assuredly, it would cause a mild scandal. In the big rooms of their crowded houses, full of sofas and chairs, sitting at tables in groups of three or four, they might shake their heads. They might even pity her, although she was not, and never would be, one of them. But it would make no difference. In the next room or in the room beyond, where the men sat in the flickering light thrown back by the logs (as perhaps men had sat by firelight when there were no houses on the empty hill) there would be talk of how her husband pulled her naked from a tree. She was not yet seventeen and yet she had learned enough to know that in most men's memories the hunt quite outshone all that succeeded it. It was going forth that stirred them, not coming home.

If they guessed the rest, they would not often turn their thoughts to it.

When she woke after midnight, the air was cold again. He had still not come for her. Elva lit the lamp and, taking out her shears, spread the pieces of Harry's coat on the bed where the man who was now openly her husband had first come to her in secret.

Although the old woman had been sitting by the door, until she spoke Elva did not notice her.

She began in a toneless voice, "He cannot help himself, is what I think. Perhaps it is wrong to defend him. But you must remember that he has my blood. The love I bore his great granddad went into him. You, on the other hand, are no more than a shadow of myself. That is reason enough to loathe you."

It did not matter that the old woman was there suddenly. Elva had seen the hedges come from nowhere. She had heard the voices in the empty air.

"Thyself!" she cried.

"Love him?" The old woman's voice was quiet and mechanical, as if she did not attach much meaning to what she said. "Once, I think. But it was all so long ago. In the years that followed, I bore him other, living sons. Still, it is hard to forget that when he found the mattress pooled with blood and picked the ewe's bones from the sheets, he was certain I had killed the child. And I never will forgive that he meant to have me burned for it."

The two women looked at one another.

Seen from a distance, there were a score of windows shining in the dark. The house was huge and rambling and, even with the wedding party gone, far from empty. It was only because he knew the room that Odlaw, walking on the hill, believed he recognized a pair of darkened figures against the light.

One patch of darkness reached out to touch the other below her waist.

"Will you call it Harry?" it asked her presently.

She shook her head.

"Arthur?"

Perhaps it was her grief that overwhelmed her. Certainly she had known unhappiness, but it was not the same as grief. And yet it may have been that in spite of her heart's pain, in a world that had overturned all she knew, she had finally puzzled one thing out and meant to hold to it at whatever cost.

"Jack," she heard herself whisper, too late to have held her tongue.

Chapter Ten

ESPECIALLY WHEN THE CHILD DID NOT MOVE INSIDE her, she would forget, sometimes for as much as half a day, sometimes only for an hour. Sometimes, after Emily had come into the bedroom, prodding and reproving her, directing her away from the window and out of a draft, she would be freed by the maid's irrepressible chatter . . . and sometimes by the color of sunlight on the counterpane . . . or by the sight of the littlest serving-boy out in the wind, brave as the Lionheart and armed with a stick, chasing his equally bellicose shadow across the sheets Mrs. Curran had hung on the line. Once, encouraged by thirteen straight stitches in Harry's coat, by the relief that she did not need to cut them out and start again, she did not remember until morning.

But it was more difficult when Emily, having searched through the closets, began laying out the wider-bellied dresses on the bed. Then, feeling the life thickening within her, it was harder to put aside the death.

Elva tried to tell herself, since her brother was already

lost, that the slip of a single word was without consequence. But in her dreams she heard his tearful voice begging her to promise, and in her thoughts, sleeping and awake, her own, which was the voice, inescapably, of a murderer.

She did not know when, any more than she knew the hour of the birth: some time far off, and yet certain. She did not know how. In a way, it was not much different from how it has always been. The life would come, as the death would, mysteriously. Only, she was just beginning to realize, she was to be the cause of both.

It was like a trap, waiting.

Each day she woke, although it was not the day, it was nearer.

There was no excuse. Her husband had never actually lied to her. He had not seduced her with promises. For if she had said nothing, after the first days when he had opened his heart to her, he had scarcely said a word. Now that she was alone, condemned and deserted, it nearly seemed without cause, unless, of course, it was because in the wood when she might have spoken . . .

In the early months of her pregnancy, whenever His Grace had gone off, she had sat on the door sill, watching the green mists rise from the fields, the life returning to the trees and plants and thought, perhaps, with the world bursting with spring, she might dare to go back and cross the wood again. But with every day she grew heavier, till she couldn't stand any more than the child inside of her and she only sat on the sill, watching. More and more, although His Grace was often away, she stayed in her room.

"She's been naughty," Emily said in the way one talked to invalids, as if Elva were no longer present, even though she was already twice the size that she had been. "She hasn't ate her breakfast."

The truth was, she was sick.

Emily added a jar of marmalade to the tray. She buttered toast.

Elva looked out the window. She saw Arthur, wrapped in his tarpaulin, fairly often. Harry was more skittish. Sensing his cowardice, the cowman chased him off whenever he noticed him sneaking around the barn. It was only when she saw the two hedges together (both still without their coats) that she was satisfied that her youngest brother had not yet fallen. Before sunrise they stood watch among the plantings on the nearer side of the gate. Fortunately, the dogs were still frightened and, while Odlaw had offered a bounty to any who would rid them from the yard, even Sam Maddox, although he pretended to stalk them, recognized they were dear to her and loaded his shells with chalk and saltpeter instead of shot.

" 'er life is rough enough, I'd say if we was asked," he said to Tommy Chorlton and arrived at the house too late and, when His Grace remarked on it, walked up too early and promptly fell asleep against the well house wall.

His Grace was not a fool: he knew the rebellion for what it was. But seeing the part he had played at the start of it, he waited; and the longer he waited the harder it was to undo.

He began riding out in the morning. Lady Milton saw him far too many times at her table. He called on Grizel Washbothem's father twice and stayed on longer than was fitting. When on the third time the old gentleman saw His Grace coming up the track, although his morals were scarcely better than his daughter's, he sent his man to say he was not at home.

"Tell him, Grizzy," he told her afterward, "for my sake, if not your own, that servants talk."

Late at night, when his sadness had become a hunger, His Grace would go for a walk to the edge of the hill, knowing, now that the door to the bedroom was locked, that all he had left was the path through the willow-girt meadow over which he had carried her like a prize from the wood.

When he was at home, he sat quietly watching the old mulberry come into flower against the bleakness of the new ploughed fields. The tree seemed to fatten as she did, and as it reminded him as well of the tree from which he had taken her, he began to dislike the look of it. From his own bedroom, when he woke in the morning, he cursed it, and when he passed it during the day he never failed to hurl an oath at its branches.

But the tree continued to bloom, grew bulky and gravid. And so before an uneasy wind blew the first thistledown out of the paddock into the empty nests of the finches, he had the trunk girdled, then cut and the logs stacked in high double cords outside the back kitchen door.

The Head Keeper's daughter smelled his shirt in disgust. "You might at least wash," she had scolded him. But after she had made him tie his roan in a grove fifty yards from the door (for he was married now), she snuffed out the light.

He did not trouble to draw the curtain, and he left the door open a crack so he could listen to the night.

He liked to hear the owls killing. His whole body shook when he heard the screams. Then, if only for a moment, his restlessness and irritation seemed to leave him.

"You're pining," she said when she found him awake.

"I am thinking of the barley yield," he answered, turning from the animal comfort of her breasts.

The summer had been hot with little rain and September had been wet. Even at that, his own fieldmen would never be sufficient for the work. Although he had increased his borrowing and offered to raise the wage, before he had thought to ask, his neighbors had received a commitment from the available men. As a favor, George Grass had pledged two of his own, but two of his oldest and then only after he was through with them. Defying his mother, Rob Milton had agreed to help the best he could, but His Grace had seen the coolness in his eyes.

"Where is she?" the naked woman asked.

"At her sewing."

"At such an hour?"

He watched her vacantly, his scalp gleaming with sweat, the sockets of his eyes hollow.

"The Devil finds work for her hands," he said.

"She be a woman as I."

"You may have forgotten," he said bitterly, "she came from the wood."

"She's your wife."

"And you are my love," he said absently. Although it was time he was going, out of habit, he thrust his hand into her. This time, adrift in her own loneliness, she did not cry out. Hating her silence, he dragged himself over her.

Shortly before sunrise, the door pulled back. The Head Keeper stood between the jambs, his big shoulders trembling. He had found the roan and had waited as tactfully as he could. But it did not accord with his dignity to be kept waiting until it was daylight, and the shadows of his child's "company" turned unambiguously into the arms and legs of a man he knew.

"Matey," he said grimly, as if His Grace were no more than a fellow he had met just that minute lurking under a bush. "You'll come out, will you? For I'll not strike a blow in me own house or with 'er to see it and bear witness against me."

For a moment His Grace lay rigid in the bed. His gaze concentrated on the young woman, he threw back the blanket. With the father watching, he caressed the pair of her dainty, white buttocks.

Then he rose and, neither dressed nor armed, crossed to the door.

All tallied and told, with everything summed and subtracted, including the pencil and the foolscap on which he worked his columns, the stamp and even the halfpenny envelope in which he had sent his complaint to the magistrate (for he had a good eye and was not a man to overlook trifles), the Head Keeper of Badger's Wood figured that he had come out short by just something less than one shilling.

"I might have walked into Stephen's Well and so saved the stable," he explained at the Royal Charles on a cold evening in October. "But if 'twas to be done, I told myself, was to be done royal. So I took me old mare."

The barman, although he seemed equally to occupy himself keeping the counter polished, grinned.

"So first is four days of oats," the Head Keeper said. "And second the fare—down into Bristol and then along from Cupheag and Metichanwon to Water Street Station itself—which were dear enough by coach, but which, I don't mind sayin', it weren't."

He made another mark.

"And the nights, from Monday to Thursday, and each of them dinners and a twelve penny glass of Spanish port besides at the finish. And this very suit, to stand afore 'em and to make his lordship and all of them hide-bound bureaucrats sit up and take notice."

He set down another line of scratches.

"And a barrister to say me words."

Tommy Chorlton whistled when he saw the number set out in black and white.

"And then a gratuity," the Head Keeper went on, "to have the final judgment writ out and sent up proper, with a constable, to His Grace. That alone were six and eight."

"So His Grace were not . . ."

"Stayed in his house, laddie."

"How's your back, then?" the barman asked.

The Head Keeper smiled, in spite of the bandages wrapped about his ribs.

"Paid for," he said, "exceptin' one shilling."

"Then let this make even," the barman said, taking upon himself the impartiality of a greater judge. And, balancing what was paid against what was still owed, he set the next round in front of every man without expense.

In the way of things, word of the beating, which until then had been kept out of the till of public opinion, now that it had an adjudicated value, was passed easily from hand to hand. It was not midmorning when George Grass's drayman, pausing at a shop in the village, left more than the price of a hand saw and a bag of birdlime to be spent after him. Lady Milton's cook and, as it now seems certain, a troop of pickers and kilnmen, passing through to the next farm, brought it away with them as change, although in the telling the amount of the fine was possibly tripled and (since any tale of somewhere else is soon brought home) the distant judge in his robes transformed into the local barman in his apron.

By evening there was a line of men against the counter of the Royal Charles, expecting that His Grace had been ordered to set things straight with all.

"I've come to see it evened up," said a pale, dark-haired man, who in the spring had mended a wagon for His Grace, been paid his full price and ever after regretted not asking more.

"Even up! Even up!" the men cried behind him.

Although the mistake was clear enough, perhaps the barman saw that he was not entirely innocent. In any event, he laughed when he pulled the pump. But he pulled it sharply, as if delivering blows himself, and the next day sent a bill for thirty pounds up to His Grace.

His Grace left the barman's bill neglected on the table. It was Rendcombe's that had made him angry, although, when it came, even he would have said, it was accurate: so much for Joe Gormley's shingles, so much more for climbing the stairs to his wife's bedroom, now once a week as her time grew near. At any other time His Grace would have paid without question. Instead he had the doctor banned from the house, and, in part, the trouble that followed came from that.

"He's no ordinary devil," His Grace went on with terrible seriousness to the old woman as they sat by themselves over dinner.

By then the afternoons were dark and the fires had to be started after breakfast to get the room warm by evening.

There were lanterns in the barn where the cowman still worked. There were lamps shining in Elva's bedroom where, while she believed there was no point in it, spurred on by the old woman, she was trying to finish the last coat for John. But she tired easily and much preferred looking over the meadow into the last of the light. Life went by the calendar, the warm weeks followed by cold. What there was of the barley that hadn't been spoiled by blights had been gathered and put away. What was left was stubble, where now, not merely at dawn but with the draining light at each day's end, she often saw her brothers (now two with their coats) and only the last and dearest, shivering.

Winter stood in the wings.

" 'No charge,' " His Grace said, quoting the hated bill. " 'Ribs strapped in Badger's Wood . . . settled by order of the Court, paid by . . . ' "

"Yourself," the old woman said.

"Indirectly."

"Paid. Subtracted from the fine."

"Done," His Grace said. "However the means. And no reason, other than his spitefulness, to mention it."

Sitting across from him, the old woman sipped at her goblet, listening to him grumble against Rendcombe. Yet for what truly cut his heart he had only silence. All the more it made her aware of the differences between them. Perhaps, because of the wideness of the gulf, as if seeking a way across it, she pitied him.

"What will you do," she asked, "when her time comes?"

"There are women, I suppose," he said, sensing betrayal. "There were no doctors when my mother . . ."

"You!" she interrupted him. "What she will be doing is clear enough."

He jabbed angrily at something on his plate.

"She is not what I expected." He stopped, appalled by the way his life had gone. "An honest woman wouldn't . . . Christ, everyone knows she locks the door."

"She must finish her sewing."

He had expected her to be fairer than that. "It was you," he complained, "who started her."

"I helped her begin. Still, it was no more than what she wanted."

"It is not even for the child!" he cried at her.

There was a moment's pause, which she let linger. "You must know," she said at last, as if reluctantly, "she already has *her* children."

The pause was longer while he turned, exchanging the sight of her for a view of the darkness. Beyond the windows, he was certain, shadows scurried . . . or held their places invisibly, ill-clad and cold in their rough-stitched wool and tarpaulin, like frost-bitten sentries.

His face flashed despair.

She did not help him.

"Can you tell me what they are?" he asked.

She did not bother to shake her head.

"More and more," he told her bitterly, "I feel I have already become a widower."

It surprised her how little needed to be done: a word here and there, a frown, a few details which, more out of memory than thought, she could supply easily. The old woman had never struggled against it; from the start she had been prepared to lift everything onto her shoulders. Her shame, the demands of the dead, her hope for the scene that, in repeating, might pass the dishonor on to the next, none of these had left her. However tender her feeling for the girl and in spite of the young man's obtuseness, she had not been turned aside by affection or by second thoughts. Only it seemed not to have mattered. Whatever drove her, piloted the world for its own sake, and would, she was now convinced, even had she recoiled from the final task, have kept on just as fiercely to the end.

The estrangement was their own doing. But while her own marriage had led the old woman to expect nothing better, there had always been the chance that the emptiness between husband and wife might have been bridged by a greater power than the simple call of sex to sex. But Elva stayed in her room and dared not speak, and the only words Odlaw's life had taught him were of honor.

In a way, it was honor that had kept Rendcombe from the house. For what was honor but the refusal of one man to tolerate the intervention of an other? The old woman had had little to do with that. Without her help, the priest, whose long memory might have proved difficult, had taken himself off. Even Rob Milton, preserving a kind of rough gentleness in the face of everything, had hurried away, as if ashamed.

And so she was only half surprised. For she had foreseen, if not the details, at least the outline. The old know it if the young do not. All life leads to ruin. It was as certain as snow in winter, as inevitable as early fires on bare November afternoons.

Nonetheless, she had never considered that one more beating would turn His Grace away from any chance of civil measures, leaving Elva at the mercy of his hurt and pain.

"And so," the old woman thought, figuring the accounts herself, "the law and medicine, the church and even his few friends are closed to him."

What remained for her were merely stage props.

Since the spring she had penned a number of dogs and kittens in a dingy enclosure at the margin of the wood and fed them indifferently to keep them small. There was

a terrier and a spaniel bitch and several more orange tabbies
than she had started with. She needed so many because
she was not certain of her skill in slaughtering nor of the
amount of blood she could extract from a slit throat nor
which bones would most resemble a child's. When she
brought out the basin and the knife and hung them on
a nail to have them ready, the dogs yelped and the cats
squeaked and hollered.

"Be still, my beauties," she warned them. "Have you
forgot the dead are silent?"

Chapter Eleven

THE CRY AWOKE THE HOUSE JUST BEFORE DAWN.
Before that, as likely as not, there had been little worrying
noises behind the door. Perhaps Elva had scratched and
clawed at the wall but she had stayed in her bed. Emily
had been asleep down the hall. Mrs. Curran, who would
have rested through the crack of doom, lay in her cot
dreaming, after all these months, of the butcher, who at
the wedding had slept in the attic and never once noticed
her. The cowman, pressing his head into the warm flanks
of Dimple and Daisy, heard nothing but the ringing of
milk in his pail. Later in the day Joe Gormley discovered
that several of the hounds, let out by the boy in all the
confusion, had come back with fur in their mouths and
mistook the blood and stink for fox. But by then no one
was thinking at all clearly.

"What is that horrid racket?" Elva had asked, for in her
dreams it did not matter if she spoke, and because it was
only dreams, the old woman answered.

"It is only me killing the spaniel," she said.

"Doesn't it mind its death?"

The old woman considered the spaniel's bulging eyes. She had coaxed it up the short steps of the well house and tied a string around its neck. Hung from the rooftree, it shook its black muzzle and wriggled its splayed-out paws.

"Certain, it misses its breath," she admitted.

"Could you not have left it in its kennel?" Elva wondered, unsatisfied.

"Might have done one thing," the old woman said, "or I might have done another. But, like my old gran, I did this."

"Perhaps it is unlucky," Elva suggested resentfully.

Unmoved, the old woman proceeded to cut off its head with a cleaver. Then she wiped the blade and employed it to sever its leg.

But it was only dreams.

If any had seen the old woman bearing a basin into the house, none saw fit to mention it. Thinking it nothing more than Mrs. Curran's sloppiness, one of the maids swept a large piece of gore out of the butler's pantry and down the back steps. She too was up and about early, before the house. The blood on the kitchen floor was simply an inconvenience. She cursed the cook under her breath.

The blood in Elva's bed, however, blotted out everything.

Emily was the first to see it. She had heard the cry out of her deepest sleep and knew at once, with a shock, what had happened. It was the noisiest, liveliest, most rollicking cry she had ever heard and, shaking with joy, she stumbled down the carpeted hall in her nightdress and ran through the door into Elva's bedroom. It never occurred to her that the door was unlocked or how it came to be so. All she saw was Elva covered in blood from her head to her stockings.

Afterward, choking and wiping her tears, Emily told Mrs. Curran, that she must have dreamed the cry. There was no other explanation. Otherwise there could have been no time, not nearly enough time for the babe to have given forth the merriest, naughtiest cry ever heard in all of Redding and the next moment, in the instant between her bedroom and Elva's, to have been immobilized, hacked into pieces and consumed.

There were some bones, with the gristle and tendons still clinging to them. But not nearly enough. There was no rib cage or skull. Even His Grace, standing on the sticky floor in his bare feet, his legs stiff and unsteady, recognized that.

"What have you done with the rest of him?" he bellowed.

But he never hit her again. He raged and he shouted but he never came near her. He had come in when he heard the commotion—not the child's cry but the screams of women—and what he saw made knots of muscle constrict under his skin.

He had gone to bed early, as he did on those few nights he was at home. After half an hour he had begun to dream of her. He had removed her trousers and fondled her in the dark. In his dream they had fallen asleep in each other's arms. He remembered happiness. But the dream, like every dream, was filled with mystery. It flowed from one place to another, changing seamlessly from the wood to the hall to the bed where they had first slept. In each place there were men and women, some of whom he knew and many he did not. Beside his bed, he recognized his father. The old Duke was standing with his barons and the sporting men, smoking his pipe and spilling tobacco and ashes over the floor. He often dreamed of his father but he had never once dreamed of his mother. Both were now lost to him, but his mother, it seemed he had always known, was Death.

"The news is you're getting married," the old Duke had said.

"I had not realized that word of it could reach the wood," Odlaw had answered.

"There is no better gossip than word of the living," said his father. "And the best of it is who among you has taken the other to bed."

"Surely that is a small thing."

His father laughed.

They had glanced warily at each other.

"Always," his father said, "it is the begetting of ourselves we most care for."

His Grace had wakened to the screaming of women.

He lay in his bed, staring at the long empty place beside him. Then he stood. Then he ran.

"Take her!" he cried to them, not certain himself what he meant by that. But no one did. No one touched her. No one brought a towel to clean her face, her legs, her arms. It was Joe Gormley, last into the room, who sent them from it and, when only she was left, relocked the door.

Elva found she could no longer remember the child, and because she still remembered the urgency of her flesh and because the pain had not left her, in her heart she believed she was unworthy. She remembered, after the loneliness of the struggle, that her damp hair had hung forward and, much later, the digging on the underside of her breast, the mouth seeking and searching and not finding. The birth had not been swift nor had it been merciful. She had pushed, but the life inside of her, if it was yet life, had seemed unwilling. She was so weary when it was finished that she was not certain if at the end she had rolled over on top of him, or whether it was the body of a child or the man. There was simply no strength in her.

But the cry had frightened her more than torture.

"Hush!" she had thought desperately, as if it was still herself breaking the oath and not something lost and pulled free of her.

The blood that seeped between her teeth was in fact his blood, not dog's blood. She had already bitten through the cord when the old woman came in with the basin.

"You did not leave the door open," the old woman said. "It was my own room once. One year to the next, I kept the key."

By then Elva was already forgetting things. Her breath had become no more than a whimper; her head swam. When the old woman lifted him, although Elva tried to raise herself, she found every limb powerless.

A door had closed and, later, opened.

The others stood by her bed.

She remembered Emily's face and decided it was not much different from her husband's, both of them rheumy-eyed and disheveled, both of their features much too thick for actual faces, but screaming or perhaps looking as if they were about to scream. She was not certain if either had managed it.

She could not tell how many eventually came into the room. There were too many, but mostly they stayed by the door.

"I'll go for the priest," someone said.

"No," a voice answered, the word whispered but unyielding, in spite of its nausea and dread, a man's hard voice, like the voice of her father.

⋆   ⋆   ⋆

Rendcombe would have seen at once they were dog bones. But morning came, bringing a low cloud out of the west and the threat of storm instead of light, and no one sent for him. His Grace sat at a breakfast he did not eat. He did not raise his eyes from the plate. Even Joe Gormley, putting aside his enmity, looked in on him and went away quietly.

There was a constable in Stephen's Well, but he was the same constable who had wobbled out on his bicycle to deliver the order for the fine. In any circumstance, His Grace would have never given his wife to such a man. Yet, except for the fine, he might have sent a wire on to New Awanux. He might have sat in his chair before the great windows waiting for strangers to come from the station, to hire a chaise and ride up the cattle track out of the town. In short, except for the fine, he might have trusted his despair to the impartiality of strangers.

Instead, surrounded by those he knew, all he could think of was blood.

But he never could sit for long. His eyes, which had to look somewhere, rested on the stump of the mulberry beyond the gate. Over the hill a few random kernels of snow, defying the pull of the ground, pocked the gray, windy flesh of the morning, reminding him it was nearly time for fires. He remembered the wood that he had ordered piled outside the kitchen door.

To do him justice, passion has usually been excused as though it were a kind of terrible accident. Presumably, had His Grace strangled her the moment he had come through the door into her bedroom, even Rendcombe would not have escaped unmoved. In fact, Odlaw waited two hours, which, except for the terrible years at school, was the longest he had sat in one place without thinking of something that needed doing out in the fields or in the barns and which, at least in some part, because he was not accustomed to brooding, accounted for the ferocity that followed.

The day already seemed a nightmare to the women of the house. None of their lives were untouched by death, but the murder of a child by its mother was an abomination that sucked the souls from their breasts. They sat numbly in the kitchen, waiting in Mrs. Curran's mountainous shadow, their thoughts robbed of everything but horror. It was Mrs. Curran herself who saw His Grace. He was out in the back with a wheelbarrow moving the logs into the middle of the yard. He did it himself, with Joe Gormley watching but not giving a hand, but not objecting either. When she had taken a long look at the piled wood and the chair set down unsteadily on top of it, Mrs. Curran turned her immense blank face back to the rest.

"I'll not say it's not his right," she said.

The between-maid, who was the youngest, looked uncertain.

But Emily took a rag and began scrubbing the well-scrubbed table until the rag was worn through and her white knuckles burned.

After twenty minutes they heard a door close. They heard His Grace on the stairs. If they had heard so little as that, the walls were not so thick or the servants' wing so far from the heart of the house that they wouldn't have heard Elva's screams as well. Her cries, echoing through the large cold rooms, would have provided an understandable prologue to the drama. They expected a prologue, as they expected symmetry and order. They were country folk and comforted that the untidiness of day-to-day existence was, by the great bold strokes of life and death, made straight and plain as tales told in kitchens, around a table or before a fire.

Until the end, they did not see that her stiff silence was essential. But they had no sense either—finding nothing comic or absurd in their own existence—that they were largely ceremonial, with little purpose but to decorate and watch the unfolding of the tale, told and retold, like all lives, over and over.

When she was dragged into the yard, Elva was still grasping the sheet she had held on to when her husband had lifted her from the bed. Her features, blackened with dried blood and already looking half charred, peered grotesquely at the wood, at the chair and the stuffing of straw strewn about at the edges. He had used the sheet to bind her. He used his belt besides, finding that it was more than ample, now that her waist was flat, to fit around her middle and buckle her to the rungs of the chair. He did not look at her. His long fingers, with which he had pulled her from the tree, (and with which on their first night, letting the blanket drop, he had welcomed her naked to his arms), never trembled.

The flames, after they had caught from the straw, danced on the wood and then on the chair leg, swaying with the startling witchery of a woman, in her finery, sweeping across a polished floor to meet him.

Yet, it had seemed to him it was the snow he would always remember, white and delicate as a child's breath, against hair black as a raven's and as slippery, when his hands had run over it, as feathers.

"Once," the old woman went on as she always did, "on one side of the wood or another, there was a duke whose wife died, leaving him alone with his sons and a daughter. But he would not accept her death and went seeking her in a wood which had its beginning and ending in one place and where, he had been told, the dead lingered. And so it happened, in spite of his courage, that he became lost and, believing he would soon die himself, he gave himself up to despair. But an old woman who had a cottage there found him wandering.

" 'My good woman,' the Duke asked her, 'can you show me the way out of the wood?'

"The old woman smiled. 'But there is a condition,' she added."

The child drew her fingers idly through the heavy tangle of her hair. The familiar figures marched through her head. Although she was sleepy, she did not protest. Since she was a baby, the old woman, who was a relative of some sort, had drawn her off by herself to whisper one thing or another.

"Thyself . . . myself," the child said, rushing the tale on. She liked the talking hedges, although it seemed hard to believe that anyone's brothers could be turned into trees.

"Must the hedges always be brothers?" she asked, because she had brothers of her own.

The old woman nodded.

"And must they be cruel?"

"Yes."

"But in the end don't they save her?"

The sky, with the snow beginning, was bitter and gray. The women appeared at last on the porch, watching the flames leaping high from the straw and catching the wood. At the corner of the barn two of the hedges, one in wool, the other in tarpaulin, crept timidly into sight. Still they shied away from the roar of the timbers and, as if they smelled the blood, from the gruesome visage of their sister.

But her husband, his old shirt open, stood close enough to feel the heat of the flames. For a moment or two he said nothing.

"Why have you done this?" he asked finally, his voice measured, as if he asked not for himself but, like a magistrate, on behalf of the women on the porch and the men standing behind him by the well house.

Elva's gaze did not appear to consider him. She was watching the sky. The light had gone out of it, leaving in its place an eerie desolation. In some unfathomable way she seemed to be waiting. A few rough flakes, skittering across her sight, caught in her hair without melting. She did not move. Perhaps, the cloud lowered. Then very quietly, without even a breath of air, across the well house and over the roofs of the barns, the snow came tumbling soundlessly out of the darkness.

By then many of the women had burst into tears. Because of the suddenness of the sound, as if betrayed, Elva turned.

At the same moment a door at the corner of the barn opened. At first Elva saw only the old woman. Then at long last, stepping from behind her, a shape in a patchwork coat, the third coat, made of bed linen and blankets, on which Elva had worked even as the pains pulled at her legs and which she had not finished, a small crippled shape—its one uncovered limb still dragging twigs and leaves—came hobbling across the yard.

It blundered past her husband. Sobbing, it leapt into the flames.

It was Joe Gormley, running swiftly from the well house, who threw in the contents of the bucket. For a long time after the wood steamed.

It took Elva some moments to collect and control herself. Not bothering to unbuckle the strap, she looked about unsatisfied, until, finally, she noticed the old woman coming away from the barn. A child, wrapped in a piece of wadmal, was sleeping in her arms.

"His name is J-Jack," Elva whispered.

She stopped and for a moment she stared at her husband.

"Even against my w-will," she continued, as though her thoughts had never left the question he had asked. "Although," she went on stammering, "they never gave me c-cause for anything b-b-but bitterness . . . even then, I had no choice and could not h-help . . . For they are my b-blood. You were only my husband."

The old woman adjusted her head-cloth.

"John lived, of course," she said. "They all went on living, for a time."

The child glared at her.

"But wasn't he the one?" she complained, for the girl was eleven and truth was dear to her. "I mean, when the Duchess spoke . . . and when she had broken her promise . . . wasn't the youngest brother supposed to die from that?"

They were sitting in the kitchen, the old woman in her favorite place by the hob. It was a cramped kitchen, but it was snug, especially with the April wind trying the doors and the windows. But it was too dark to look out on the hill where Harry and Arthur, men once more and, toward the end of their days, uncles and granduncles many times over, had their graves. Still, the old woman often walked there and every spring, with a chopping stick, uprooted the first green sprigs of the hedges that poked above the stones. But she never went down beneath the house where the old Duke rested, although sometimes she thought of the boy who slept in the gray, dry vault beside him.

"Who am I to explain it?" the old woman said. "There were other sons. But it was only the youngest who was allowed to recross the wood. It may be that courage had something to do with it. Or perhaps it hasn't. It may be that love, in spite of the best evidence, never gives up hope. I can no longer judge. But by now that son would have married. And his sons, surely, would have had sons of their own, one in particular, my dear, who, dreaming, looking out across the cattle track toward the grim trees . . ."

The Twelfth Duke stood in the doorway. He was tall and long-shouldered but, although he had been a widower for some years, his breath did not yet smell of malmsey. Seeing the hour, he had put aside a pamphlet about increasing the barley yield and come away from the library. In one hand he held a torch, ready for the flame. Propped against the door, he had rested a pike. Disregarding the wind and the hour, he meant to go at once with his sons to spear eels in the river. Only, he wished that the old woman were more reliable.

"Shouldn't you be taking her up to her bed?" he asked, unwilling to hide his impatience.

At the thought of the stairs, the old woman, whose small feet bore the scars of some long-forgotten burning, sighed. Nonetheless, she gathered the child to her skirts and limped toward the door. But it happened, as they passed him, that the Duke reached out, touching gently a glossy mass of loose hair. His breath caught unexpectedly.

"Good night, Elva," he whispered.

And at this last moment, although either might have turned, only one, the wonder and terror waiting ahead of her, did.

Ridgefield—Niantic
July, 1991